Editing: Kim Campbell of Proofing the Pages

Cover Art: Get Covers

Naked Cover and Endpapers by Sophie Jade illustrations

Special Edition Jacket Cover by Anrl Light

Night Blooming

VICTORIA WREN

"There is a crack in everything. That's how the light gets in."
— Leonard Cohen

TRIGGER WARNINGS

This book was written with an upper YA audience in mind but I hope that adults will also enjoy this book. This is a dark, gothic horror and fantasy, but my reader's mental health matter to me a great deal so I would like to take the opportunity to warn you ahead of time about any triggers to expect.

Please be aware of scenes involving and alluding to sexual assault, grief, trauma and death of a family member through cancer.

ONE

"**M**r. Raggerty will catch you, and he'll eat your heart all up," her brother James told her when he was five and she was three.

Images like those stuck around in your head and slowly grew into nightmare fuel.

When Mr. Raggerty appeared in the field outside Marianne's window every year, it was a sure sign fall was coming. The leaves would turn crisp and brown, and the wheat would bleach to dazzling sun gold. The corn grew tall; a sea of green and yellow for miles. Mari had never liked the scarecrow; with his crinkled plaid shirt, glossy button eyes, and sack for a head. It didn't help that James used to tease her and say he looked through her window at night, peering in and scratching the glass with his straw fingers.

The thought turned her stomach to mush, and now, even at nineteen years old, the sight of him hanging limp from his pole every September made goosebumps rise on her forearms. But James wasn't around to tease her now.

One year, when she'd been small, she'd begged her father to tell her the truth. Was Mr. Raggerty real? Did he really come to life at night and run around their yard playing with their swing set? Her father chuckled and promptly explained none of that fairy tale stuff was true. It was made up to get you to buy theme park tickets and princess costumes. And scarecrows didn't come to life. The way he processed and explained things helped control her rampant, childish imagination.

He was a professor at Meadowford, where he taught science and had a logical way of thinking. The year after, he'd left them. Mari preferred his way of dealing with the darkness and monsters under the bed. Still, his leaving to start another family, in another town, left a bitter sting.

More than anything, she was annoyed he'd left her with her brother, the self-proclaimed 'man of the house.' The title didn't make him any more mature. It seemed to give him more rights to make her life a misery. She thought she should miss that about James, but she didn't. Dead for four months, his unusual sense of humor often lingered in her memory.

Mari hit send on the email, dispatching her client the last of the edits. She had a long check list of fixes for him to make on his latest project. It was a novella set in a ruined castle in Scotland. Some of the research Mari had delved into was really interesting and made for some grim reading.

Somehow, over the last few months, she'd fallen into a professional and easy working relationship with her 'client,' Eric Summers. He was eccentric and wrote horror and fantasy novellas, usually set in the real world. Mari was his fact-checker. When she dropped out of college, she'd listed her services online. She had to do something to keep herself busy, and make some money, yet she hadn't expected an actual writer to find her among the hundreds of listings out there. Eric claimed he liked her sensible, methodical, and no nonsense profile.

His work was dark; sometimes a bit gory and spooky, but he kept coming back, which meant he didn't see her suggestions as too nitpicky. Mari could be *nitpicky*, and she was good at it. But it helped that he didn't know who she was or what she looked like, and vice versa. It kept things professional and at a good, internet sized arm's length.

Tossing her books aside and shutting down her laptop, the shadows of the sun slipping below the trees made her yawn and stretch her back. Bending to peer out the window, Mr Raggerty spun on a stiff late afternoon breeze, and Mari winced and hunched her shoulders.

She needed to grow up. It was a bundle of straw after all.

Tiny feet skittered across the hardwood floor, and Mari grinned, stooping to scratch behind Bear's ears. The sandy-colored terrier nudged his snout into her palm, winding between her legs. He peered up at her, brown eyes, glossy and full of yearning. His wiry fur tickled her legs as he darted through them, back and forth.

"I know what time it is," she said with a sleepy yawn, turning to the mirror to pull her long dark hair into a low bun. Grabbing a hoodie, she yanked it over her head. "Same time every night, Bear."

He whined, jumping a foot from the floor, begging for more scritches, and she playfully dodged him, her socks sliding on the polished floor as she grabbed for her sneakers. Outside, the breeze played with the trees, brushing through the ripe wheat, as it was growing dusky. Shivering as the old scarecrow twirled on its pole, Mari yanked the drapes closed. She didn't want to return later and see him still gawking up at her. It was enough to give her nightmares.

Motes of dust hit the air as she yanked the drape across, her dark eyes catching a gleaming light across the cornfield beyond the small cluster of trees where the imposing Rosewood

Hall sat shrouded in shadow. Rosewood was an expansive estate, hidden among the trees and brambled, long overgrown. It was a building of the eighteenth century with gothic turrets and columns and stone statues lurking in the vast gardens. Like a sleeping, stone giant, the building was half eaten by moss and brambles, hidden behind a wrought iron gate with the Rosewood emblem blazened into the metal. It was also derelict, and no one had lived there for as long as she could remember. James used to play over there with his friends, hiding in the ruined, winding halls.

Mari frowned and poked her head through the gap in the drapes.

There was a light on inside Rosewood.

"Ha," she murmured in surprise. She was sure the old place had been condemned. She'd read it somewhere online; or in one of the local papers. Unsafe. Unfit for human visitation; or something. There was no electricity, or so she thought.

Mari and her mother lived in the estate farmhouse right out in the back end of nowhere. The house was on the edge of the old colonial town of Winstone, MA. There wasn't much out here besides corn and wheat; and, of course, Rosewood Hall. The ancient building that once belonged to the town founders. Marianne lived in one of the only houses that used to belong to the Hall—vast and open space stretched for miles, nothing but farmland and forest. The estate was separated by nothing except one large corn field and its infamous straw-headed resident.

"Mom?" Mari called as she hopped into the darkened hallway, her voice floating down the polished, wooden staircase. "Did you know Rosewood has a tenant?"

Mari paused in the dark, waiting for a reply, and part of her heart hardened. She wasn't sure why she expected her mother to take an interest. Bear barked as he shot ahead of her down the stairs. As Mari hit the hallway downstairs, she was greeted by darkness and the glare of the television bleeding through the door. The volume was down to zero. She wet her dry lips. "Mom?"

A cold wash of fear iced her palms as she stood at the family room door, finding her mother on the couch, blonde hair splayed across one of the scattered cushions. Her heart thundered in her ears, until she saw the gentle rise and fall of her mother's chest and the magazine lying open over her belly. Gently, the mother's eyes fluttered open, stifling a yawn.

Bear jumped for attention, licking Mari's knuckles.

"Did you say something?" she asked, blearily. The room smelled stale, and Mari forced herself not to look at the waste paper basket, even though it was full—filled with cans and begging for her to see it.

"Uh…Rosewood." Mari blinked and shook herself. "There are lights on over there."

Her mother's brow lines grew deeper. "I thought that old place was condemned."

Mari shrugged, sweeping to the window and peering outside. The top of the Hall was barely visible from this angle, and Mari craned her neck.

There were no lights on now. Whatever it'd been was gone. Maybe it was just kids playing around? It was nearly Fall, and kids loved cycling on their bikes along the Grenfell River. The house had plenty of warning notices dotted around its perimeter, but it didn't stop them. An old, condemned house with its dark, winding corridors was far too tempting. And this was Winstone, where there was nothing else to do, other than troublemaking.

Mari rubbed her arms, shaking off the strange sense of apprehension. She had spent too much time inside this dark old place, staring at a laptop screen and proofing tales of witches and ghosts. Eric's latest yarn about a witch buried beneath an oak tree had tickled her imagination.

"Never mind," she muttered as the sky grew dark. "Have you seen the flashlight? It's getting dark early now, and if Bear breaks off again like last night..." Mari tutted, throwing her hound a playful glare. "He likes chasing rabbits."

Mari's mother yawned, running a hand through wiry blonde curls. "It's…" She paused. "I think it's in the den."

Mari paused, her blood freezing as their eyes collided. Her mother shuffled to get off the couch. "I'll get it."

"No, it's fine," Mari said, holding her hand. "It'll be fine. I can find it. You stay there."

Her mother's eyes grew watery with relief, and she slumped against the cushions, expelling a pained breath as though it hurt. "I need to clear that room—"

"You don't have to do anything. It's fine," Mari butted in with an authoritative wave of her hand. "I can get it."

Compelling her spine to remain iron and locked tight, she forced on a breezy smile and backed out of the room; tracking across the dark hallway to the shut-up room just off the kitchen. Mari had lost track of how long they'd lived like this.

In the dark, shadows spilled out of empty doors and shapes in the rooms. It was just a habit they'd grown into when James got sick. The light had hurt his eyes, so they shut them off. They shut everything off for the six months it took for him to die.

Balling her fist, her nails embedded in her flesh as she cracked open the door; the stale smell of old sheets wafting across the room. She wrinkled her nose. How long since they'd aired out this room? The sight of the bed, unmade and covered in old sheets, made her gut lurch, taking her back four months to the morning he'd been wheeled out in a body bag.

The first Mari knew of it was the swift diagnosis. *Cancer.* It'd struck her how fast something could rip up and gut out a healthy twenty-year-old young man. A good-looking guy with a life, friends, and a scholarship to play football. Those words seemed to take hold, festering and rotting him from the inside out until the boy she'd grown up with, the guy who liked to poke fun and tease her was a husk. He'd become a hollowed-out shell she no longer recognized—a boy who'd sucked their mother into a strange, living death alongside him.

They made the den his bedroom when he couldn't walk up the stairs. Living in the dark and quiet, Mari got used to the shadows.

Holding her breath, she crossed the room. Sweat built upon her neck as she rifled through the dresser drawer until her hand closed around the flashlight. Spinning on her heels, she fled the room, locking it tight. Bear waited in the hall, his lead in between his teeth.

She smiled in relief, bending to cup his adorable face. "You know how to make me smile," she said, grabbing her coat from the rack in the hall. She called over her shoulder. "Back in an hour, Mom," she called.

Her mother chuckled darkly, "I see Mr. Raggerty is back on his pole. Don't let him follow you home."

Mari rolled her eyes. It was something her brother would say. "Funny, Mom."

Dead leaves swept across her sneakers as Mari trudged the darkened lanes back through town. Winstone was a tiny, sprawling farm town; barely existing outside of Lincoln, a larger neighboring town known for its land preservation. They had exactly five hundred residents, most of whom were over fifty. She'd begun college in Meadowford, but after James's diagnosis, things had gone south.

James needed a caregiver, and her mother needed backup. James hadn't been the easiest of patients. Cancer stole his body and his humor, leaving a dark, angry young man confined to a bed. Gone was the playful banter, and jokes often bordering on cruel jabs. All that had been left was a bitter, foul-mouthed half-skeleton of a man.

Mari had dropped her classes and gradually faded away, like her brother. She was nineteen and needed an income, with a talent for proof-reading, editing, and fact-checking. Setting up a freelancing job online had worked well, and she didn't have to admit she got anxious leaving the house anymore. It was disconcerting just how comfortable the shadows had become. A place where she could be unseen. She wasn't a scared child needing a nightlight to keep away monsters waiting under her bed. She'd inherited her father's logical brain, and the dark was a safe place to hide.

"Bear," Mari called to the dark woods ahead. The patch flanked the farm lane where the road turned off onto the dirt track, which led to her house, a road dividing hers from Rosewood. "Bear, this is not funny."

In the distance, the moon rose over the trees, glinting off the leaves. A scuttling noise rushed towards her, and the tiny hurricane bounded out of the bushes. A frightened rabbit darted into the wheat field, and Bear wasn't far behind.

Mari scowled. If she lost him in there again… She wasn't sure why she was so jumpy. Maybe it was the story she'd been proofing. The words had somehow crawled under her skin—a witch and a curse and an old oak tree.

"Bear, you little…" she cried as her dog leaped the fence and vanished into the thick corn. Stuffing her hands into her coat pockets, Mari lost track of how many times she'd stood rooted to this spot, waiting for Bear to have his fun. "Come on," she drawled with growing impatience.

She traced the beam of light over the wheat, hoping it'd catch his eye and interest. Late September was cooling into a dry, nippy fall, and Mari took a deep breath, loving the smell of this time of year. She loved pumpkin lattes, the smell of caramel candles, and how all the storefronts in town changed to Halloween décor. She used to love Halloween. A prickle of fear touched her scalp.

Trick or treating with Zara. A ghost of a smile played on her lips. Had it been a year since that night? She rubbed her neck, trying to recall the last time she'd seen her friend. But the memories were dark and fragmented, and a nagging fear clawed her gut.

You should have called her. You should have made it right.

Swallowing, she pushed away the thought, flicking the beam higher. "Bear, come on!"

They'd grown out of trick or treating years before, but that didn't stop them crashing James's party at the house. He'd been so pissed they'd invaded— his uncool little sister and her best friend. It didn't stop his friends from ganging up on him, inviting them in and letting them at his alcohol stash.

"Bear!"

Okay, enough was enough. It was getting cold, the chill nipped her fingers, and it was too dark, even for Mari, who'd existed inside darkness for months.

Mari gritted her teeth and hiked a leg, grazing her inside thigh as she climbed the wooden fence. Growling, she trudged through the corn, grown to head height. She waded through it like water, tossing the beam around as she searched for her errant pup. "Bear…I swear to God!"

The beam of light hit a face, twisted and dead-eyed, and her heart nearly damn exploded. She clutched her chest. Mr Raggerty twirled on his pole, watching as she waded through the crops as though casually interested. The back of her neck prickled, supremely uncomfy with her back turned to him. So she twirled in his direction only to find he'd pivoted to face her.

It was only the wind. Everything in her rational mind told her so. But it didn't stop her feeling majorly creeped out. James used to say to her Mr. Raggerty was looking for his wife. The thought made her gag.

Something furry sprung past, brushing her leg, and Mari shrieked, shrill enough to crack glass.

"Holy shit, Bear!" She grabbed him and tackled him in a chokehold, all while he frantically licked her face as she wrestled him back on his lead. "You scared the crap out of me! Let's go home."

Sweating, she jogged back to the fence, crawling under this time. She set the beam to full with shaking hands as she hit the dirt road. A spark of adrenaline still coursed under her skin, and she let out a brave, almost crazed laugh, wondering what the hell had got her so spooked.

Lifting the beam, it sailed through the trees, illuminating the eerie outline of Rosewood, visible as she walked the dirt track with the house on her left. Pausing, her jaw dropped. So she hadn't been imagining it. There were lights on, in fact, *several* of them. They flickered, casting shapes on the ceilings visible through the windows. Who would want to live there? James told her it was rotted through. It was a death trap.

Her palms prickled as she turned to the road, letting the beam guide her home. Mari's heart jolted so violently she swore for a second it stopped. She nearly dropped the flashlight, and at her feet, Bear cowered.

In the middle of the road a man cloaked in shadows, waited for her.

TWO

The flashlight danced in the air, flying wild-ly before it rolled and landed at her feet. Mari grabbed it with trembling fingers, aiming it at the man's face.

He winced and held up his hands, blinded as the light touched his eyes, reflecting like a cat. Mari held her breath. He was taller than her and about her age, maybe older.

"Whoa!" he cried, shielding his eyes. "I'm not here to attack you!"

Her mouth was oddly dry, and her lips slack. How long had it been since she'd spoken to anyone other than her mother? The emails with her clients didn't count. She aimed it at his chest with a shaky hand. He wore a white shirt and a light tan jacket over the top. His hair was fair, the color of sand.

"What the hell are you doing stalking around in the dark?" she yelled, tossing her eyes to the wide expanse of the field to her left. "There's nothing out here!"

"Take it easy," he said, lowering his hands. Mari caught a glimpse of dark eyes under thick lashes. "We live here."

Mari didn't respond, her brain fuzzy and too startled to think clearly.

"Over *there*." He nodded through the trees. To Rosewood. Mari hopped from foot to foot, suddenly needing to pee out of fear. "We just moved in."

"You live in there?" she asked. "Nobody lives in there."

He smiled, and it was slow, deliberate, and easy. "We own it....well..." He looked bashful. "My family does. The Rosewoods. Perhaps you've heard of them?"

Mari rolled her eyes. How dumb did this guy think she was? "The Rosewoods haven't lived in that place for..." she counted, "like twenty years. It's derelict."

"It's perfectly livable," he said evenly. "And yes, I *know*. We're the Martin contingent. Hunter Rosewood was my Grandfather."

Hunter Rosewood had been the last resident of the old place and had died long before she was born.

Mari aimed her beam; it caught on his jaw, which was strong, with a proud chin and straight nose. He didn't look much older than her. Nice looking, *more* than nice infact, but Mari argued that she hadn't been surrounded by guys lately. Last week, she thought the Amazon guy was cute.

"Martin," she repeated.

He took a careful step nearer, holding out his broad palm. "Ash Martin. I'm one of the *non-murderous* descendants of the old Rosewoods, and we just moved in this afternoon—my sister and I. I saw you earlier walking your dog and thought I'd try and catch you."

His lip quirked at her reaction to the non-murderous line. Of course, a murderer would say the exact same thing.

Mari wished she'd made an effort with her hair, outfit, or anything. But how often did she run into anyone out here in the middle of nowhere after dark? Apart from her scarecrow voyeur who'd twirled in their direction.

"Catch me?" She winced inwardly. She must sound like a parrot. She was out of the practice of conversing it seemed.

He grinned, a little sheepish, and, god, it was adorable. "The electric company isn't turning on the mains until tomorrow, and we have exactly three matches left in the pantry. It's like a cave in there."

Mari didn't mind the dark. "So, you need candles?"

"Candles... matches—anything that'll let me see three feet in front of me." He whistled, tossing his gaze over the corn. "I'd forgotten how bleak it gets out here at night."

"You've lived here before?"

Darting a careful look back at her, he shrugged, hands in his pockets. "Oh, years back."

Mari bit her lip, whistling a low breath, glad for the shadows as she burned under her jacket. "We have matches." She carefully stepped past him, keeping him in her eyeline as Bear followed. The pup had gone oddly quiet. "We live across the field. At Kellers."

He fell into step with her as they walked side by side up the dirt path. Mari's sneaker caught on a knot in the road, and she stumbled, only to find his hands on her upper arms, steadying her. She snaked out of his grip, shaking her head. She realized she hadn't taken his hand when he'd offered it. "I'm sorry," she said with a reedy laugh, holding out her hand. "I didn't introduce myself. I'm Marianne Fox."

His lips pinched, a smile forming as he took her outstretched hand and shook it. She smiled. It'd been a while since she'd touched someone else.

"Marianne Fox," he repeated, like her name sounded good aloud. "Nice to meet you."

"Just Mari," she corrected him, her tone curt. "Come on—we're up here on the right."

The orange hue of the lamp flickered from her bedroom window as Bear darted ahead, ducking to sneak under the old chicken fence with a yip as he tore up the short drive. It was an impressive colonial farmhouse, and Mari's parents owned it for years before she and James came along. It used to be pristine, with whitewash cladding and a low-hanging porch roof. Ash smiled in admiration as they approached. "Always wondered who lived here. Looks so cozy."

"Just me," Mari said, clipped and tight as she nudged open the gate, the smell of honeysuckle fragrancing the air. "Me and my mom."

He didn't say anything, following her to the back door, and waves of apprehension tickled her neck. She didn't like turning her back on him; his footfalls were stealthy and silent on the gravel as she wound up the small path, where her rebellious hound waited with his rubber turkey in his mouth. Ash chuckled and ducked to his knees, scratching behind Bear's floppy ears.

Mari pursed her lips. Bear was a traitor and a flirt. *But* if he liked him, then Ash couldn't be too bad. Her hand paused on the door, casting the stranger a careful glance over her shoulder, the invite to come inside dying on her tongue. "I'll just be a minute."

Opening the door, she flung on the kitchen light, and Ash squinted. Mari rushed around the kitchen, looking through drawers, her hand closing around a bunch of candles tied with a cord. "Will these do?"

Ash lifted his chin. "That's great, thank you."

"Matches," she muttered, slamming and opening drawers. Flicking her eyes in his direction, she allowed an inch of guilt to creep in as he stood at the back door with his hands in his pockets. He didn't press to come in, and she wouldn't ask. There was a lingering scent of vodka in the air, and from the glare spilling into the hall, Mari guessed her mother was asleep on the couch.

"Meadowford is kind of a trek from here," he said, and she looked up at him in surprise. In roundabout way she guessed that was his attempt an icebreaker.

A smile fleetingly touched her lips. "I'm not in college if that's what you're asking." Stooping to the cupboard under the sink, she rifled through cleaning fluids and old rubber gloves.

Ash let out a short laugh, scratching the back of his neck. "Guess I'm not very subtle. Do you work in town…nearby?"

"From home," she answered, keen to shut this down wherever it was headed. "Are you in Meadowford?"

"Ah, no. I've not been in college for a long time…it's just me and my sister."

Though her curiosity piqued, she wasn't going to show it. Her face burned behind the cupboard door. This was coming close to an actual conversation, more words than she'd spoken aloud in a long time.

"How old is she?" Obligated, she asked the question. Standing straight, she caught him smiling, still stood on the doormat.

"Uh, about your age, seventeen."

Mari fought not to scowl. "I'm not seventeen."

"Oh—sorry. You look…" Embarrassed, he shuffled from foot to foot, a blotchy rash crossing the bridge of his nose.

"Young, yeah, I know," she said. "I'm not." She knew how baby-faced she was. It was the freckles on her nose, the roundness of her cheeks.

"Sorry." He held up his palms in defence. "I'm an idiot. I don't get out much."

Yeah, me, either.

"It's just me and Clover. It's been that way for a while." His smile dropped, and a melancholic look crossed his face, something sad and full of longing. "I'm about as transparent as glass." His lip quirked, as though his game was up. "I was prying—because you look around my sister's age, and she could do with the company. And it feels like the stars aligned when I saw you heading out with your dog earlier."

God, he's trying to set us up, like a grown-up play-date. Mari's palms burned with anxiety, her chest tightening. She slid open the cutlery drawer and mercifully saw the matches hiding in a cubby compartment at the back. She plucked the box out and handed it to him along with the bundle of candles.

"My sister kind of has…challenges," he gritted out, dropping the candles to his side like it was hard to talk about. "She doesn't go outside."

Mari didn't answer, and they locked eyes, waiting for him to continue.

"She *can't* go outside."

"Can't?"

"Yeah…have you heard of that illness? The one where sunlight hurts your skin?"

Mari didn't reply. She had heard of it. Maybe in a book? In one of her dad's old medical journals she'd kept for fact-checking.

"It has a longer, more technical name, but trust me, it's the worst. I've been her carer for, well…forever."

Forever. She knew something about forever. Visions of James's final days filtered back to her, the smell and the never-ending dark.

"I'm sorry," was all she could say. A stiff breeze crawled around her legs, reminding her it was growing late, and Bear needed a feed, and they were still standing at the backdoor.

Ash ran his tongue over his lip, weighing up his words. "I know we just met, but when I saw you out there…" He sighed heavily. "What are the chances of moving back here and finding a girl near her age across the field? If you ever feel like heading over and spending some time…"

Okay, enough is enough.

"I'm sorry," she mumbled, her hand fumbling for the door handle. Ash took a wide step back in surprise as she grabbed the door and pulled it inward. "Good night."

Locking the door, her fingers trembled as she fled the kitchen and switched off the light, leaving Ash Martin, her new neighbor, in darkness on the backdoor step.

THREE

With morning came the sun and a stream of emails from Eric overnight. Mari huffed as she opened the laptop, scanning through them with her glasses perched on the end of her nose.

She breathed a steady sigh of relief. Eric had a flare for drama, which often spilled into his notes and stories. Her lips curled in a smile when she read some of his feedback, rambling notes he'd written more for himself than her benefit.

Thumbing through, she got to one of the last emails he'd written at three am.

"You know, we really should make one of these meets in person. Could we do Zoom, or could I make the drive from Boston? It isn't too far, and I feel bad we've never met."

Mari clenched her teeth and closed the email. "Don't feel bad—I certainly don't."

She liked the vast, anonymous, cyberspace between her and her clients. The faceless aspect of this job suited her just fine, and no matter how much of a close and professional relationship she'd developed with them, she wasn't into meet-ups in cafes.

Treating herself to a few mindless minutes of scrolling through social media, she leaned her chin on her palm and thought of Ash Martin. Guilt tickled her conscience. Her gaze crept to the window, where rain rattled the thin pane of glass. Peering over the sill, she spotted her straw nemesis whirling in the pelting wind. A van had parked on the grass at the side of the road outside the old Rosewood Hall—an electric company van.

So maybe the building wasn't condemned after all? She fired up the search engine on her laptop, and it didn't take long to see the old hall's lease details online. Mari frowned, confused as to why anyone would *want* to live in there. It had to be a wreck inside.

Mari bit her lip. Maybe she'd been too hasty in shutting the door in his face last night? He'd been polite, after all, asking for a friend for his sister, for god sake. A knot in her belly tightened. Mari didn't need friends. She didn't need college, Eric Summers, or the extremely hot stranger and his sister across the field.

Bear wound between her legs, and she flicked to Eric's email, about to type a curt but polite and resolute thank you but *no thank you* when her screen flickered and went blank.

She stared at it dumbly for a few moments, as if it would magically blip back to life. But when it didn't, it was time for random button smashing. Fear held her in a cool grip as she impatiently flicked buttons and finally ducked under her desk to the plug socket. Then she looked at Bear.

"Are you kidding me?" she cried, dismayed at the chewed laptop wire. "Did you do this?"

He cocked his head, eyes shining with mischief as though he would answer. Mari took an even breath. Eric's changes needed a response, and another client was lined up for a consult. Chewing her lip, she paced the room, her choices blooming before her as she stepped into the hall. Outside, the wind rattled the doors, and the sky was thunderous and grey.

There were only two choices here. Either she went into town and bought a new cable or went into James's closed bedroom door and dug through his old stuff. The second option made her breath catch in her chest. When had he last slept in that bed?

Mari crossed the hall on wooden feet, her bravado slipping as she touched the door handle. The muscles in her hands seized, and she backed away, sweat beading on her lip.

She couldn't go in there. If she went into his room, she'd see his stuff, his discarded shoes. His laundry basket still full of soiled clothes. Then she'd be forced to remember.

"Is there gas in the truck?" she called as she jogged down the stairs. In the kitchen, her mother stood soundlessly over the stove.

"Are you leaving the house?" she asked, surprised and weary as she tightened her robe.

"Goddamn dog chewed my cable," Mari thundered, grabbing her coat from the rack. She stuffed her arms into the holes. "I can't work without it. Is there gas in the truck?"

It was pointless asking. Her mother hadn't driven since…Mari questioned when was the last time she'd driven. She took the keys from the pot on the mantle in the hall and fluffed her hair out of her coat. Spikes of apprehension hit her belly, and she paused before opening the door.

"I'll be an hour," she called over her shoulder, shielding her hair from the rain as she ran the short distance to the old red truck parked on the grass verge. It still smelled like tobacco in the cab, and she jammed the key in the ignition, praying the thing would start. It roared to life, and she smiled in relief, trundling out of the drive and onto the dirt track. Her gaze swept to Rosewood and the electrical truck still parked out front.

Slowing up, a pang of guilt hit her as she spotted lights on inside the house, the upper floor illuminated.

She can't go outside…

Would it be so bad to converse with another human being? Another human who wasn't her mother?

Driving past, Mari's eye caught a flicker of movement at one of the top windows, and something inside her stilled. A flash of white, too quick to process, and it was gone. A shudder rolled through her shoulders, and Mari couldn't imagine being stuck inside a place like that with no one to talk to.

Speeding out of the drive, Mari clicked on the radio and daydreamed while driving to Lincoln, parking the truck near the old town museum. Hudson's tech sat on the corner, and Mari did a speedy job of getting in and out as fast as possible. Inside, it smelled like new carpet and cables, walls lined with the latest computers and phones.

"Is someone chasing you?" the clerk joked as he swiped her card on the machine. He was about thirty, with a round, wholesome face, and Mari glanced up in surprise.

"Excuse me?"

He laughed it off, shrugging as he slid her replacement cable into a carrier. "You keep looking over your shoulder."

A short and breathy laugh stuttered and died on her lips before her mouth turned down. "Thanks for your help."

"Hope you get home safely."

She was about halfway to the door when he said it, and her shoulders hunched. When she looked at him in confusion, he pointed to the shop window and the leaden sky outside. "The storm?" he prompted.

"Oh…" Mari hadn't checked her phone. She had no idea a storm was heading their way. "Yes. Thanks, you too."

Her hands gripped the wheel as she climbed back into the truck. Peering over the dash, she assessed the sky, heavy with grey clouds. When a few raindrops hit the windshield, she turned on the wipers and headed out of town. The back roads from Lincoln to Winstone tended to flood, and the Grenfell river banks sometimes spilled over toward Mickleford. Glancing at the dash, she spotted the fuel gauge, and her heart sank. She tapped the glass, hoping the needle might move. Had it been low when she left home?

"Shit," she muttered, the engine sluggish as she drove out of Lincoln, hitting the quiet, rural back roads. Hank's garage was up ahead, and her heart vaulted, fear creeping up her neck as the sign appeared just as the heavens opened. Sheets of rain plummeted from the sky, bouncing off the dash, and the wipers worked frantically. Mari pulled into the station and hopped out, the soft toes of her canvas shoes absorbing rain.

Looking over her shoulder, she sensed relief that no attendants seemed to be on duty, proba-bly all inside, hiding from the rain. She grabbed for the Diesel spout when a shadow moving inside the gas station caught her eye. She dropped the handle, her arms going slack.

The blonde hair piled up in a shabby top knot caught her gaze, and when the girl turned and they locked eyes, Mari saw the familiar flash of blue. Throat knotting, Mari bolted for the cab as Zara bounded for the shop door. "Mari—*wait!*"

Shaking and wet, Mari strapped in and started the engine, pulling away as Zara ran to keep up with her. Her best friend hammered on the passenger's window with her fist, her fine, blonde brows pulled in a scowl. "Mari, what the hell is wrong with you?" she yelled through the glass. "Talk to me."

Her arms were like jelly on the wheel, sweat slick on her palms as she roughly shoved the truck into drive. The engine roared as she pulled away, leaving her old friend in front of the station, gaping at her open-mouthed.

"It's okay," she whispered, glancing at the rearview mirror, Zara's shape fading like a ghost in the rain.

Something was wrong with the truck, and Mari seriously regretted her rapid decision to flee the gas station without gas. The roads were bumpy and wet, and rain pounded the windshield. Inside the cab, it was stuffy, and Mari's phone lay on the passenger seat, the signal as bleak as the weather.

"Shit," she muttered for the second time. *What the hell is wrong with you?* Slapping the wheel with her palms, she shook her head miserably as the car sped through the storm, trundling over potholes. Up ahead, to her surprise, she spotted a guy in running gear. Yellow and black lycra.

Okay, he's a little crazy. Slowing down, she carefully pulled alongside him, catching his eye. He was distracted, ear buds in, red-faced and sweaty as he ran, his hood pulled over curly brown hair. Mari bit her lip. She didn't have to talk to him, but he was heading into no man's land. Once she passed the turn-off for Mickleford, it was nothing but fields and meadows for miles.

She wound down the window, slowing the truck. "You shouldn't be out here," she cried over the engine drone and the rain. "It gets pretty bad out here and if the Grenfell River floods…"

The guy made a face, indicated to his earbuds, and yanked them so they dandled around his neck. "Huh?"

Mari tutted in exasperation "Turn *back,* it's too wet to be out here running."

Impatience and stress made it come out more sharply than she intended and he didn't seem to be taking her seriously. "I'm nearly done—a couple more miles—but thanks."

Mari flushed, annoyed he'd brushed her off. This guy clearly wasn't a local, because otherwise he'd be indoors right now, like she should be. "Don't go further than the Mickleford turnoff. There's nothing out there."

He smiled thinly, humoring her, but she wasn't sure why she'd bothered. She wouldn't be so keen to talk to a stranger next time, even if he was an idiot who would likely end up in a ditch. Winding up the window, she pulled away, a sense of fear eating at her conscience as she watched his shape get smaller in the mirror.

The old battered sign for the colonial town of Mickleford approached on her left, and she turned in the other direction, praying the old truck would have enough fuel to make it another ten minutes.

Tension crowded her shoulders, making her neck ache as she thought of Zara. She hadn't seen her since the night after Halloween last year. Briefly allowing her lids to flutter shut, she suppressed the memory of that night. It'd been the last night she'd seen James laugh and she recalled the hangover the following day and the mud on her knees. Memories of that night were fragmented, and she blamed the alcohol. She'd woken up outside, in the cold.

The engine lurched, sputtered, and died, everything dulling to a quiet hum in the cab, with the rain pounding the roof. "Oh—crap." This was happening. She'd run the truck dry. Staring at the key idiotically, as though it'd suddenly spring back to life, Mari sniffed and pressed the heels of her hands to her eyes.

Do not cry. She didn't have time to wallow in self-pity, even though every part of her wanted to curl up and sob. *Goddam Bear.* This was his fault for chewing the cable.

Mari was about a ten-minute jog from home, and even then, she'd have to pray the Grenfell River hadn't burst its banks. It usually swept away the dirt track, leaving a boggy causeway from the main road to the farmhouse.

Gritting her teeth, she pulled up her hood, grabbed the cable and her phone, and left the truck on the grass. Cold air turned icy in her lungs as she ran, shielding her head with her arms. Water soaked the hem of her jeans, and she was drenched within minutes, the rain sticking her hair to her head.

This was a disaster, and she made a mental note never to leave the house again. She'd not even had the chance to respond to Eric, leaving him on read all morning, impatiently waiting for her feedback. Slipping on loose, wet stone, Mari's ankle twisted, and she cried out in pain, a sharp, burning agony sprawling up her calf. Hobbling, she gritted her teeth and dragged her sorry ass to the well-concealed turnoff for the farm. She only got a few yards before her sneaker sank ankle-deep in mud, and she feared the track was washed away, leaving the farmhouse looking like a ship at sea, floating on a mud tide.

Gripping her hoodie around her face, she fumbled for her phone, her thumbs slipping on the touch screen. She glanced up at their house, wondering if her mother had noticed she'd not come back. She tried to dial as a bolt of lightning zigzagged across the sky.

"Marianne!" a voice called from behind. "Marianne Fox!"

Trudging in the direction the voice had come, Marianne thought her humiliation was complete. Ash Martin waved frantically from the porch of Rosewood, peering at her through the trees like she was a lunatic. "Get over here!"

Pain throbbed in her ankle, and she bit back tears taking a few steps before she slipped, sinking to her ass in the mud. Ash sprinted off the porch, shielding his head as he jogged through the trees.

A cold sweat broke on her back, her breath hitching as he reached her side, sinking into the mud beside her. "Why the hell are you out in the middle of a storm?"

As though all the muscles in her face had frozen, any attempt she could make for a good reason died the moment he cradled her injured ankle in his hand. Wet, blonde hair fell in his eyes, rain dripping down his face. Daylight turned his eyes hazel, framed by dark, thick lashes. Mari grabbed his shoulder and bit her lip in agony when he pressed her skin.

He winced. "It's swollen up like a grapefruit. Did you walk on this?"

"Hmm," she hummed in pain, and then, to her horror, he scooped her off the ground in one fluid motion as though she weighed nothing. Humiliation complete, she hid her face in her jacket as Ash cast his eyes to her house on the brow of the hill. He shook his head. "I don't think we should risk the mud." Face inches from hers, his breath fogged as their eyes collided, and he laughed, his face creasing adorably. "We'll both be stranded."

"Well…I…"

"I'll take you indoors." He gestured to the old manor with a bob of the chin, and she went cold. Her face must have betrayed her because he laughed.

"Don't worry, we've got light and heat," he said. "Stay with us till this storm passes."

"Okay," she said, with no other choice ahead of her. Cradled in his arms, Ash carried her bridal style through the deep, draping willows, his feet hitting the gravel path that led to the wide oak door of one of the oldest homes in Winstone.

She gripped the back of his hood, and he gave her a reassuring smile.

"Welcome," he said, carrying her sorry state through the doors of Rosewood Hall.

FOUR

It smelled of church, like dead flowers and wilting lilies, abandoned in a chapel after a wedding. The scent hit the back of Mari's nose, and she sneezed into her cocked elbow, one arm gripping the back of Ash's shirt.

"Sorry," she mumbled, even though the cloying scent of florals made her nose itch and urged her to rub her eyes. Rain pounded the porch, and Ash kicked the heavy oak double doors shut with his toe.

Embers from the fire in the large hall spilled across the room, casting a rusty glow. Mari looked over his shoulder at the peeling wallpaper revealing rotted, damp plaster, and the dust sheets draped to conceal old, musty furniture.

The hall went all the way up, right to the tall rafters, revealing a large, poorly patched hole in the roof, where drips of rain fell from the heavens and leaves fell through the gap, drifting to the floor and making a pile. Ash nodded to the staircase, heavy oak banisters leading up to the first floor, and a wide galleried landing. "You're freezing. You could catch a chill."

Mari sneezed again, opening her mouth to tell him it was only the heavy fragrance in the air. What was it? Jasmine? Roses? Either way, it reminded her of death and funerals. Briefly closing her eyes, she snapped them open as he ascended the stairs, cradling her like she weighed nothing.

Blushing hotly, she stammered, "I can probably make it, seriously—you don't have to—"

"Have you seen your ankle?" he remarked, and she shut up. Carrying her across the hall, over a faded rug, smashed-out windows caught her eye.

Ash noticed her looking. "Kids," he said, rolling his eyes and heaving her through a bedroom door. "Leave a place empty for too long, and exploring this old place becomes a fun game."

Candles lit the bedroom, and Mari wondered where the lamps were. Hadn't the electric board been there only today?

"It's all too damp," he said, answering her unspoken thought. "We have to dry everything out."

Water pelted the thin pane of glass of the window overlooking the front of the house and its view across the field. "A great big hole in the roof isn't going to help," Mari said as he set her down on the edge of a plush bed. It was dark wood, a sleigh bed with heavy navy sheets. Running her hand over the satin, she shivered. Ash made a face. "I'll get you one of my sister's robes—wait here." He paused at the door, giving her a wry smile. "No running off."

Mari quirked a brow, an amused smile on her mouth despite her situation. She nodded at her ankle. "Couldn't if I wanted to."

Okay, this hurts. She gritted her teeth and hissed when he'd closed the door, easing up the hem of her wet jeans to reveal the damage. The skin was swollen and hot and an unpleasant mauve. "Damn," she muttered as the door opened, and he was back with something white and silky over his arm.

"Here," he said, laying the robe in her lap. "Leave your wet things over the chair. The fire will dry them out." Mari noticed the ornate mantle piece, the focal point of the grand bedroom. It was chipped stone, dusty, and lit by two candles burning low. The fire crackled in the grate, and the heat felt good on her damp skin.

"I take it you don't need any help."

Mari looked at her feet, biting her lip in embarrassment. "No, I'll manage."

The moment he closed the door, she shuffled to her feet and squeezed out of her wet jeans, folding them and putting them on the back of the chair. Her pink fingers ached as she quickly unbuttoned her shirt, weaving into the robe, thankful it was warm.

Jasmine.

She sniffed the fabric, and there it was again. Settling in the chair, she turned it to the fire and plopped back down, stretching her calves and wiggling her toes. She winced in pain. Something outside caught her eye, falling leaves pelting the glass. From here, she had a near-perfect view of their farmhouse. It sat, nestled on the brow of the hill. She could even see the lights in the living room while the rest remained in darkness. It struck her how lonely it looked, cold and isolated from this grand old bedroom in Rosewood, that she'd looked upon all her life.

How was it possible this old place felt warmer? When it'd sat empty and neglected for years, it had a hole in the roof and drafts coming in through smashed windows.

Mr. Raggerty, ever-present, whirled in the wind. His spindly plaid body spun on the pole, and he turned directly to face her, almost as if he'd spotted her up here. She shuddered.

"It looks like you have a stalker," Ash said beside her. She jumped in fright, letting out a shaky laugh.

"Sorry," he said, handing her a ceramic mug full of coffee. "Bad habit." His eyes landed on Mr. Raggerty again. "It's almost like he's watching you."

Mari snorted. "Don't even make jokes about that—he's given me nightmares for years. My brother used to—" She snapped her lips shut, and if Ash noticed, which she was sure he had, he cleared his throat instead.

"Do you know his story?" Ash said, his hazel eyes alive and teasing as he pulled up a chair beside her and laughed at her confused expression.

"Hmm, he started life as a pile of hay?" she joked. Mr. Raggerty had always been there for as long as she could remember.

"My grandpa used to tell me a story." Ash linked his long fingers around his mug as it rested on his knees. "About the *old* Rosewoods .Tobias was the second in line to inherit this old place, and was forced into an arranged marriage to keep him in line. This was back in the 1800s. There was a rumor he was a complete womanizer and was having an affair with a woman in Mickleford. You've heard of the Mickleford Witches, right?"

Mari nodded gently, intrigued. She'd grown up here, and everyone knew the stories about Mickleford. It was supposedly the real Salem, where actual witchcraft took place. "I think you'd have to go a long way before meeting someone who didn't know about that story."

They were two sisters, and the eldest killed eight men. She was hung in Cedar Wood, one of the neighboring towns, but the younger one vanished, and was never seen alive again.

"Well, old Toby liked to court a bit of danger. He liked a party and often threw them here, drinking and causing havoc, the usual over indulgence—he was having an affair with the witch, the one who was hung. Things got a little intense, and she wanted more—like for him to kick out his wife and kid and move *her* in." He looked away, almost a little uncomfortable. "She claimed she'd lost a baby—*his* baby and that's when things started to get too much for Toby, especially as his wife was expecting again. Before he could break it off, when the rumors began to spread...he vanished, never to be seen again."

Ash licked his lips, chuckling as Mari's eyes bugged. "Nice guy! Was he one of the eight she killed?"

"No...he just went missing. But then, oddly enough...guess who showed up in the field the day after he disappeared?"

They locked eyes for a long beat before Ash broke into a laugh, and Mari let out a relieved sigh. "Are you kidding me?"

"You should see your face," he teased, grabbing a small vial out of his pocket and getting down on his knees in front of her. "It's a good story, right?"

Mari shifted in the chair. Her spine straightened as he took her injured ankle and drew it into his lap. "Your grandpa certainly had a dark sense of humor."

Ash narrowed his eyes, took her swollen ankle, and lay it carefully on a towel. Mari wasn't damp and cold anymore. Suddenly, her skin was alive and covered in goosebumps. "It's halfway true…but the guy on the pole has been restuffed several times since the 1800s."

She let out a shaky laugh as he tipped a dark oily substance into his palms, briskly running them together and then laying his hands on her skin. She flinched, and he smiled up at her kindly.

"We don't have ice in the house…but my sister made this. She's good at the botanical stuff."

"Oh," she breathed as he massaged it gently into her skin. Her toes clamped, and he looked up sharply.

"Am I hurting you?"

"No," she answered honestly. He wasn't. Her skin felt warm and tingly.

He rubbed the oil in circles, and she watched him work, his long fingers on her skin. His lashes were so dark and long, they cast shadows under his eyes.

"Where is she?" Mari asked, looking over her shoulder as the fire burned low and crackled. She was so warm, so numb, she could almost drift off to sleep. The wind howled against the pane of glass, and she let her shoulders slump.

"Oh," he said. "She's in the ballroom… maybe even the Library. Then, at Twilight, she'll head to the orangery."

It sounded like something out of a period drama or something Eric might write. She winced inwardly, remembering his notes and unanswered emails and how utterly out of kilter her day had become. She raised a brow curiously. "Twilight?"

"Yes." He looked up, eyes stormy. "She has a condition called Icaria Disorder. It's a rare blood disorder…"

"Yes, you said I'm sorry," she interrupted, shaking her head sleepily, the deep, earthy scent of the oil making her drowsy. "I forgot. It's a sun allergy, right?"

"Hmm. It's severe. It's more than an allergy. There's nothing we've ever found to make it any better. It's just better that we stay out of the way. We lived in an Alaskan town near the Northern Hemisphere…you know…"

Mari nodded. "The one that only has a few hours of daylight." It made sense. She could have some kind of existence.

"Yeah, but Clover had no life there, no real friends. So my boss was happy to let me transfer here so I could work from home." His voice strained, and he faltered before clearing his throat. "I found out this old place still sat empty all these years later. And here it's dark and big. With so many unused rooms, she can have for herself. It was perfect."

Mari thought *he* was kind of perfect, gazing down at him with heat rising in her chest. He was gentle and loved his sister. And his hands on her skin were making her warm in other places. "Apart from the big hole in the roof."

Ash laughed. "That's tomorrow's job."

"What do you do for work?" It sounded so strange to ask out loud, so long since she'd met anyone new. Ash blew out air like he was about to bore her to tears.

"Data analyst for a food tech company." He rolled his eyes. "I know—so interesting. I look at data, and report on it. That's about it."

"Well, I work from home too," she piped up. "I fact-check, and proofread for writers."

He laughed. "Now that *actually* sounds interesting."

"The guy I work for is pretty interesting, me not so much. I think I annoy him most of the time."

"I can't imagine you annoying anyone." Their eyes locked, and he carefully withdrew his hands. "How's that feel?"

"Better," she admitted, easing it to the floorboards to put weight on it. It hardly hurt at all, just a dull ache.

"You want to come down and meet Clover?" he asked. "Like I said, she's about your age and dying to talk to someone who *isn't* me."

Mari nodded keenly, allowing him to link an arm around her waist. Blushing, she looked away, her eyes drawn to the rattly glass window, and Mr. Raggerty watching from the windswept field. "I'd love to."

He nodded to leave her clothes to dry, helping her to the door. The dark hall was lit by glowing wall sconces, their flickering light casting eerie shadows over the cobwebbed ceiling. Mari clung to his arm, finding whatever potion Ash had massaged in her ankle; it was miraculous. When they reached the mouth of the staircase, the faint tinkling of a piano greeted them out of the gloom. Light spilled from the hole in the roof, along with falling leaves and droplets of rain.

"That's Clover," Ash mentioned as he helped her down the stairs. "She loves to play."

Mari's mouth dried up. Recognizing Hubert's symphony, the piano's keys were sharp and brittle, like it needed tuning. They edged around the puddle, murky rainwater dotted with golden leaves, and Ash leaned her on the wall to fling open the double doors, revealing an expansive ballroom.

It was like something she'd seen in a book; opulent and decadent. The room was draped in deep maroon velvet, with old rosewood paneling lining the walls and floor-to-ceiling windows. The floor gleamed with polish, untouched by rot or damage. The music from the piano swelled, and a girl appeared out of the gloom—a pale girl in a white ruffled nightgown with long, blonde ringlets.

Mari wanted to tell him that she thought this was magical; and the girl at the piano, with her small, pretty, face pinched in concentration, was like something out of a dream. But all of the words died on her lips.

As the girl noticed them watching, she looked up, the music rising, chasing to the finale. On top of the piano sat a small gold music box, with a ballerina in a white fluffy tutu of feathers twirling along as she played. It looked like an antique, and the tinkling music sounded tinny, like it'd been unused for years.

Clover met Mari's gaze; all she could think of was how small the girl was; delicate and fragile like a little trapped bird. It sparked something in her chest, something she'd not felt for a long time. Longing, like she'd want to protect her forever, and for some unknown reason, tears sparked in her eyes, unsure where this burst of emotion was coming from.

She glanced at Ash, who gazed fondly at his sister, and she took his wrist to grab his attention.

"What happens to her?" Mari whispered urgently. "What happens to her in the light?"

Ash's expression drew grim, his mouth pinched, and eyes haunted, lost. The music stopped abruptly.

"She burns," he said. "She burns alive."

FIVE

She burns…

Mari swallowed, her throat parched, and she wished she'd drank the coffee Ash had handed her a while back. Cold seeped through her bones, but as the young girl approached, gliding over the polished wood, her long nightgown whispering as it swept over the floor, it was impossible not to return her smile.

Clover Martin was hypnotic; her eyes glassy and wide with an almost golden chestnut hue and flecks of golden amber. Framed by long dark lashes, she looked similar to her older brother, but her hair was two shades lighter. Her bleached wheat locks falling in brushed-out waves down her back.

Her pale pink lips parted in a smile, lifting her already hollow cheekbones. Dark shadows swept below her eyes, and Mari wondered if this was the result of the sickness. The strange allergy to sunlight she'd only briefly heard of before. As their eyes met, Clover's smile dropped.

"You're cold," she said, her eyes darting to the goosebumps on Mari's bare forearms. She looked sharply at her brother. "You could have gotten her more than a silk robe."

Ash rubbed his chin thoughtfully. "We haven't fully unpacked, Clo. It was all I could find."

"It's fine," Mari insisted, waving off her concern. She was flushed with embarrassment. Her feet were pink, cold, and bare. She must look dreadful, especially if her hair had frizzed in the rain. "I should probably leave soon."

Clover's eyes clouded with disappointment. "How's your ankle?"

It was the first time since walking into this ballroom that she'd paid attention to her ankle. Testing it with her weight, she winced slightly, but it was nowhere near the dull throbbing ache that had left her unable to walk. "Well, whatever you did—it worked a treat. You should bottle it and sell that stuff."

Clover beamed, looking at her brother with eyes shining full of appreciation. Like a little girl who was told her dress was the prettiest at the dance, it made Mari warm to her more. Ash smiled wistfully, nodding his head. "The worst of the storm has passed, so I can walk you home—"

"Wait—I can show you where I make my potions." Clover blushed. "I mean…my remedies. I know they're not *potions*, but I sometimes pretend they are. I don't…." She breathed out a small laugh. "I don't get out much."

The three of them exchanged an awkward laugh, and Mari couldn't fight her rising anxiety. This was the longest she'd been out of the house in…forever. She wondered if her mother was even awake or noticed she was missing. One little soul in the house would've missed her. Bear would be desperate for a walk by now.

Despite that, her curiosity won out, compelled by the shadowy corners of the house, begging to be explored. Her gaze caught an old oil painting down the far end of the hall, and her brow rose. It'd been covered with a black veil, masking the subject beneath. This was like a place out of Eric's books. "I'd love to see where you make them."

"Great!" Clover burst with excitement. "It's this way…off the ballroom."

Ash made a face at Mari, a brotherly, don't encourage her face, but Mari made one back. "Whatever you're growing, it smells amazing."

Clover pirouetted on her bare feet excitedly before taking Mari's hand. "That's the Jasmine you can smell," she explained. "It's night-blooming."

Clover's palm closed around hers, and something in Mari froze. Like a fragment of ice had touched her heart. Clover's hand was bone cold and thin, her skin like paper against hers. Like there was no blood rushing through her veins or even a heart to make it pump under her skin.

Mari tensed and instantly tried to brush it off. It was reading all of Eric's spooky manuscripts. It'd gotten to her.

She pulled away to hide her reaction, shoving her hands under her armpits and feigning a shiver, hoping Clover or Ash hadn't noticed. By the strange look Ash tossed her, Mari guessed he might have. "It's this way," Clover chimed, skipping ahead and throwing open double doors.

Mari watched in interest as Clover backed against a wooden paneled wall and tiptoed around a pool of light touching the floor as it spilled through an open drape. Ash ran ahead, holding his sister back with one arm as he yanked the drape closed, sending motes of dust flying into the air.

"It's a cloudy day," Clover complained, and he shook his head.

"Not until Twilight, Clo."

Pouting, Clover waved Mari across the room, where the smell got stronger, and her nose started to itch. She sneezed, and it echoed to the rafters.

"Sorry."

"It's fine. Are you allergic? Because that might be a problem," Clover asked.

Mari's heart jumped a little. "Uh, not usually." She stepped over the threshold into a vast, lofty, Victorian orangery. Her eyes raked skyward, where ladders led to a second galleried floor, vines covering every metal railing on a rickety spiral staircase. She gasped—no wonder she was sneezing. It was covered in foliage. Flowers were crowding in every available space, and moss was overtaking the stone floor. Bursts of white, pink and yellow filled her vision, curling across every surface. It clearly hadn't been cared for in years; wildly overgrown, and ruinously beautiful.

"This is incredible," she breathed, becoming used to the scent, finding it no longer tickled the back of her throat. Every corner she looked at was filled with roots, as well as pots spilling with blooms and vines crawling to the light. It was like something out of a fairytale. Above, the light had been sealed by two enormous blinds.

"At night, we can open them and see the stars." Clover grinned. "And the smell is amazing. I can go outside then. Where I plant the night-blooming flowers."

"There's so much." Mari gazed at a huge oak apothecary table set up with old papers and books stacked high. On the countertop stood hundreds of vials filled with oils and creams. A massive cork board was littered with notes, recipes and botanical illustrations.

Clover skipped around it. "It's a hobby."

"An expensive one," Ash joked.

"Botany?" Mari asked, her senses overwhelmed, too busy nosing around tumbledown pits. Ruined urns overflowing with ivy. A flower with small white petals garnished the stairwell that led to the gallery above. This was the jasmine she could smell.

"What kind of plants do you have in here?" Mari asked in awe.

"A bit of everything," Clover said as Mari sank onto a plush red velvet chaise. She fanned herself, sweat beading on the base of her spine. It was humid, and her nose was draining. "I gave Ash an oil blend of geranium, black pepper, Jasmine, and sage to help with your ankle."

Mari lifted the hem of the robe, her toes nearly normal size. She smiled at Clover, who slipped in beside her on the chaise. "Like magic," she said.

Clover sparkled when she laughed, or rather, the air tinkled around her. It was a pretty sound and made her face look less drawn when light hit her eyes. Clover inched into place, and Ash cleared his throat.

"I'll just go see what state the roads are in now," he said, hands deep in pockets as he turned on his heels, aiming to get them both alone to talk. Mari watched him go, the heavy stoop of his shoulders, eyeing his defined back and shoulders. Clover was staring at her so intently that she flinched when she eventually tore her eyes away.

"He's always trying to get me to make new friends," she said wistfully. "When he told me we'd moved in across the way from someone my age, he was excited." She licked parched lips. "He worries."

"He's sweet," Mari agreed, wishing James had possessed a fingernail width of Ash's gallantry. "How old are you?"

"Seventeen." Clover edged nearer, and Mari could see every speck in her eyes. Too close, and she stilled her breath. There was a scent, something she couldn't make out—airborne one minute and then gone, masked by the closing Jasmine.

Mari tilted her head. "I'm nineteen—twenty in a few weeks."

Clover's face crumpled in disappointment. "Oh."

"That doesn't matter, though," Mari jumped in, eager to wipe the melancholy off her face. "I don't get out much, either— as you can probably tell."

"Aren't you in school? Or work?"

"I work from home…I dropped out of college six months ago."

Clover didn't pry, but the silence she left between them made Mari start to sweat, making her want to fill the void. Her words stuck. "My brother died."

"Oh," Clover gasped. "That's so sad. How did it happen?"

"He had a rare type of bone cancer—it was over fast. But since then, I dropped out to take care of my mom. She hasn't really…."

Noticed I'm still there…

"It hit her hard," Mari admitted, swallowing a lump, recalling the blonde, bubbly woman who'd brought her up and the shadow of a person she'd faded into.

Clover gripped her hand, surprisingly strong for someone who looked like she couldn't climb a flight of stairs. That bone cold chilled her again like icy veins threading through her blood. "Of course it did. She lost her son…and so fast. What was he like?"

Mari huffed out a shaky laugh. "James? Well…"

Her heart thundered, and her temple spiked with pain, a dull throb rushing down her neck. She blinked dizzily, remembering the taste of Whiskey sours and how it burned going down. And wet, sludgy mud clung to her boots so she could hardly run.

"Are you alright?" Clover asked, alarmed. The girl brushed a strand of hair out of Mari's eyes and she finally came back to clarity. Whatever that was, it was over.

"Sorry, I'm fine," she said, a little unnerved. "I must be tired."

"You were going to tell me about your brother, James?"

Mari looked up, meeting Clover's eyes, twinkling and glossy in the dimmed glow of the orangery. Her cheeks were almost rosy, and Mari wondered if it was the room's heat. Maybe the plants and the aromas did Clover some good.

"Well…he was twenty-one," she said. "A football player, not studious—not like me at all. My mom used to say you'd never believe we were related. He was blonde and athletic, and he liked a prank…"

Clover looked keenly interested. "I bet he was good looking…did he have a girlfriend?"

Mari's heart thundered under her robe.

"Mari, what the hell is wrong with you?"

"Mari?"

Her eyes snapped up. "Uh, yeah, he was pretty cute, as far as brothers go."

God, it was stifling in here. Mari wasn't sure if it was the greenhouse warmth or the hundreds of candles, but she was sure she'd need a shower when she got home.

"I couldn't imagine what I'd do without Ash," Clover said, pretending she hadn't noticed Mari's stuttering response. "He's my world."

"We weren't close," Mari said, her bluntness surprising her. "James could be cruel sometimes and….he had a temper. But I loved him, of course. He was my flesh and blood." Mari smiled, trying to wipe away that sad look on Clover's face again. "Your brother came to my rescue like a knight in shining armor. My brother would've tricked me into the mud and then watched me sink....before he'd finally take pity on me."

He could be cruel...

"Every family is different, I suppose," Clover mulled it over as though sibling rivalry was something she couldn't comprehend. However, it'd never been the rivalry between James and Marianne that divided them. You couldn't rival what you couldn't touch. They'd been set on different courses since birth, and sometimes, she wondered if her mother wished she was the one who died. "Do you miss him?"

Can you miss pain?

"Of course," Mari said, feeling like she was lying when she wasn't. Of course she missed him, he was her blood, her brother. In a way, he was still in the house; his essence, his smell. Living in the darkened rooms of their farmhouse, Mari felt like he'd not gone. Abruptly, Clover rose from the chaise, her nightgown tumbling down as she walked. She dashed to her workbench and plucked a tinned candle from a pile. She unscrewed the cap and gave it to Mari, who immediately sniffed it.

"Oh, wow, that's good!"

Clover grinned. "It's Frankincense, Jasmine, and lemon—it'll be good to clear your home of old, tired energy. Frankincense is a spiritual oil."

"And Jasmine?"

Clover burst out laughing. "I have a lot of it." She waved her hand at the tendril draped over the stairwell. "As you can see. But it's a good one for lots of ailments. I make them and if you promise to come back and see me, you can have as many as you want."

They both laughed, and Mari's shoulders relaxed. "You don't need to bribe me to come back."

Clover took her hand, and this time, to Mari's surprise, it was warm, like the girl's pulse suddenly burst to life. Her expression darkened. "I get the feeling you've been hiding away in that farmhouse for a while," Clover said, and Mari couldn't help the involuntary gulp she took. Clover shrugged. "And it's not like I'm going anywhere…I can only make so many potions before I go bonkers. I'd love you to come back."

When Mari didn't respond instantly, she blurted. "And it's not like we'll be living like this forever…I swear we're going to hire a decorator."

"You do have a massive hole in the roof," Mari agreed.

"And it's not only me who gets bored…Ash is your age, although sometimes you'd think he was fifty with his overbearing attitude."

Mari blushed. The thought of seeing him more regularly wasn't unappealing. He appeared as though he'd been mind-summoned, his long legs taking vast strides as he crossed the room. He had her jeans and shirt draped over his forearm. He fanned himself. "How you don't suffocate in here is a mystery," he joked, turning his hazel eyes on Mari. "The road looks clear, and your things are dry…not that you have to leave…"

Mari stood, swaying a little, heady from the heat and blood pumping in her cheeks. "I really ought to get home. But thank you so much."

Clutching the candle, she scuttled after Ash, who showed her to a side room to change. Mari wondered how many little rooms were hidden away from corridors. This one was a small wood-paneled room, with one portrait hung at the rear end of it. It was windowless and dark, and once again, as Mari hurried into her clothes, she spotted a black, filmy veil covering the painting's subject. Zipping up her hoodie, she took a step nearer, itching to see the painting beneath, but Ash's voice at the door distracted her.

"Everything okay?" he asked as she opened the door.

Smiling, she handed him back the robe, surprised as he made to follow her. "What are you doing?"

"Walking you home," he said with a wink. Mari snorted out a laugh.

"It's across the corn! I think I can make it."

Ash had a twinkle of mischief deep in his hazel eyes, and she went beat red. "I don't like how that scarecrow looked at you."

Flustered, she peered over his shoulder, catching the shape of Clover scuttling through the darkened hall, head bowed as her feet moved soundlessly up the grand staircase. Mari frowned, watching her flee, and seconds later, a door banged upstairs.

"Is she okay?"

Ash showed her to the front door. "It takes it out of her—she loses energy quickly. In a few hours, she'll be back down, fussing with her flowers and repotting something. But meeting you today has made her year, trust me."

SIX

"You can lean on me if you need to," Ash said as a blast of cool air hit Mari's chest. She drank it in with relief, cooling her red-hot skin. The mid-afternoon sun, now burning away storm clouds, shone off his hair as they walked side by side.

Something about his expression convinced her that she could lean on him, not only physically. Strong, dependable, in a good way. Not in a brotherly way like Clover relied on him. That wasn't what made her warm.

"Thanks." She gave her ankle a test. "It's much better."

Leading her through a thicket of trees that spanned the perimeter of the Rosewood estate, he held back a sapling branch with his arm and motioned her ahead. The road between the corn fields was still wet and slick with mud, and Ash grabbed for her arm. She chuckled. "Careful, I might take you down with me."

His hand folded around hers, and it was warm. "I'll risk it."

She smiled, feeling giddy, and realized she probably looked a little goofy. It'd been too long without anyone to talk to, and casting her eye over at Rosewood in the distance, it suddenly didn't look so cold and uninviting, now she'd met the inhabitants.

They reached her porch steps, careful not to slip on wet, leaves on the wood. She climbed the steps and looked down at him. "It looks like no one's home," he commented, like he was vaguely concerned. "All the lights are off."

"Oh. My mom is in there. We just keep it dark, that's all." When he frowned, she clicked her tongue, rushing to make an excuse. "Money saving and all that."

"Ah." He nodded, unconvinced, as his gaze raked the house from top to bottom. It made her anxiety rise, prickling at her chest. He was looking too closely, and that wasn't a good thing. Now, she itched to get inside.

"Thank you." She clutched the candle. "And say thanks again to Clover for this—it's really sweet of her."

He smiled. "She does have a talent." His knitted thoughtfully. "Perhaps you'll come back to see her?"

A wave of heat hit her, and she didn't want to blush. She wished her body wasn't so treacherous, reacting like a teenager with a crush. "Only her?"

He looked down, shrugging. "I'd love to see you again." He cast a glance at the farmhouse behind her. "But I have a feeling when you close that door, something grabs hold of you and doesn't let go. I'd like to know who or what kind of power it has over you."

No one had ever spoken to her like that before. "I don't know what you mean."

He looked at her for a long time, too long, and Mari fumbled with the candle, fidgeting with her hands. It was clear he was waiting for her to fill the void.

"My mom needs me."

"Maybe," he said, tilting his head thoughtfully, glancing at Mr. Raggerty, who looked limp and soggy after the storm. Strings of hay hung loosely from his shirt sleeves, making it look like his fingers clawed the ground. When he glanced back at her, she averted her eyes, shining with tears.

"Are you alright, Mari?"

She sniffed hard. "I'm fine—it's allergies."

"No." His tone made her glance up. "I mean…are you alright? In *there?*"

"I'm fine," she lied, even though the truth must be emblazoned all over her face. "I don't know what you're talking about."

"I live in the dark because I have to protect Clover. I feel the darkness is protecting you in there, and you use it like a shield."

Flushed, the truth burned on her tongue, and her words got stuck and thick with emotion.

When was the last time someone asked if she was okay?

"In the end, my brother couldn't stand the light," she stuttered, her anger rising. Who did he think he was, giving her an on-the-spot analysis? He didn't *know* her. "It physically made him sick, with the cancer treatment...so we turned off the lights....and..."

We didn't switch them back on.

"I get it. You do what you have to for those you love." A sad smile crossed his lips, and he jerked his chin at Rosewood. "If you light the candle, leave it in the window...and I'll do the same. I'll see it and know you're okay."

She laughed sadly. "From over there? You'd see it."

"You'd be surprised how far light travels," he said. "If I see it burning in the window, at least I know you're not completely alone in there."

"I'm not on my own," she insisted, although her heart felt numb. And the thought of stepping back into enforced darkness made her skin crawl. The familiar sound of Bear scratching at the porch door made her smile and nodded in his direction. "See?"

"I know…your mouth is saying one thing…but your eyes say another." He looked away like he could no longer stand it, as though the sight of her made him unhappy. She narrowed her eyes, letting out a reedy laugh.

"Really? What about my eyes?"

Ash turned a shoulder and made to walk away. "You've seen something you either want to forget…or bury." He cast her a grave look. "You're haunted, Mari."

Mari's nostrils flared the moment she opened the back door. She was greeted by a darkened kitchen, Bear sitting by his bed, and a guilty look on his face. She spied the puddle on the kitchen tiles and groaned. He wound through her legs to greet her, and she scratched his ears.

"It wasn't your fault," she said, stooping to kiss him between the eyes.

How long had she been gone? Bear wasn't used to being left for hours at a time. Clearing up the mess and dumping the soggy paper towel in the trash, she peered around the door. "I'm home, Mom."

The television was on low in the family room, and Mari's feet left damp paths from her wet shoes as she trekked across the hall. Her heart vaulted, slipping into her throat momentarily when she saw the dining room door open. The shape of her mother moved in the shadows, and she trod carefully, not wanting to startle her. Still in her bathrobe, her mother stood motionless in the dark room, staring at the hospital bed that James died in, which still needed to be collected.

Gently, she put her hands on her mother's shoulders. "Shall I fix you some dinner? When did you last eat?"

Mari cursed herself for leaving, but now she was back and wouldn't be venturing out anytime soon, even if the occupier of the mansion across the field was possibly the best-looking man she'd ever set eyes on. Settling her mother on her couch, she covered her with a blanket and fixed her a sandwich, pressing it into her weary hands. Her mother's nails were bitten to the beds.

"You missed a call while you were gone."

Plumping a cushion from the couch, Mari jolted with surprise and stared at her hard. "For me? On the house phone?"

No one called the house. Mari wasn't even sure where the house phone was; she dimly recalled it on the hallway table under a lamp and a pile of mail. Anyone who needed her emailed, and that was the only way she'd been contactable for months. She'd long since frozen her socials.

Her mouth went dry. "Who was it?" she asked, even though she had a nagging suspicion she already knew.

Mari's mother sighed vaguely, staring at her sandwich as though it confused her. "Your *friend*—Zara."

Her heart sank into the pit of her stomach. Her mother looked up sharply, her usually dull eyes suddenly fiery. "I don't know why you even still talk to that little witch after what she did."

"I don't," Mari spat, unable to control the trembling in her fingers. Grabbing up another cushion, she turned to the window so her mother wouldn't notice. "I haven't seen her since…"

"…what she did to your brother…to a dying boy…" Mrs. Fox wiped her eyes, and let the plate fall into her lap. "The lies she told about him…"

Mari squeezed her eyes shut, the images of the last night she'd seen Zara threatening to overwhelm her. "Don't get upset."

"I don't understand why she'd even be calling the house…"

"I saw her today at the Gas station…" Mari trailed off, spinning on her heels, but her mother had sunk into the pillows, her mouth drooped, and her eyes hooded. She stared at the television and said nothing, and once more, Mari was alone. The lights that had temporarily fired the woman had dulled to embers.

The afternoon was wet and muggy, and Mari made use of her lost time by emailing Eric's notes back. She gritted her teeth while they exchanged their usual back-and-forth.

It would be great to meet you one day, he wrote feverishly. **Or at least we could talk on Zoom.**

Their faceless and voiceless arrangement suited Mari far more than he'd ever be able to understand. Later, when she trekked back through the corn fields with Bear, taking him for his long overdue walk, her thoughts turned to Ash and Clover.

Casting her eyes past Mr. Raggerty, always on the peripheral, she caught sight of a light flickering in one of the top windows. How long had it been since anyone had cared if she was alright or how she was feeling?

Light the candle, and I'll know you're okay…

It was possibly the most romantic thing anyone had ever said to her, and she wondered what he was doing in that decaying mansion and if Clover was still sitting in her humid orangery, surrounded by her plants and oils. Something about it had seemed magical, ethereal. The smell of jasmine was almost enough to make her eyes droop, and she'd struggled to focus there.

Bear ran ahead through puddles and rivers in the field, his claws scraping the porch steps. Mari laughed, rushing after him and unlocked the door. A shrill ring from the hallway phone made her pause at the door, and she stared at it, her mouth drooping.

It rang and rang. And rang. And gradually, her blood turned to ice. She should have guessed that Zara wouldn't leave things alone. She'd always been stubborn. Doggedly, unrelenting when she believed she was right about something. Mari had known her since she was four, since pre-school. Through school, they'd been one another's shadows, inseparable. James accused her of being jealous when he took an interest in Zara. Her friend got tall, lean, and pretty, and it didn't help that she had a massive crush on James.

Everyone liked him. He was James Fox, blonde, gorgeous, and determined to go far. But Mari had never been jealous of their relationship. How could she? It was her best friend and her brother, the two people she loved, who were together, and that only made her happy.

The phone stopped ringing, and she breathed with relief, the caged sigh spilling from her lungs. She'd been holding her chest that whole time. Instead of heading to her room, she snuggled next to her mother on the couch, pulling a blanket over them while the rain pelted the window. A black and white movie played on the television, and she leaned her head on her mother's shoulder. Mrs. Fox said nothing, and Mari wasn't sure if her mother sensed her there, but it was times like this she liked to pretend that all that had passed was a dream and the vibrant woman who'd brought them up still existed.

Mari lost herself in sleep, her neck crooked at an uncomfortable angle, when she woke to the shrill ring of the house phone. Eying the space where her mother had sat, she got up awkwardly; her mouth fuzzy and eyes blurry. It was past ten.

Stumbling into the dark hall, where shadows spilled and the light of the moon shone off the mirrors, she stared dumbly at the phone, its shrill cry like a piercing scream. Mari inched forward, her feet like lead and her fingers trembling as she reached for it, anything to make it shut off. She cradled it to her ear. "Hello."

Zara's breathy sigh whispered down the phone. "Thank God you're alright—I've been so worried."

Mari blinked, sleepy, and pinched the bridge of her nose. "Why would you be worried?"

There was a beat of silence before her old friend answered. "When I saw you at the gas station…you drove off so fast… it was like you'd seen a ghost."

I had seen a ghost. "Don't call the house, Zara. You upset my mom."

"I had to check you were okay…Jesus, Mari…you're my best friend."

Her throat clogged, and she couldn't speak. The silence urged Zara to keep ranting.

"For god sake. Can't we talk about this? We grew up together!"

"Do not call here again! It only upsets her…." Frustrated tears burned her eyes. "I can't deal with this right now."

Zara huffed, and Mari could envision the face she was pulling, the one where she blew her hair off her forehead in frustration. "Maybe you can cut me off, Mari. But I don't have the heart to do that, even after James…"

"Stop!"

"No! I was worried, okay? After you drove off, there was a report on the news about a guy going missing in the storm…"

Something in her veins iced, and she shook her head as though shaking away a memory. "Who?"

"I don't know—some guy, going for a run. No one has seen him, and his wife reported him missing a few hours ago. I just…" She trailed off, exhausted. "But you're fine. You're home. That was all I was worried about."

Tears threatened to spill over her lashes, and Mari clutched the phone to her ear, her knuckles white. She'd seen a man out running. She'd wound her window down to warn him to go back. How could someone just vanish?

"Don't call here again," she said, her voice quivering. " I have to take care of my mom."

Zara scoffed. "Your mom should be in a hospital, Mari. No one has seen her in months. That's not taking care of her."

Heat rushed to her face, and her temper, usually slow to rise, rushed to the surface. "I can't…I can't do this."

"Can't do what? Face the truth?"

Mari slammed the phone down hard, so hard it rattled. Breathing heavily, she fled to her room, where the shadows waited. She carefully sat on the edge of the bed, gazing out over the wet corn and the bedraggled scarecrow hanging limp on his pole. Maybe it was old Tobias Rosewood watching her? The thought made her shudder. She remembered how he used to freak Zara out, too, and how she always insisted the curtains be closed when she slept over.

The runner she'd seen was gone, swept away like a branch in a gale. Tomorrow, she'd watch the news again. Surely someone else would have spotted him?

Mari's gaze found Clover's candle, prettily encased in its tin. Twisting the lid, the scent of jasmine and geranium floated under her nose, and she breathed deep, willing back tears. She'd never wanted to lose Zara. How had everything gotten so messed up?

She placed the candle on the sill, and sank into the window seat, the glass cool against her skin. She took a match and struck it. The first one burned out, but then she struck another, its glow reflecting in the window. She lit the wick, watching as it flickered, sending its message to someone watching her over the field.

SEVEN

A dull throbbing in her temples woke her from sleep. Sitting up, her stomach gurgled, and for a horrifying moment, she thought she might vomit from the pain behind her eyes. The smell in the room was intensely perfumed, causing her gut to roil. The candle on the sill had burned to nothing, just some left over wax at the base. She gaped at it, mortified at her stupidity.

Everyone knew you didn't leave candles burning all night, but apparently, that was what she'd done. Pawing at the sheets, she didn't recall climbing into bed. Her last memory was barely closing her eyes as she gazed across the darkened cornfield to the top window where she knew Ash slept. She must have dozed off, her forehead pressed against the window.

Had yesterday been a dream? Her time inside Rosewood, though fleeting, seemed like it'd happened years ago and to someone else. Stepping over the threshold to her own home seemed to jolt her back to her lonely reality. She longed to return to the fairytale and magical existence Clover lived in.

Blinking against the hard sunlight as it burned through the clouds; she got up, her vision a little off as she went downstairs. It was quiet, apart from Bear, who leaped from his plush bed by the back door and bounded to her feet. "Hey," she greeted him croakily, her throat dry. Gulping down water, she leaned on the kitchen counter, lost in thought, as she gazed out over the field. The day was bright and fresh, and Mr. Raggerty had recovered from the storm, his plaid shirt billowing in the breeze.

Mari fed Bear and laughed as he followed her into the family room, knowing he'd whine for some of her breakfast. Dropping to the couch, she flicked on the television and thumbed through to the local news, where her worries rushed to greet her.

Swallowing, she leaned forward, keeping the volume low. She checked herself, shaking her head. There was no one to keep the volume low for. Her mother wouldn't rise till noon, and James was gone. When he was sick, tiptoeing around him became a habit that'd become a way of life.

A news crew had been in the town, reporting near the gas station where she'd seen Zara and, not long after, the runner she'd warned to turn around—the man now missing. The reporter told viewers his name was Dan Wheeler, and he was forty-two. He was staying in the local motel for work, and when his wife in Toronto didn't hear from him, she called the police.

Everyone in Winstone had seen him. Hard to miss in his running gear, in yellow and black, but there was no trace of him, no tracks. And as yet, no one had come forward with what direction they'd seen him travel. Dan looked nice from the picture plastered on the screen, and he had two boys. Mari's stomach tightened.

She'd *warned* him to go back. Dan hadn't listened, and now he was gone. Was it possible she could have been the last one to see him alive?

To distract herself, she found herself typing Clover Martin's name into the search bar of her laptop. Nothing came up, apart from an old Tumblr page with a cartoonish avatar that vaguely resembled Clover. Thumbing through it, Mari's eyes blurred, scanning through many photos of Clover's flowers, her hobby more of a lifestyle. She had followers and had last been online a month ago, probably before they moved. Satisfied, Mari searched for Ash next.

It didn't take long to find a very poorly maintained Instagram account. Ash's profile picture was hazy, only half his face showing in the shadows of a badly taken selfie, but she could see it was him. He mainly posted photos of his view, and by the looks of it, he'd had many of them. There were tower block views, isolated beaches, and lonely, misted mountains. The last one was of a bleak outcrop of trees nestled in a valley with the caption.

"Never does the sun shine here in Fairbanks."

Mari frowned, scrolling the comments, of which there were none. It looked like an isolated place, solitary, like his Instagram grid. She clicked it off before she got tempted to start nosing at anyone else's profiles, like Zara's—some things needed to stay buried.

"You look like you've seen something…"

What he'd said irked her, probably because he was skirting dangerously close to the truth. Tapping in Fairbanks, the first result was about a local school teacher and the ongoing search for her whereabouts. She stiffened, her mind circling back to Dan Wheeler.

"Shit," she muttered. The reporter urged anyone watching who might know something to come forward, even if it were a dead end.

I might know something.

The thought plagued her. It nagged at her while she showered and washed her hair. It gnawed at her while she drank coffee at her desk and answered Eric's latest email. When she went downstairs to feed Bear, she was convinced *she* was the last person to see this irritating human who had thought it was a great idea to run in a storm. A man who had a family, a life he loved, and people who needed him.

A sweat built under her shirt, and her fists balled so tight she'd drawn blood on her palms. The very last thing she wanted to do was leave the house again.

Then she laughed out loud. *The car!* She shook herself, a surge of relief washing through every cell of her body when she realized she'd abandoned her truck on the side of the road. She couldn't get into town without a car.

That's settled then, she thought, passing the long hall window. What she saw captured her breath. It was sitting there in the drive. Throwing open the door, she dashed outside, finding her truck parked in its place, full of gas, and the keys switched off in the ignition. Mari spotted a letter tucked behind the wheel and snatched it up.

"I'm here to help. I thought you might need this. Ash." The note read.

Her heart fluttered, heat in her cheeks making her smile, but it faded quickly.

"Yeah, thanks for the help," she muttered.

For the second time in many months, Mari drove into Winstone, and not because she wanted to. Guilt surged her forward, eclipsing her like a wave, and she couldn't get Dan Wheeler's idiot face out of her head. With Bear happily at her side, his tongue darting out and tasting the breeze, she trundled into the main town, narrowing her eyes as the sign for the Police department appeared on the right. Pulling into the lot, she tensed, her body wracked with fear.

You've got to do this, he could be dead and you were the last one to see him. Bear scampered out and wound through her feet the moment the door opened. He wasn't used to car rides, and this proved to be exhilarating for him. Tugging his leash, Mari crossed the lot, the morning sun warming her hair, the air balmy. A man looked up from his desk as she entered, and somewhere in the building, a phone was ringing.

The man, rotund, balding, and around fifty, eyed her with interest. "Miss?"

Mari's voice stuck in her throat. Yesterday at the store she'd had more conversation with the clerk than she'd had in months. It's funny how Ash hadn't intimidated her like this. It was the way the man looked at her, with growing irritation.

"Yes?" he prompted when she said nothing for the longest time.

"I was in town yesterday," she stammered.

He frowned. "That's...nice."

Mari blushed. "No, I mean...I don't usually come out." The longer she looked at him, the more her blood rushed, and she thought she might recognize him from somewhere. She was sure this guy coached football at her old school, or at least, he did once.

Her heart vaulted, that uneasy sickness building in her stomach. "What I mean is I came in for an errand, and as I was driving home…I think I saw the missing guy."

His brows pulled and lifted in surprise. Grabbing for a notepad, he waved to the chair she was leaning on. "Please take a seat. We need all the help we can get—people don't just disappear around here." He chuckled darkly. "This isn't Cedar wood."

Mari faked a tight laugh, unsure what he meant, only that he was referring to the town nearby, a place she hadn't spent a great deal of time in. It was a cute forestry town on the colonial route through Massachusetts, a place of historical significance linked to witchcraft, like Mickleford.

Mari edged into the seat and then immediately stood like her ass had caught fire. "I can't stay." Blood rushed in her ears. "I only came to say I saw him, heading east…out towards the town limits…out where I live."

He snorted a laugh. "And where would that be?"

"Oh. Right. I live at the old Keller farmhouse, right near Rosewood Hall."

His lips pursed in surprise, and he smiled and wagged a pen at her. "I thought you looked familiar—you're a Fox."

His mouth dropped as if he realized his blunder. "You're James Fox's sister…oh my." He cleared his throat awkwardly. "I was so sorry to hear he passed. James was on the football team at Randal."

Mari nodded, numb and acutely aware of Bear whining by her feet. "Can I go?"

"Hang on," he said with an impatient wave. "You said you saw a man matching his description?"

She nodded again, eager to get this over with. "It was him. I remember the running gear. I was nearly at the turn-off for Mickleford when I saw him. I stopped by him and told him to head back…I know how the Grenfell River can flood those old back roads." She shrugged. "I guess he didn't listen."

The man tutted with growing impatience. "A damn shame. But thank you…that gives us a heads up. We can continue extending the search out that way."

"Right. Well." She backed up, aware he was watching her with interest. "I hope you find him."

Now leave. Her feet picked up speed, and her clammy palm was on the glass door when he called after her. Her stomach rolled, lungs craving fresh air.

"I was sorry to hear about your brother," he said, raising his bulk from behind his desk. The phone rang next to him, but to her surprise, he ignored it. His features had softened, and he was making *that* face. The *"I'm sorry"* face. The one she'd been subjected to at James's wake repeatedly. "Maybe I shouldn't say this…but hell, this town is small, and you know how people talk."

Mari's hands tingled, and she leaned on the door for support, already foreseeing what was coming as the blood slowly drained from her legs. "Oh?"

"I never believed what that girl said about him—you know—the rumors? I don't believe it. James was a good guy. A *decent* guy. And it sucked that she said all those things...and the poor guy isn't around to defend himself." He coughed. "It's just cruel, is what it is."

"I have to go," Mari whispered, the door opening behind her as she leaned against it. Willing strength to her legs, rather than get in the truck, she walked Bear the length of the main street, sucking clean air through her nose.

Wiping her eyes, she paused by the bookstore, heart pounding in her ears.

She remembered the taste of whiskey sours and tracking mud into the kitchen the next morning after the Halloween party. But then there was nothing, and it hurt to try to piece it all together—one big, frustrating mess.

Squeezing her eyes tight, she faced the shop window she'd stopped by, opening them to see displays of old vintage books arranged with candles and dripping wax behind the glass. Clover's face popped into her mind, and she was struck with sorrow. How might she like to visit a place like this in the daylight? Mari spotted a frayed vintage tome in the display, edged yellow and worn. She pressed her nose against the glass.

The Hedgerow Apothecary.

Mari smiled. If Clover couldn't come out to shop, maybe she could take this to her.

EIGHT

You're being a good neighbor, Mari told herself, clutching the old, worn book to her chest. It smelled perfect, mothy, and eaten like the pages had been flipped and thumbed through a thousand times. After she'd paid for the book, Mari drove Bear home, fed him, and found herself taking a less than casual stroll across the corn, weaving in and out of the mazes of stems rising high above her head.

It's the decent thing to do, she reiterated firmly, as she stared at the iron gates woven in an intricate pattern of an old rose. After all, Ash had gallantly hauled her off her ass, they'd taken care of her, and he'd brought back her truck.

Part of Mari couldn't face going inside Kellers again because what Ash had said was true. Once the door closed, something unseen drained her soul. James was dead and gone, but so was her mother, and Mari feared she'd be sucked in with her.

The gate squealed on its hinges, and Mari left enough gap to wiggle through. Ahead, the door caught her eye, big and thick, and a panel in the wood had been uncovered. It was a stained glass representation of a winged Angel, his light beaming in a halo around his head. In the morning sun, the glass shone with bold, vibrant blues, red and orange colors. The angel stood at the edge of a rock pool, pouring water from one golden goblet to another. Mari had never seen this before, and she stared at it in wonder.

When no one answered, Mari peaked around the porch, peering through the grimy glass to see if she could spot them inside. Taking a hesitant step off the porch, she wandered around the building, avoiding bramble patches and moss-eaten tree stumps. The woods crowding the building were dark and shadowy, flanked by a low stone wall. It was once an ornamental garden but was long overgrown with bushes and weeds. Mari's foot cracked on a twig, and she spun, facing a stone maiden, a life-sized statue hidden in the trees.

Mari shrieked and clamped a hand over her mouth in embarrassment.

The statue was beautiful, a young maiden with long braids clutching a rose to her chest, but a detail made Mari's neck hairs rise. The maiden's face was ruined, covered in deep gouges, making it impossible to decipher her features. Frowning, she stepped closer and, this time, yelled in fright as several black crows exploded out of the trees, sending up a flurry of dead leaves in their flight. Mari nearly let the book slip from her hands.

"Hey!" Ash called, jogging up behind her. "Are you okay?" He steadied her as the birds took off out of the bush, leaving Mari stunned and shaking. "Crap! That was a lot of crows."

"A murder," she gasped, catching her breath, hugging the book hard.

"Huh?"

"That's what it's called—a murder of crows. Meaning a *shit ton* of crows."

They looked at one another and burst out laughing. An adrenaline rush flooded her blood, relieved she wasn't alone. Ash scratched the back of his neck, nodding with feigned interest. "You learn something new every day, I guess."

Mari giggled, mortified and feeling a little foolish. "Sorry. It's kind of my job to know weird stuff like that." Her attention drew back to the maiden with the gouged face. "What happened to her?"

Ash looked surprised, peering over her head. He gave a noncommittal shrug. "No idea…blame the crows, maybe?" He stared at it, then looked away like it bugged him, grinding his teeth. "Teenagers?"

Mari didn't mention the covered portraits inside the house. The scratches over the maiden's stone face left her unsettled, but when she glanced up, Ash was watching her intently.

"Having a look around?" he teased and her tense expression melted into a smile.

"I wasn't snooping. I was looking for you."

"In the yard?"

"You didn't answer the door."

He nodded, grinning like he didn't believe her. "If you'd have gone any further, you'd have ended up in the old Rosewood crypt." Ducking his head, he peered through the trees. "See that there? That old ruin?"

"Oh." Mari followed his gaze, though it was hard to make out through the overgrown hedges and light mist on the air, broken by shards of sunlight. There was a small building with stacked columns and a broken-up stone angel with her hands raised to the heavens. "Is everyone buried in there?"

Ash looked thoughtful. "I mean…all the Rosewoods that lived here in the early years." Taking her arm, he helped her back through the undergrowth, where the house waited in the shadows, and this time, the door was open. Mari pointed to the stained glass panel in the door.

"This is new?"

"Had it uncovered this morning." Ash stood casually, watching her with interest. "It was boarded over—something the first founders put in. Think the guy who built it liked religious symbology—there's one like it in Cedar Wood somewhere."

"Oh." Mari feigned interest, distracted by the sun in his hair, and his sleeves rolled high. He was also covered in paint, and she nodded as though she'd heard every word he'd said. As if guessing by her vacant expression, he brushed a hand over the stained glass and laughed. "Sorry—a bit of a history nerd."

He looked embarrassed, and she rushed to fill the awkward gap, thrusting the book under his nose. God, what was the matter with her? "I saw this and thought of Clover," she blurted. "And after yesterday…you coming to my rescue and all…"

Ash smiled, his face creasing. Inside, she wilted. She thought she must have *really* missed male company to be such a mess over the first decent-looking guy who'd ever been nice to her.

"You didn't have to do that—it's so kind, and she'll love it."

"And you didn't have to bring back my truck, but you did."

"Anyone would have done the same."

"No…" She tilted her head, smiling. "I'm not sure they would."

He looked at her strangely, almost sad, before waving his hand toward the door. "Come in and see her for yourself." The door opened inward with a satisfying squeal.. "Your visit really lifted her spirits yesterday."

Mari dipped her chin, greeted by the smell of damp plaster and roses as she walked in behind him. Leaves tumbled from the hole in the roof, billowing to the ground and gathering in a mass on the rickety floor. Ash looked sheepish. "I'm not sure how I'll ever get up there to fix that."

"It must be so hard for her—for you both," Mari circled back to his sister, her mind focused on his sister's miserable illness. Ash glanced at her over his shoulder.

"Some days are harder than others. It's the lack of companionship that worries me. I mean…I'm hardly stimulating company."

"I'm sure you entertain her just fine."

Ash sighed. "She has her flowers and her books. And sometimes…I think it'll all be alright."

Mari caught sight of another veiled portrait over his shoulder, nestled in a dark corner near the stone fireplace. This time, she had to ask; her curiosity had piqued. "What's the deal with the covered paintings?"

He looked surprised she'd asked, glancing over his shoulder, his brows raising quizzically. "It's kind of creepy, right?"

Mari nodded. "I wasn't going to say creepy—more mysterious."

"*I* think it's creepy." He looked uncertain, hands deep in his pockets, as he jerked his head for her to follow. "I'll show you something."

Clutching the book, Mari tailed behind him down a narrow corridor lit by wall sconces. There was a faint smell of oil in the air, and she guessed they were oil-fired lamps, so the electricity was still out. Decaying paper peeled off the wall in chunks. She was sure she'd not find her way back through here alone. Ash paused, taking a clanging set of keys from his jeans and slipping one into the door. The double doors opened and revealed a long, dark dining room. There was a long table in the middle crowded with high-back chairs. When her eyes adjusted, she saw more portraits hanging around the room, their gold frames visible under the delicate black veil.

"Okay," she gasped. "That *is* creepy."

"I haven't cleared this room yet—but I'm not sure I should disturb it."

Mari walked ahead, passing a large cracked vase of dead flowers, her eyes drawn to the portraits. Something about it was eerie, and she did not want to see what subjects lay underneath the veil. It felt like a bad omen. "I think you should lock the door and leave them where they are," she said with a short laugh. "Why cover them all up?"

Ash leaned in the door, his expression unsure as he spoke. "You remember I told you about Tobias and how he vanished?"

Mari nodded.

"Well, his widow…kind of went insane, and she demanded that all the portraits in the house be covered up. She said they were watching her and that Toby was trapped inside the paintings. She lived with it for ten years—until she eventually threw herself off the tower on the roof."

"That's awful!" Mari backed away, holding the book like it was a shield. Ash's lips twitched in a smile before taking her hand and leading her back into the corridor.

"Let's go find Clover," he said. "Sorry if I spooked you." Mari followed him, hopelessly enthralled by him and the feel of her hand tucked in his.

The smell of jasmine clawed her nose, but she found it wasn't as irritating as before. It made her chest swell, like she'd walked into a home. Clover was at the piano in the ballroom, a crescent of music filtering through the halls, lifting to the rafters. It was almost magical with the sun shining through the hole, lighting the motes of dust of gleaming rose gold.

"Mari!" she exclaimed, leaving the safety of the piano. She skipped across the floor and edged around the sunlit hole. Her hands found Mari's, and she tried not to wince at the feel of those dry, cool palms brushing hers. "You came back."

Mari thrust the old tome under Clover's nose, and the girl's face lit up. Her delicate blonde brows pulled into a confused frown. "You bought me a present?"

Mari blushed furiously as Ash stared at her profile. "Well, I was in town anyway, and I happened to spot this in the bookstore window—and thought of you."

Clover gazed down at the book as though it were made of spun gold. "This is so nice of you."

"Thank you for rescuing me," Mari said, and Clover's eyes shone with mischief, jerking her chin at her brother.

"That was Ash's doing. Does he get a gift too?" she giggled, and Ash rolled his eyes, spinning on his heels.

"Think I'll leave you both to it," he said with a wink, and Mari avoided eye contact, already feeling like a sixteen-year-old as it was. Clover tugged her hand, dragging her out of the gloom of the opulent ballroom, where the scent of rose and jasmine grew stronger. Mari slipped out of her cardigan as they went into the orangery, and she swore it was hotter in here than yesterday. The storm had cleared the clouds, and the sun had warmed the glass over their heads.

Instead of heading for the chaise, Clover led her under an arch of white and yellow flowers with vines that wove between the metal. The arch revealed a small ornamental pond, filled with lilies and a small, trickling fountain. There was another plush red sofa, and Clover ushered her to sit. Mari noticed the gloves again and, more vividly, the small patch of red, burned skin that was revealed on her wrist.

"Clover!" she gasped, grabbing her hand and turning her wrist over. The welt was deep, a nasty open burn and the girl squeaked and yanked her hand away, tucking it under her arm. "You should go to a hospital."

Mari wasn't sure what a third-degree burn looked like, but there was a slight scent of rot as Clover had whipped her hand away. Her nose wrinkled.

"It's fine—just an accident."

"It looks painful. What happened?"

The girl's eyes were glassy and melancholic as she gazed at the dark, oppressive blinds shielding them from the daylight. "I got too close."

"Let me see it."

Clover's laugh died. "My potions help—a few days, and it'll be gone. Please just forget it."

The stricken expression on Clover's face made any protest die on Mari's lips. She recognized the traits, the hiding of symptoms, the way James had locked himself away for so long before he'd admit anything was wrong. Mari wanted to push, but she didn't know Clover well enough. Instead, she smiled.

"Well, listen, I've got a whole pharmacy back at my place—think we have just about every-thing—if you need something."

Clover whisked her hand away, tugging the glove further up her wrist. "A few days, and it'll be fine. I'm used to it. But thank you."

Mari tucked a leg under her. Something about the trickling water and oppressive heat made her yawn. "How long has this been going on?"

Clover licked her chapped lips, and the dim light in the room cast shadows under her eyes. "As long as I can remember."

She burns alive.

"And it's anytime you get too near the light?"

"It's called Icaria Disorder," she said, tight-lipped. "I was born with it, the doctors say, and there's no cure."

"So why did you leave Alaska?" Mari asked. "It's dark half the day. Wouldn't that be perfect for you?"

Clover's watery gaze cast around the lofty room, and Mari followed it, catching the sight of creeping pond tulips opening to bloom. "Ash found it hard to work there. He tried for a long time to make it work, but that kind of climate can drive you insane—the constant dark. He couldn't work or really socialize, and when we found out that this place was still here, it seemed perfect."

Mari nodded in understanding. "I'm kind of used to the dark—when James got sick, we turned off all the lights, any noise—it hurt his head, made him…"

Angry.

"Really sick," Mari finished.

Clover let her hand rest on top of Mari's, over her knee. "Beauty can grow in the darkness. I've never minded it much, and I love my flowers and plants. But Ash…he's sacrificed a lot for me, so it was time for me to give him a break." Her eyes twinkled. "It'd be good for him to make some friends."

Mari's lip twitched, aware of what she was alluding to. "Speaking of your plants…what else was in that candle? The scent knocked me out."

A little too well.

Clover laughed. "Jasmine can be sedative, and Frankincense too."

"I haven't slept that deeply in…" Mari shook her head, and her new friend beamed.

"I'll get you another! I've got tons—come see this!"

Suddenly dragged to her feet, Mari stumbled around the pond, hand in hand with the younger girl. Beaming with excitement, Clover led her through a murky, stained-glass door filled with the scent of roses. A light sweat broke on her head, and she fanned herself, the atmosphere cloyingly hot.

"Over here." Clover tugged her past an array of potted roses, thorns poked out dangerously from the stems. Ahead was an open glass case, and inside sat a pewter pot sprouting with a cluster of small flowers. In the center sat three tightly closed buds, waiting to bloom.

Clover bit her lip, edging Mari closer, gazing at her with expectancy, like she should know what she was staring at. "What's this?"

Clover beamed. "It's mine."

"Yours?"

"I mean—I *made* it."

Mari threw her a confused smile. "You mean you grew it?"

"No, I mean, I created it. It's a hybrid—of my own creation."

Mari nodded, feigning awe, not wanting to admit she didn't have the first idea about plant life, roses, or anything. She'd been an English major and proofread books for a living. "Oh…that's cool."

Clover's expression clouded. "I guess I shouldn't be surprised. You don't look that impressed. You have the same look as Ash does when I talk about it."

"No, really…it is cool. It must take a lot of work. Why?" She looked at her new friend. "Aren't there like a thousand types of roses out there?"

"Over three hundred actually." Clover wound her hands behind her back, her white dress pulling at the narrow waist. "But none like this. It's a hybrid of three types of rose."

"And what makes this so special?" Mari asked.

Clover looked at her tiredly, disappointed her new friend hadn't erupted in excitement. "It only produces three buds—and they only bloom at night once a month. But that's not what makes it so important...important to me."

Mari licked her lips, struggling to keep awake. The air was dense and suffocating and she felt like napping. When she didn't answer, Clover rushed on.

"It's the oil you see...its properties. I can add it to my potions." She cradled her wrist, the one gloved and with a hidden burn. Mari's eyes widened with understanding.

"You mean... it's healing? It'll help heal the burns you get from the sun."

Clover's smile took over her face, full of hope. It sparkled in her eyes. "Not just that. This..." She swallowed. "This is my cure."

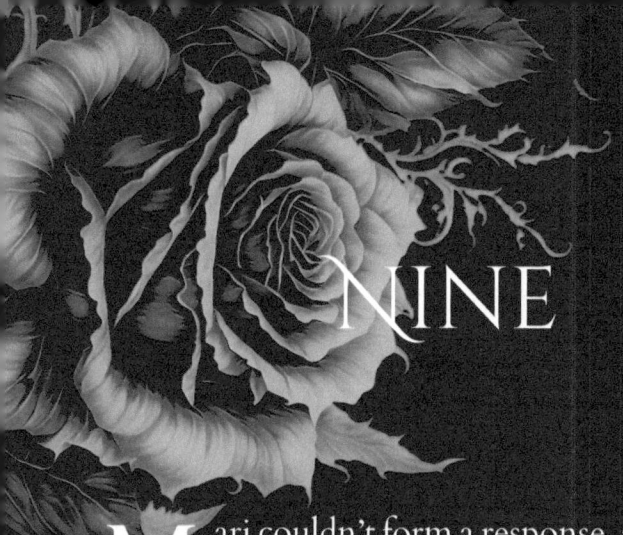

NINE

Mari couldn't form a response, at least not a good one. Fascinated, she stared around Clover's workroom. At the labels and potion bottles lying discarded on the workbench. The dresser was overflowing with books and notes. An old-fashioned chalkboard on the wall littered with math, recipes, and Latin names of plants she didn't recognize. Dumbly, she repeated, "A cure?"

"I mean…" Clover faltered, a little shaky with excitement. "Not entirely…but it's a step forward. I could…" She waved her hands around the room. "Leave this house in the day—maybe walk in the sun."

Mari shook her head in disbelief. "How did you do this?"

"Its breeding and blending of plants. Different species fused—in a beautiful mutation. It's taken a long time." Carefully, she rolled off the glove, and Mari got a whole look at the wound. It looked worse revealed, her skin puckered and raw, oozing with infection. "I've been testing it."

"That isn't good," Mari snapped, memories of James flooding back. "You're hurting yourself. How do you even…how does it work?"

Clover motioned for her to sit on a bench. "I use the oils taken from the petals and dry them into a tea…then I drink it. I can put the oil in lotions and creams, candles too."

"Does it have a name? This mutation of yours?"

Clover's smile waned as though she sensed Mari's disapproval. "I call her the Night Witch. Here." She rose swiftly and dashed to her work-bench, pulling out a drawer and appearing sec-onds later with a flask. "Taste it—it's nice."

Mari carefully unscrewed the cap and sniffed it gingerly. It wasn't unpleasant, just rich and fragrant, the unmistakable undercurrent of Jasmine brewing in the lower notes of the base. Tentatively, she took a sip, then licked her lips. Then another. It slid down too easily. "It's okay," she agreed. "Not bad. What'll it do to me?"

Clover smiled. "Short term—make you more focussed, give you energy, all good things. Increase your metabolism—"

"And long term?"

"It heightens your melanin production, increases blood flow to the skin, purifies the circulation."

"Melanin?"

Clover nodded, taking a moment to gather her thoughts to launch into an explanation. By the time she'd finished, Mari still wasn't sure if she understood.

"Cell renewal…new oxygen and blood to the cells. It repairs the skin, protects it, maybe…it could act like a shield," she tried to explain, and Mari nodded in encouragement. "The light burns me because my condition means I don't produce enough melanin. That stuff in your skin makes you tan in the sun. I possess none of that. Melanin hides deep within the tissue, and with gradual sun exposure, your skin color will change over time. Intensive exposure means you burn quickly, and the melanin does not have enough time to rise to the surface levels."

Mari nodded thoughtfully. "So…yeah, like a bad case of sunburn?"

"Exactly. Except for me, I don't have any melanin…or it never rises to the surface. But this could stimulate production."

Letting the knowledge sink in, Mari shook her head in wonder. "Clover, this is amazing—if it works. But in the meantime, you're hurting yourself. That burn needs hospital treatment."

Clover pulled her glove back on, oblivious as sweat rolled down Mari's neck. She'd started to breath shallowly, and dizziness made her pinch the bridge of her nose. It was too hot in this room.

"Does Ash know?"

"Of course he knows—that's why we came back," she admitted. "The weather conditions—the light." She broke off, her eyes widening in panic. "Are you alright?"

Tipping forward, Mari breathed deeply and put her head between her knees. "I'm dizzy."

Alarmed, Clover hauled her carefully to her feet. "It's my fault!" she cried. "I know it's too hot here. I'm so used to it—I'm always so cold."

Mari tried to wave her away, but she swayed sickly, her stomach sloshing, and the tea she'd drank burned in her throat. "No…I'll be fine."

"Let me take you to the ballroom…you can lie down there. It's cooler."

Mari's vision blackened, and the need to breathe clean, cool air was almost unbearable. Blindly, she held Clover's arm and lost herself for a while before she sensed her feet leave the floor. Turning her head, she opened her eyes, and a feeling of safety fell heavy as she met Ash's cool gaze.

He carried her to the ballroom while Clover muttered and fussed behind them.

"Trust my sister to nearly boil to death the first visitor she's had in months," he joked, lowering her to the soft couch. She gripped his shirt harder, and he gave her an affectionate smile. "Easy, I'm not going to drop you." He lay her down, her head and eyes so heavy she had no choice but to close them. "Maybe she bored you into a coma with all her science jargon?"

"Shut up, Ash!" Clover wailed. "I'll take care of her. I'll open the window—"

"You'll stay the hell away from any open windows, Clo. You've done enough." His voice faded as sleep clawed at her eyes, and her lids fluttered closed. "I'll watch over her." There was a pause, and they moved around her, their voices fading in and out of her conscience. "You didn't give her any of that disgusting junk you've been brewing…?"

Was it the tea that had done this? Or merely the heat? All at once, the fight was over, and peace, numbing and oppressive, stole her away, and she slipped into a dreamless sleep—at least she thought it was dreamless. She woke with her toes cold and a stiff breeze from the dark, open window fluttering the thin blanket across her legs.

Sitting up, the moon's light spilled off the polished floor of the ballroom. Surrounded by giant veiled oil paintings and nothing but shadows, Mari looked around for Ash, but he was nowhere to be seen. Shivering, she swung her legs to the floor, wooly-mouthed and drenched in a cold sweat.

She had sworn she'd heard a man crying out for help. His voice had startled her from her sleep, or maybe it was a dream.

A loud knocking came from above, and she was on her feet. Her blood iced. It was above, loud footsteps from the floor above, and then it came again. A man screaming for help. Mari stumbled forward and clutched her chest, dashing to the heavy door and dragging it open. "Where are you?"

The grand staircase swept up to the lofty first floor, the boards worn and old, creaking in the wind. Leaves fell from the gaping hole in the roof, red rowan leaves that pirouetted to the ground like droplets of blood. Mari's legs drained of blood as the man screamed again.

"Where are you?" she cried, her voice echoing.

A shock of ice flooded her blood as a pair of hands clamped on her shoulders. Gasping, she spun into Ash's arms. "Easy, easy…you were sleepwalking!"

"No, I wasn't…there was a man…a man crying out for help!"

Ash brought her to her knees, trembling in his arms, fighting waves of dizziness. "I wasn't…"

"Mari, I've been following behind you all this time…you were under. I'm so sorry…it must have been that crap Clover thinks is going to cure cancer!"

She held his strong arms, her eyes finding him, and suddenly, the world seemed right. Her stomach stopped churning. She reddened with embarrassment. "How long…?"

"A couple of hours," he said with a gentle smile. "I'm so sorry. She gets so carried away…and it's my fault for indulging her."

Breathing hard, she sank to her knees. "I'll be fine. I just…" She couldn't believe she was about to say this. "Think I need to get home."

Ash smiled kindly, and it was impossible not to trust him. He radiated warmth and reassurance like a lighthouse in a storm. She reached for his hand, and he pulled her to her feet.

"I'll walk you home."

TEN

She'd heard a *man*. A man's voice floating in the darkness. She was sure she hadn't imagined it, but with her head so wooly, it was hard to know for sure.

Mari leaned hard on Ash's arm, not minding when he slipped it around her waist. He gave her a mischievous half-smile. "Clover might have blown my chances of seeing you at the house again."

They reached the steps of Keller's Farmhouse, the breeze sweet and cool on her skin. She drank it like water, starved of oxygen, and could think clearly. "It wasn't her fault."

Ash looked skeptical, allowing her to walk the steps alone. "I'm so sorry…if it was anything…"

Mari put a hand up to quiet him. "I think the heat got to me, that's all. The tea was nice, and

I barely drank any of it. I'm not used to getting that hot that fast."

He pressed his lips thin, gazing up at her, then darted his eye to the small windows on either side of the door. Mari heard Bear scratching to get out, her presence enough to send him into a frenzy. Ash grinned. "Someone missed you."

Mari laughed, turning her shoulder and unlocking the door. Bear bounced to freedom, jumping to chin height, glad to see his best friend home. Mari laughed and scratched his head and under his chin. Ash knelt, and Bear bounded for him, greeting him with licks and snuffles under his jaw. He laughed, giving him a good scratch. Mari smiled in admiration. "He certainly likes you."

"If I take him home with me, then Clover will want to keep him." He met her eyes briefly, cagily. "At least then you'll come back."

"I'd come back," Mari promised. "You need to stop worrying about me. I overheated, and that's all."

Truthfully, she wasn't sure what that was, only that she'd woken from the strangest dream she'd ever experienced. And that voice was calling for help. In the twilight, as evening rolled across the fields, draping them in an orange glow, she couldn't begin to process what she'd heard. Had it been real at all? The memory of the voice made goosebumps rise on her arms.

Bear scooted out of Ash's arms and went indoors, dutifully finding his leash and trotting back to the porch, where he dropped it at Ash's feet. Mari gasped. "Traitor!"

Bear's tail wagged expectantly, and Ash hooked the leash into his collar as though he'd done it every day of his life. "Think I have a job to do."

She grinned, feeling better in the fresh air. "You've been chosen."

Mari glanced over her shoulder at the darkened house, where the television glow lit the family room. Ash looked past her into the darkness of her hallway. "Unless your mother already took him out?"

Mari closed the door. "No. She won't have." Stuffing her hands in her pockets, she joined him, and they quickly fell into step. For a while, they walked in silence, easy and comfortable, and she darted sneaky looks at him out of the corner of her eye. The grooves between the corn wove into intricate corridors at head height, and they took the route out past Rosewood, where the sun dropped below the yellow wash of light.

Ash gazed at her profile. "You aren't the run-of-the-mill nineteen-year-old, are you?"

"Huh?"

Bear tugged the leash, determined to keep them on track. Ash brushed a hand through his hair. "I mean…no phone….no social media…"

"How do you know I don't have social media?"

"I may have done a little research…you know…" He blushed.

Mari hadn't been on her socials since James's funeral. After the funeral, she'd shut it all down. Sometimes she scrolled, but it was anonymous. It hurt too much to peek in at her old life. Even flashes of Zara. Her old life popping up on her phone would leave a hollow ache in her chest.

"I'm not a stalker, I swear!" he laughed and it broke her out of her train of thought. She'd looked up plenty of guys over the years, so she could hardly blame him. She'd looked *him* up, only to find his lonely-looking profile with all the views from various windows.

"I stay offline as much as I can. I only have a profile for my work, and it's a made-up name."

"Nineteen, working from home, no phone, no socials. Are you in hiding?" He laughed at his joke. "Witness protection?" That word sent a flurry of goosebumps up her arms for some reason.

She squirmed uncomfortably, hating that he was skirting close to the questions that seemed inevitable. Gazing out over the field, she paused, unhooked Bear, and let him run free. The pup tore into the corn, vanishing out of sight. How could she ever explain?

"I'm taking a break," she said, clipped.

"From life?"

"Maybe." When she didn't elaborate, she glanced up, and his eyes were hot on her face. "Is it so unusual?"

Ash looked thoughtful. "In this day and age…yeah, kind of."

"I don't see your sister all over social media," she accused. Ash laughed sheepishly.

"That's because she's socially inept. How many friends do you think she's had over the last few years?" He looked annoyed suddenly, tired. "How many kids do you think turned up to her tenth birthday party?"

Mari swallowed her retort, feeling a blast of guilt and sorrow. "Poor Clover."

"It's not her fault." He walked ahead, the corn brushing his jeans, with hands deep in his pockets. "She's not had a normal life—no school, friends. The only people she talks to are the geeks on the plant forums."

That just made her heart heavy, and for a moment, she thought of Zara and the life they'd had together before James died. "That's so sad.

Do you…?" She chose her words carefully. "Do you think what she's trying to do will work?"

Ash met her eyes incredulously. "Do you?"

Mari looked skyward, expelling air. "Not really."

"If modern medicine can't give her some kind of life, do you think I believe a weird concoction of roses and plants will? It's crazy," he admitted. "But it keeps her going. Hope is a powerful incentive."

And a dangerous one. Mari remembered the day of James's diagnosis. The utter look of disbelief on his face was enough to freeze her to the core, a memory she could not forget. Her mother begged for anything—a cure, hope the size of a grain of sand…anything. But he'd sat there, angry, confused, and shocked. His life was over, and there was nothing he could do.

"She said that was why you moved here…so she can keep studying."

He nodded. "The climate is better here for her ridiculously expensive hobby," he sighed out. That wasn't what she'd meant. "And once we're up and running indoors she can continue her homeschooling online."

"No, I mean…*you* moved here." She paused, the dying sun bouncing off his skin, lighting up his face. "*You* left—to make her happy."

They locked gazes, and for a second, she thought she was in freefall again. His throat bobbed. "Of course. She's my baby sister, and I love her. She has no life, and here I can give her…something. Wouldn't your brother have done that for you?"

Mari scoffed a little too hard. "No." Her expression made him frown, and he narrowed his eyes, rephrasing his earlier question.

"What are you hiding in that house, Marianne Fox?" he asked. "Or are you hiding from someone?"

Whistling out a breath, her vision spun, and she distanced herself by stalking ahead and calling for Bear. When he didn't appear, she quelled a spark of panic, the kind she always got deep out here in the corn. Towering over her head, it went on for miles, touching the border of

Lincoln, and she feared her raucous pup would keep going and going.

Ash called after her, but she ignored him, blood pounding in her ears. Zara's voice on the phone haunted her, gnawed at the edges of her mind. "Mari...wait."

"Bear!" she called, relieved when he appeared, running between her feet. Dropping to her knees, he dropped something at her feet, and she narrowed her eyes, quickly bending to retrieve it. It was a patch of fabric, a lycra piece of cloth that had been torn. It was no more than a scrap, but her hands shook. Ash called after her, and before he could catch up she darted into the corn corridor Bear had sprung from. Her feet pounded the dirt as her pup ran ahead, barking. Then he crouched in the dirt and whimpered.

The ground had been disturbed here, and the dry mud raked over. Mari's breath hitched. There were sneaker prints in the tracks. She gazed down the length of the long, narrow rivets between the stalks, spotting the shadow of Rosewood in the distance.

"Mari?" Ash called, and she stuffed the fabric into her pocket. She forced a smile, quick to hook Bear on his leash.

"Think we should walk back," he said, taking her arm. "Kind of eerie out here at twilight—and I should get home for Clover."

"Of course." She caught up, dragging Bear and not minding his hand brushing hers as they returned. She walked fast, feeling unseen eyes on her back like something else was out there with them.

When he reached the steps of the farmhouse, he took her hand, his thumb grazing her knuckles. "Please say you'll come back," he said like he was using all his courage to muster the strength to ask. "You light her up, and that makes me happy."

Mari stared down at him, their fingers entwined, and she thought she might melt. His hazel eyes were hypnotic and hard to refuse. "Of course, I'll come back."

"I'll get an air conditioner in there," he joked, and she laughed. "Just...don't give up on us. Don't give up on me."

"Why would I give up on you?"

He looked melancholic. "Most people do."

She was hot again, but not from the heat. "I feel you have many secrets, Marianne Fox, and I'd like to know you better." The word made her world spin on its axle. "It's not only Clover who needs a friend."

He was good with words, *too good*, and she swayed a little nearer. If only he knew the ghosts of her old life were keeping her prisoner. Inside, she was molten, staring at him, at his mouth for too long. "I'll come back...to see Clover. I have a feeling you bore her to death."

He grinned, and it was dazzling. "Well, okay. I'll look forward to it."

"Fix the hole in the roof."

He saluted. "Yes, Ma'am."

Wrapping her arms around her waist, she waited until his head vanished into the field of corn before she turned around and withdrew from her pocket the small scrap of lycra.

Black and *yellow* lycra.

Dan Wheeler.

She fingered the scrap of material she was sure had been ripped from a man's body: running gear and sneakers in the dirt.

Mari was sure she'd not dreamed it. A man was crying out for help in that house, and the memory caused goosebumps on her flesh. Ash glanced back and waved, and her heart leaped with fear, curiosity, and longing. God, what has she walked into? Could it be possible that Ash was involved in this? And why did he have to be so damn perfect?

She had not lied to Ash. She'd go back to Rosewood Hall. Part of her longed to be in his company, and part wanted to wrap herself around him and wipe the sadness off his face.

One way or another, she had to return to Rosewood. But this time, Mari decided she'd go at Twilight.

ELEVEN

A blush pink haze dipped below the trees as Mari made her way through the corn fields later the next day. Clutching some old science magazines to her chest, which had belonged to her father, she hoped it would buy her a good excuse for visiting so soon. Before he'd left them, Mari had vague memories of her dad in his study, pouring over his journals and magazines, often holed up in his office for hours. He let her sit by his feet and cut some up for scrapbooking. She enjoyed making pictures with vivid photographs printed inside. The memory made her chest ache, and she forced it away.

She hadn't seen her father for ten years. He'd shown up on her fifteenth birthday, but James and her mother threw up a barricade. Mari was sure she'd seen a man in a long coat at the rear of the crematorium at James's funeral, but he'd run out so fast she couldn't be sure.

Corn husks brushed her bare legs as she hopped through the treeline and wove up the path to the iron gates of Rosewood, still slightly ajar. The house appeared gloomy without the sun shining on it, casting an oppressive shadow that she was reluctant to step into. Mari wasn't sure exactly what had gotten into her.

She'd socialized more in the last forty-eight hours than in five months. Working at her laptop today, she was distracted, her gaze drawn to the old manor hidden in the trees, and she tapped her fingers repeatedly, casting her eye at the torn scrap of material.

Dan Wheeler's face flashed before her eyes. Not only was she possibly the last one to see him, but she was positive that this scrap was from his running gear. And she couldn't get the voice crying out for help out of her head.

So, Mari's knuckles wrapped the stained glass panel, a little shaky as she waited. After a few moments, Ash's voice floated out through the door. "It's open."

When she poked around the door, she saw why he couldn't answer it. She spotted his powerful jean-clad legs first, then his torso. Overhead, he'd built a scaffold. It was enormous, stretching all the way to the lofty roof. He peered down at her. "Builders came to put it up this morning. Want to climb up? The view is amazing."

His voice echoed, and Mari laughed. "Uh, no, thank you. I'm very happy on the ground. What are you doing?"

He gazed at her, framed by pink light pouring in through the gaping hole, as tiny leaves tumbled down. He waved his hand. "Doing what you told me."

She clutched the magazines harder. "By yourself? Don't you have help....or a hardhat?"

He winked, his eyes twinkling in mischief. "Thanks for the concern. Have you ever tried to get a roofer out here at short notice? In the back end of nowhere? It was do it myself or get used to the forest floor in the hall." He nodded to the magazines she held. "What are those?"

"Reading material for Clover. They're my dad's old science journals. I thought she might be interested, you know, for her projects."

Ash wound his body down through the metal bars. His brow was dusted with sweat and grime. Mari braced herself, using the magazines as a shield between them. Something happened to her insides whenever he came too close. She wished she didn't like him as much as she did, especially with this Dan Wheeler problem hanging between them.

He rolled his eyes at the mention of Clover's project, wiping his hands on his jeans. "Don't encourage her even more."

"I'm only helping her...you said she needed company."

He licked his lips, casting a glance skyward. "She's in the orangery, waiting for the sun to set. She'll be glad to see you." He turned, placing one foot on the metal wrung, his knuckles brushing hers. "I'm glad to see you too. I thought." He scratched his neck. "I thought maybe I was too pushy last night—asking too many questions."

Yes, he *had* skirted too close to home, to where she lay her secrets and buried them. But she liked him, and she felt he was someone she could talk to. "No, it's okay. I'm just not used…."

"To guys you hardly know asking personal questions—I get it!" He nodded toward the long corridor that wound down to the ballroom. "Go find her. If you're lucky, you'll get to see the show."

Mari's brows rose. "The show?"

A secretive grin touched his lips. "You'll see."

Hugging the books, Mari left him, casting a shy glance over her shoulder as she headed down the wood-paneled corridor. The giant doors to the ballroom were thrown open, and the scent of roses, night phlox, and vanilla tickled her nose. Gentle light spilled from the glass doors to the orangery.

As she stepped inside, she was struck by a wave of stifling heat, but there was a faint relief of breeze in the air, and she quickly spotted why.

All the massive blinds had been thrown wide, allowing the sunset hues to drip in, casting a violet glow on the girl dancing below, accompanied by the tinny tune from her music box.

Mari hung in the door, fascinated as Clover pirouetted on pointe, her ankles flexing with ease as she balanced in a ballet pose, elegant and graceful; like a bird. Unaware Mari was watching, Clover brought her arms over her head, twirling and spinning on her toes, her white high-neck nightgown floating around her legs.

Mari watched in silence and awe as the girl spun and dipped with grace and poise and bathed in ethereal light from the open blinds. Pausing and righting herself, Clover's face broke in a grin when she spotted Mari lurking in the shadows. "You came back? Quick!" she beckoned with her hand. "Come here. It's about to happen!"

Letting the magazines slip onto Clover's workbench, she hurried to her side, struck by a scent of overpowering rot that made her nostrils flare. It was gone instantly, masked by jasmine, as Clover tugged her under the setting sun. "Won't this hurt you?"

In the starkness of the pink glow, Mari hid her disgust. Clover was beautiful and delicate, but she was not only pale; she was near transparent, and it made her heart jolt. Purple veins clawed up her neck, visible through the paper-thin skin of her hands.

"It's twilight…it won't hurt me."

Mari stumbled after her, immediately breaking into a sweat. "Where'd you learn to dance like that?"

Clover smiled as though she were forcing away a pang of sadness. "I've had many years alone to learn."

The statement tugged at her gut, and Mari felt guilt creeping in. Suddenly, her reasons for being here, Dan Wheeler, and everything she thought, seemed ridiculous and idiotic. Following Clover under the open blinds, she gazed up as the sun slowly crawled into a far corner of the window. "What are we looking at?"

Clover squealed in excitement, squeezing Mari's fingers as she held out her hand. "Wait ...any second now."

"What?"

The sun vanished, setting behind the house, and the room was bathed in an eerie glow. A chill tickled her neck as she looked around, up and down at every conceivable nook and cranny draped with vines, spider webbing over their heads.

Everything came to life. Mari held back a gasp, unaware of what she was seeing as petals opened and buds sprung open, lifting their drooped heads to the dark. It was like the room breathed slowly and deeply, and leaves arched their necks as stems straightened, crawling to the shadows where they bloomed.

Mari gasped. "Oh…"

"Do you like it?"

She shook her head in awe. "I've never seen anything—" her words caught. The smell hit her, making her sway. Exotic, spicy, and rich, every scent mingled under her nose, strong enough to make her eyes throb, like a particularly pungent perfume. She was reminded of trailing through a department store at Christmas and being sprayed by shop girls.

"Whoa…that's intense."

So, this was what Ash had meant. While beautiful, and magical, the smell was making her dizzy. She stepped out of range.

"Let me show you something else," Clover, unaware of her reaction, dragged her around the Ornamental pond and through to the workshop. Mari pinched the bridge of her nose, glad to be out of the onslaught. In its glass cage, the small buds of Clover's hybrid lifted their heads, seeking the shadows.

"Watch," Clover gripped her hand, caught in a heated, almost feverish glare. "Watch it happen."

As if it knew they waited for it to open, the bud opened carefully, elegantly one petal at a time, stretching to the darkness. Mari's eyes widened, fascinated by how gently it turned, its leaves trembling with new life. It was black inside, spotted with deep mauve like it couldn't decide what color it wanted to be. There was a snip, and it dropped, and Clover plucked it out of its earth, holding it up to the light.

Mari's smile dropped. "Oh, that's a shame." It didn't seem fair to cut it when it'd barely bloomed.

Clover frowned. "It's no good to me behind glass." She hurried to her bench and began ruthlessly plucking off every single petal, and Mari gazed at the ruined flower, a little deflated. Clover gathered the petals and laid them out on a fine sheet of wax paper. "This has a job to do."

Carefully, she laid out each petal one by one for drying, and Mari folded her arms and watched with interest. The canisters of the tea were already made, ready, and lined up. "How's your experiment going?" she hated to ask, having a feeling she knew where the scent of dead flesh was coming from.

Clover flinched, fingering the lace neckline of her gown. "Not very well, I'm afraid." She peeled away the lace briefly, and when Mari gaped in horror, she quickly buttoned it up. "It's not too bad."

"Not too bad?" Mari cried, her nostrils flaring. Clover's skin was broken open, a wound riddled with green pus. Mari covered her mouth. "You need a hospital!"

"It's fine!"

"It is not fine!" Mari argued. "At least…" She broke off. "At least let me treat it properly—and not with a handmade ointment, something *antibacterial*."

Clover's face crumpled, fear and pain etched in her eyes. "My potions are good—they work—look!"

She rolled up her sleeve, revealing the patch of skin that had been open and festering the day before. Mari edged closer, her eyes narrowing in wonder. The skin was healed, still red, but any sign of infection was long gone. She flicked her eyes, meeting Clover's, where the girl looked at her imploringly. "See?"

"I don't care," Mari said, spinning on her heels. "You must have a first aid kit somewhere in this building. Where are the old kitchens?"

"W-wait…"

"I'll find them." Mari walked out of the oppressive gloom of the workshop, her throat itching as she ran through the orangery. A house like Rosewood would have had serving kitchens at one point, and as she crept through the corridors, she spotted a narrow oak door with a light burning. She pushed it open, instantly smelled coffee, and took the narrow steps two at a time, finding herself in a wide, stone room in the basement. It was a depleted old kitchen. The oak doors practically fell off their hinges, but it had a stove fired by oil.

Ash clearly used this room, and she spotted used cups and plates in the sink. She found a pantry door and rifled through cupboards and shelves, her hand drifting over a dusty box. Grinning in triumph, she pulled it out and blew away an inch of dust.

She couldn't sit across from Clover, knowing what lay beneath that nightgown, and not try to do something to help her. The kit was old, but it had clean bandages, sterile wipes, and antibacterial cream. It would do, and if she was so determined to use her 'potions,' then that was on her.

Lost in thought, Mari took the stairs up to the ground floor, the walls coated in peeling wallpaper and wet plaster surrounding her. Momentarily, she lost her way, heading left out of the kitchen rather than right, then turned herself around. Prickles of fear wound around her heart as she darted through hallways and dark corridors, half expecting a wraith hiding around the next corner. Stamping her foot, she realized quickly she was lost, but she was determined not to panic.

That determination lasted all of five minutes. Every walkway and every hall looked the same. She thought she must be walking in circles, trying to take mental notes of unused lamp fittings the occasional cobweb hanging from a dusty corner. Her heart jumped from one beat to the next, knocking in her chest as she hurried along, her legs slowly draining of blood. How could she have lost her way that quickly? The ground floor wasn't that large.

She parted her lips, ready to call for help when something cut her short. Her neck blazed with heat as she strained to hear what she thought she'd heard.

A voice. Goosebumps erupted over her arms. She followed the ghostly echo down a narrow corridor adorned with faded floral prints. "Hello?"

It was there—a man's voice. Faint and fading, but it was there. Mari's knees trembled as she rushed forward, spying a spiral metal staircase at the end of the hall. She'd forgotten she was carrying the first aid kit. It weighed nothing in her hands. Her steps faltered as she headed for the stairs, her fingers closing over the cool metal wrung. "Where are you?"

She stared up into a lofty cavern, wooden broken slats above her head, a death trap. It was a back staircase for the servants to pass discreetly through the upper floors when this house was full of the old Rosewood family. The stairs looked like they'd crumple if she stepped on them. Mari stared up into the dark space, and something flickered. Eyes shone in the dark.

Was there someone up there? His voice sounded weak, and her heart thundered. Casting an eye down the empty corridor, checking she was alone before she placed the box at her feet. Carefully, she stepped on the first wrung. "I'm coming," she whispered. "Are you hurt?"

Whoever hid in the shadows gasped in pain, its shape darting away, bleeding into the shadows. Was this her mind playing tricks?

Her vision swam, the world spinning as she lost her balance and rocked back to the floor—a spike of pain shot through her temple so dazzlingly that her stomach rolled with nausea. Something itched in her nose, and she wiped it on her hand.

Mari saw stars, her legs giving way as an engulfing wave of dizziness washed over her.

"Mari?" she heard Ash, his voice, high pitched in alarm as she slumped to the ground in a haze. It was that awful, cloying smell. It itched her nose and her throat. Her eyes throbbed. She scratched her nose, and blood stained her fingers.

Darkness swept in, and she saw Ash's face hovering above her as she slipped into a dreamless void. She swore she heard someone, his voice in the air, and he'd whispered a warning.

"Get out—leave this place while you can."

TWELVE

Mari woke, wiping at her bloodied nose. The eerie gloom of the ballroom settled, lighting the glittering motes of dust on the air. Above her two worried faces hovered. Ash visibly wilted with relief, and Clover let out a long sigh. "Thank goodness."

Mari sat up too fast and saw stars. She clutched her head. Ash steadied her shoulder. "Not so fast."

Mari pulled away, blinking. "Where is he?"

Clover and Ash exchanged a confused look. "Who?" he asked, narrowing his brow.

"Don't pretend you didn't hear it—the man *crying* out for help?"

The look that passed between them only made Mari shrink. Clover's lip twitched as though she was suppressing a laugh, and Ash chuckled lightly. "Mari…"

"Do not laugh at me!" she cried, jabbing her finger, unsure where this venomous outburst had come from. Their mirth vanished, melting into concern.

"Take it easy," Ash said, rubbing her shoulder. "We're not laughing at you."

"I know what I heard!" She swayed and pinching the bridge of her nose. "I'm not crazy. I *heard* him."

Ash and Clover looked gravely at one another, and Mari's temper frayed short. She was about done with the teasing. When she went to fire another shot, Ash held up a finger. "I might have an idea of what you think you heard."

"I don't *think*—I know. It was a man. Someone was trapped up there in the roof…on the second floor." Dismally, she scratched her head, unsure exactly what she'd seen. Ash nodded in understanding.

"We do have a bird problem."

"It wasn't a bird." She fell back on the arm of the couch, her throat unbearably dry. She glanced at her fingers. There were no specks of blood in sight.

Get out while you can...

"It wasn't birds," she repeated miserably. Ash dropped to the couch next to her, his hand on hers.

"Give yourself a few minutes to feel better. And then I'll show you—I think I understand."

"Oh?" She wasn't about to let her temper drop, and he smiled wanly, nodding to Clover.

"Yeah. Just rest for now." He tilted his head, studying her with interest. "The imagination is a powerful tool, Mari."

Mari closed her eyes, her cheeks flushed and hot. She wished she could sink and evaporate into the cushions. It wasn't the first time her mind ran rampant. Adopting her father's methodical, logical way of thinking was the only thing that kept the monsters from under her bed as a child. The only shield she had to keep Mr.

Raggerty on his pole and not at her window tapping to get in.

She pinched the bridge of her nose again. "Shit. I'm sorry."

"Drink this," Clover urged, pressing a hot mug into her palm. Mari sipped it gingerly.

"What is it?" It tasted floral, and sweet, with a tang of bitterness. "One of your potions?"

Clover frowned at her sarcasm. "No, it's chamomile…from the pantry."

Mari gulped, and it coated her tongue. "Sorry. I…overreacted."

Ash puffed out air, rising to his feet. Then he planted the wooden first aid kit on the chaise beside her. "This place is like a maze, all dark, winding corridors. It's no wonder you got lost. No wonder you freaked out."

"I did not—"

Clover's scoff made her clamp her mouth shut. Instead, Ash flashed her a knowing grin before taking off into the hallway. Through the gap in the door, she spotted him climb into the scaffold in the hall, winding his body with ease through the metal rungs.

They sat in comfortable silence for a while, Marianne sipping her tea in deep thought and Clover tinkling at the tinny piano keys. After a while her head cleared, and her stomach ceased churning like a washer. Clover slipped from behind the piano and took a seat beside her. "Feel better?"

"Hmm." She wasn't sure how she felt in this house, only right now she could nod into a deep sleep. The faint aroma of decay wafted under her nose, and she remembered why she'd been poking around in the lower halls in the first place.

She turned her attention to the box and clicked it open, pulling out the sterile wipes and a bandage. Clover whined. "Marianne...I'm *fine*!"

"You are not fine."

Whatever was happening under the thin layer of lace at her throat made Mari's nose wrinkle as she pressed closer, carefully unbuttoning the collar. She revealed the wound and forced herself not to gag. It was rotten, the smell of infection strong enough to make her reel. Carefully, she cleaned it with the wipe, and Clover surprised her by remaining perfectly still, her wide eyes open and fixed at something over Mari's shoulder. "Does this hurt?"

"No, not if I don't think about it," Clover said through gritted teeth. "I should be used to it by now."

"I wish you wouldn't do this," Mari said, taking a clean wipe and removing old, dead, festered skin and pus.

"The next time will be better. This rose was *good*. It was strong."

Mari wasn't about to play along, but her heart ached for the girl. She carefully applied antiseptic ointment, and Clover quickly slathered her own mixture across the wound. It smelled sweet and heady, like lavender. She smiled. "It *is* magic."

Mari rolled her eyes and cut out a square piece of padding, fixing it in place with surgical tape. She patted it carefully. "There."

"Thank you." Clover studied her as if assessing what to say next. She nodded at the pile of magazines on the small polished table by the chaise. "That was really kind to think of me. Did they belong to James?"

"My dad." Mari cleared her throat, apprehension growing whenever she spoke about the man who'd walked out when she was five. Clover raised a brow, inching closer.

"I'm guessing by the ominous silence he's no longer around."

Mari snapped the box shut and flicked the catch. "Not for a long time."

"I'm sorry. That's hard."

"Well, I was young, so…you can't miss what you never really had."

"Don't say that." Clover laid a cool hand over Mari's settled on top of the box, and she glanced up in surprise. Clover was warm, her cheeks flushed, and her eyes gleamed in the dim light. Mari was cold. "It must have hurt."

Mari blinked, still a little fuzzy. She managed a shrug, as nonchalant as she could be about that time. "My mother isn't the easiest person to live with, and when he went away, she kind of…made James the man of the house. A role he enjoyed—a little too much."

Clover's pulse beat under her skin, hard and fast, so much that Mari could feel it through their joined hands. The girl tipped her head in interest. "He was cruel?"

Mari's head throbbed, and she steadily slid her hand out from under Clover's and brushed back her hair, feeling her scalp break into a sweat. As if sensing her discomfort, the girl rapidly changed the subject. "What made you think there was a man up in our rafters?"

"Oh." Mari laughed, feeling a little absurd. "I don't know if you watched the news, but a man went missing and…" She broke off and met Clover's wide, haunted gaze, and her mouth snapped shut, her brain zigzagging in a different direction. She didn't want to mention the scrap of material she'd found in the corn. "It must have been on my mind."

Clover looked thoughtful. "We still don't have our television set up. It's driving me a little insane."

"I bet."

"So I didn't hear about that…that's such a shame."

Mari dipped her chin. "It's sad. He just vanished after the storm." Clover went to reach for her again, but she slid away, unsure why her touch made her neck prickle. She liked Clover, *really* liked her. But something was a little off in this place, and she wanted to speak to Ash alone.

"Thank you for the magazines," Clover said, interrupting her thought. "It might help."

"Speaking of that," Mari said. "Can you promise me something?"

"What?"

"When you test the experiment again, can I be there?"

Clover laughed, relieved as if she'd expected Marianne to grill her again. "Of course! I'm not sure why you'd want to, though."

"I don't want you to get hurt," Mari answered truthfully, jerking her chin at the wound under Clover's nightgown. "What you're doing to yourself is not good, and maybe I can help…maybe pull you back if things go too far?"

Clover's eyes filled up, her chin wobbling. "You'd do that?"

"Of course! I want to help you. When were you planning to test again?"

"A few days…at least until this burn has healed. The pain does take it out of me." She looked uncertain before she continued. "I know you think I'm crazy. Ash hates it, and he makes it clear how he feels. But the doctors have tried everything, and nothing works. I don't want to live in the dark, Mari. Can you understand?"

Mari nodded weakly. "I get it."

"I can't not try. I must believe I'll leave this place and walk with you outside someday. And if they can't find a cure, why can't I?"

"Then promise you'll wait for me?"

Clover smiled. "I promise, Mari. I will."

As it happened, Ash wasn't hard to find. Mari stood below the carefully put-together scaffold, straining up into the dark. The moon was high over the house, sending a beam of light through the hole. He appeared above, smiling as he wove through the metal rungs, backlit from the moon. "Feeling better?"

Mari tried not to react to that smile and those eyes, but it was hard when her heart leaped at the sight of him. "I'm fine. It's not me that's the problem here."

He made a face, settling on the rickety wooden platform above her head. She folded her arms, gazing up at him. "I had a feeling this was coming." He rubbed at his chin.

Mari scoffed. "Ash—you can't let her keep doing this. Why would you agree to go along with her..." Mari lowered her voice conspiratorially, casting a wary glance over her shoulder. For a second, she thought she'd seen a flash of blonde hair out of the corner of her eye, a figure scuttling along the corridors. "...with this torture? She's hurting herself."

Ash crouched, looking miserable. "What would you like me to do?" he asked. "Take her to more doctors? I can show you the reports. It's been Clo and me for years, and all I want is to make her happy. This thing...I know it'll never get better."

"Then why would you let her put herself through this?"

Their gazes collided, and his eyes were stormy, dark, and regretful. "Do you know what it's like to watch someone you love live without hope, Marianne?"

The question threw her, and she stepped back, recalling the smell of disinfectant and hospital wards, and James's face when he knew it was over. She took a shallow breath. "I do know what that's like. It happened to my brother."

Ash nodded as though he understood, gazing at her through his dark lashes. "I'm sorry, but it's a little different. Your brother died, and forgive me if that's harsh. Clover will live with this forever, with no end or hope in sight. Your brother may have suffered, but it wasn't long. Clover has a lifetime."

His abrupt answer cut right through her wall, her stony exterior, and her throat bobbed with a knot of emotion. He was right, but she shook her head. "It still doesn't make it right. Frying her skin off her bones is no way to handle this...there has to be another way."

"Your friendship is a way," he said. "Clover always had trouble connecting. Bonding with anyone, and the last few days are the happiest I've seen her."

Mari sighed, as if that didn't make her feel incredibly guilty about snooping around. Friendship? She'd removed herself from her friends, her old life, and Zara. She wasn't sure what she had to offer Clover. She lifted her chin. "Then I'll come back if that helps her."

"We'd both love that." He cleared his throat and caught himself as if he remembered something. "Oh, wait! I was going to show you this. Give me your hand, and I'll pull you up."

"What?" Mari folded her arm to her side. "I'm not getting on that thing. It looks like it'll collapse."

"It's perfectly safe. I want to show you something." He flexed his forearm, reaching down, fingers splayed. "I've got you, trust me."

Tentatively, she reached for him. "What's up there?"

"I'll show you. Come on."

Mari's palm brushed his, and he clamped his fingers around her hand. Putting a foot on the bottom wrung, she gritted her teeth as he heaved her up to the first platform. "You go first. I'm right behind you if you slip."

Shakily, she took the rungs of the ladder. "You better be."

Her knees knocked as she climbed, her biceps straining as she climbed the rickety ladder into the rafters of the old building. It was dusty up here, but cool night air billowed through the gaping hole. "Do I keep going?"

Ash was right behind her. "Right to the next platform."

Her elbows wobbled, but she crawled onto the next wooden platform. Her torso was level with the hole. She was surrounded by wooden slats and shingles where Ash was patching it. He'd left his hammer and nails up here. It rocked a little as Ash climbed beside her, and she shrieked, the breeze tangling in her hair. "Oh, my god."

"Take my hand and stand up."

"N-*no* way!"

He laughed. "C'mon, trust me. I won't let anything happen to you."

Mari took a deep breath and, clutching his hand till her own drained of blood, she stood, her head poking through the top of the roof. It was quiet, and the night was full of glittering stars. In the distance, she spotted her house, the living room light on low. She saw Mr. Raggerty twirling on his pole. Ash was behind her, his hands on her waist.

"Okay, close your eyes."

"What?"

"Come on, you've gotten this far. Trust me."

It was difficult to think clearly with his hands on her waist and his breath on her neck, sending shockwaves down her spine. Her eyes fluttered shut. "Okay, now what?"

"Wait and listen."

His fingers were warm and firm, and she relaxed against him, a surge of heat flooding her body as she felt his ribcage breathe into her back. Then she heard it, and her eyes snapped open.

A man was crying and moaning. "Oh…!" she gasped in fright, her heart vaulting. "What is that? Where is he?"

Ash chuckled, and it rumbled in her ear. "Mari, it's the wind in the wooden slats…listen."

She strained to hear, and when the stark breeze hit the open rivets on the roof, she heard it again. Relief flooded her system, and she let out a low, shaky laugh. "It sounds exactly…"

"I can see why that freaked you out," he admitted. "We have to listen to this all night."

Standing under the stars with his arms around her, keeping her safe, it was hard to recall why she'd been so afraid. Ash rested his chin on her head. "Did anyone ever tell you that you have a great imagination?"

Tears sparked in her eyes, and she was glad he couldn't see her from this angle, even though her voice grew thick. "I was a bad sleeper as a kid. Eventually, I taught myself how not to be afraid of…" She snickered. "Well…everything. Trust the facts."

"I get it."

"There usually is a logical explanation for everything," she said aloud like she was convincing herself. "That was my dad's doing. Now I don't feel scared of the dark…or monsters under the bed."

"Well, as Clo reminds me daily…beauty can thrive in the dark." She tilted her shoulder, lifting her chin to look up at him, her eyes on his bottom lip.

You're a moron, she told herself, feeling every inch a fool. God, she'd let her fear take over, all the spooky things she'd read in Eric's manuscript getting to her. It got all tangled up with this strange new reality. She clutched Ash's hand, which had woven around to rest on her ribs. She tipped her chin to look up at him, and her heart thundered. "I'm so sorry."

He brushed a lock of dark hair out of her eyes. "Don't be sorry. It's a spooky old place with a ton of stuff that goes bump in the night." He smiled gently. "Can I walk you home?"

She bit her lip, nodding shyly, as he went back down the hole first. He wove through the bars, always looking up, checking that she was okay as he held out his hand. Finally, when he reached the bottom, he put his hands out and lowered her down. He let her slowly sink to the floor, her breath shaky and a little lightheaded from the climb. Ash, however, was beaming. He looked radiant under the moon; it shone off his hair.

His thumb casually brushed her cheekbone, and she turned away bashfully into his hand, her heart too fluttery to meet his gaze. She wasn't sure what was happening; only she was woozy and filled with blood pumping rapidly around her body.

"I hope we can be friends, Mari," he said, brushing hair off her shoulder. "I wonder what you'd say if I asked you out sometime. Just us?"

Blushing, she turned away, unused to this intensity of attention, of kindness. "Then you'll have to ask me sometime, and you'll find out."

THIRTEEN

S he was slower this morning, groggy and fuzzy headed. Mari squinted against the screen's glare as she pressed send on her reply to Eric— a list of fixes and adjustments for the last ten pages she'd read. Yawning, she'd consciously tried to sound enthusiastic in her amendments, with 'this is great—but try this' and 'I feel like I get what you're going for here, but…"

She scowled at her suggestions, thinking she was the one who needed an editor.

Less than ten minutes after Mari hit send, her phone lit up with a reply from Eric. She groaned inwardly, pinching the bridge of her nose where a headache had formed from sitting hunched over the laptop all afternoon. In truth, she was exhausted. Eric was used to prompt, timely responses, usually free of typos.

With a huff, her chin rested on her fist, and she clicked the email.

Are you okay? This doesn't read like you.

Mari sniffed, a little taken back. She quickly thumbed a reply.

Of course, it's me. I'm fine! Just a little tired, that's all.

A few moments later, he came back with, **I'd love to discuss these notes properly. Can we arrange a face-to-face call?**

Ice flooded her veins and she pulled away from the keyboard. She knew he awaited her answer, and she paused, hesitating before she finally typed a reply.

I'll see what I can do. Have a good weekend, Eric!

She hit send and shut the laptop down, hating that niggling feeling that somehow was disappointed with her notes or suggestions. Eric was a fantastic client when he wasn't trying to get her live face-to-face.

A permanent headache rested on her brow, wearying her eyes. Next to her the phone vibrated, and she jumped in fright, staring at it in dismay. Eric didn't have her number. Grabbing it in her clammy hand she breathed easy when she spotted the caller ID. She swiped to answer, clearing her throat. "Dr. Conners!" she greeted him as breezily as she could. "Thank you so much for calling me back."

The deep chuckle vibrated through the phone at the other end, and she imagined her family doctor with his ochre skin, dark eyes, and crinkled smile. "How could I resist my favorite fact-checker?" he joked. "What tropical disease has your author friend written about now?"

Mari smiled, thinking of how often she'd emailed and called her family doctor for feedback on Eric's work. Eric had a habit of inventing gruesome illnesses for his characters, and it was Mari's duty to keep him realistic. Dr. Conners had looked after her family for years since she'd been little, and he was there when James passed away.

Mari crossed her legs and threw back in the chair. "It's kind of a rare one. Icaria Disorder? Have you heard of it?"

"Hmm." He paused at the other end and she could hear his chair squeal as he shifted. "Ah yes—*Icarus*, the boy who flew too close to the sun. It's a rare allergy to sunlight. It can cause a nasty case of hives."

Mari's brows rose. "Hives? I've heard this is a bit more serious than Hives."

"Oh, it can be, for sure," he said, tapping the receiver with his fingers in thought. "It can range from mild blisters and itching to a full-blown rash."

Mari sucked in the air, thinking of the patch of ruined skin under Clover's night dress. "Is it curable?"

"I'm afraid not. It's manageable though—you can wear protective clothing and stay out of the sun of course…"

"Does it…" Mari fought for the words to describe what she'd seen. "Can it get worse than a bad rash?"

"In some cases—over a long exposure, it can cause anaphylaxis." He sounded amused. "What has your author come up with this time?"

Mari chuckled. "Oh, he made it much worse than what you're describing. So it's a blood disorder?"

"No, it's an autoimmune condition," he corrected her. "It's the body reacting to histamine in the skin. Look I have a friend over at Dermatology who could give you a call. He might know a little more on the subject."

Mari was on the brink of refusing, that guilty feeling creeping in when she thought of how she was going behind Ash and Clover's back, asking questions. They hadn't asked for her help. All Ash wanted for his sister was friendship. But she changed her mind and grabbed her pen. The questions would only eat at her. She thought of the rose—the Night Witch, and she gave a sheepish laugh. "Can I ask something else?"

"Of course." He sounded resigned at this point, and over the last couple of months, she'd emailed him a lot of crazy stuff. "Can Botany help it? Like…you know…herbs and oils and that kind of thing."

He chuckled, which should have been enough of an answer. "Ah, Pseudo-science?"

She frowned. "There has to be something in it. I mean, medicine comes from plant life, doesn't it?"

"Some do."

"So you don't believe it? That plants and flowers can be healing?"

"Oh, I didn't say that. I think if the patient *believes* it'll help—then there can be a very positive effect. But if you're asking if I would swap it from modern medicine? Then no."

Mari tapped the desk. "So, can it be a placebo effect?"

He cleared his throat. "Botany has had a huge impact on modern medicine. I don't wish to enter into that debate. It has its place. But if you want to know if plants can cure Icaria Disorder—then no. As it stands, right now, there is no cure. But talk to my friend at Meadowford General—he'll have a far deeper understanding."

When she jotted down the email, the doctor steered the conversation in a direction she didn't want to travel.

"How are you, Marianne?"

She rested her hand on her chin, staring out at the corn and the rain pelting the glass of her window. She thought about lying, saying she was fine, but it was easier to be truthful. "We're coping."

"I need to arrange to see your mother."

"I don't think she wants to be seen right now."

He sighed deeply. "Marianne, it's been four months. I worry she's not taking care of herself."

Mari balked, her spine straightening. "*I'm* taking care of her."

"And who is taking care of you?"

Mari's eyes flicked to Rosewood, longing for Ash and his arms around her. In an odd way, she even missed Clover. Days had passed since her last visit, and after humiliating herself so thoroughly, she wasn't sure she wanted to return for another round just yet. "I'm okay."

"Look. You know where I am if you need anything or anyone to talk to. You don't have to cope with this alone, Mari." He paused, clearly waiting for her to refuse, and when she remained silent, he went on. "I notice that you're having your mother's medication delivered to the house. Why don't you collect?"

Mari scoffed. "Why *not* deliver?"

"Because it gets you *out* of the house."

I don't want to be out of the house. She swallowed thickly. "I've just been busy working here—it's convenient."

"I worry you're becoming reclusive. You're a young woman, Mari, and you dropped out of college and life…you had friends…"

"I have friends!" She gazed at Rosewood, already deciding what to do for the remainder of her afternoon. "You really don't have to worry."

Sounding unconvinced, Doctor Conners wrapped up the call by promising to contact Mari soon. Mari quickly emailed the dermatologist he'd recommended and spent the afternoon battling Eric's manuscript and pretending that she wasn't daydreaming of Ash Martin.

Not long after that day, up on the roof, more of Dan Wheeler's clothes were found in the grate of the Boxford tunnel out near Lincoln, miles from Winstone. Even though it was horrible news, it settled her fears. The police called off the search.

She still held onto the scrap of material and tried to envision why it was out there. Could the storm have carried it in? Mari was happy with the facts; even though something still nagged at her gut, her logical and methodical brain was satiated—for now.

She yawned and stretched, gazing out over the fields as late afternoon approached. Downstairs, her mother lay napping on the couch, her hair splayed over the cushion, and Bear nestled against her belly.

I'm taking care of her…

"Mom? I'm going for a walk," she said, her voice throaty. Her mother lifted her head, giving a brief nod before falling asleep.

Taking care of her mother meant taking her to see a doctor. It meant getting her to admit her problem and get real help. Right now, her mother was draped in a thick blanket of grief. A place where she existed comfortably, numbly, and happily isolated. A place where she could pretend the last four months didn't happen. Mari didn't want to yank her out of that existence, where she'd have to grieve properly. Grieve and admit James was gone. It wasn't time.

Bear yawned lazily and seemed content to keep her company. Mari bit her lip; the urge to see Ash and Clover had become like an itch under her skin. Grabbing her coat against the rain, she locked the house and headed to the gloom of Rosewood Hall.

FOURTEEN

The first thing she saw as she squeezed through the gap in the gate was Ash outside with a large scythe. Peering through the heavily laced trees, she ducked and followed his path around the side of the house, near the old crypt, where she heard a loud chopping noise splitting the air.

He spotted her through the mist, and straightened. Brow beaded with sweat, he wore a shirt revealing his toned arms. He wiped his brow and waved a gloved hand. She stepped carefully over the thorny remains of the trimmed hedgerow and vines he'd cut. "Gardening?"

He jerked his chin in the direction of the crypt. "It's so overgrown you can't even get near it."

Mari glanced briefly at the small stone structure with the angel guarding the door, hands heavenward, her hair tumbling down her back. "Are you planning on burying someone in there?"

Goosebumps rose on her arms. The small structure gave off a vibe, an air of malice floated in the mist around it. She shook herself. Of course it gave off an odd vibe, it was a *crypt.*

He gave her a wink. "Maybe." When she looked confused, he laughed it off, wiping his forehead on the edge of his shirt. "I'm *kidding.* We have a water main running through here somewhere, and there's a leak in the house. It's destroyed the kitchen downstairs— water everywhere. I called a plumber but he can't get here till next week."

Mari let a shudder roll over her body. "Oh." That seemed logical, as she cast her eye over the crypt, ignoring the crawling sensation it gave her.

Ash raised the scythe and whacked through the undergrowth. "You know you *can* get electrical versions of those? Things that were made this century," she teased. He made a face at her.

"No electricity, remember? I haven't watched television for weeks."

She folded her arms. "Don't you have work to do? I thought you'd been transferred." It occurred to her then that he'd never spoken about his time in Fairbanks or what he'd left behind to give Clover a better shot at a normal life.

Ash smirked. "I'd love to. Someone has to fund Clover's crazy hobby." His smile dropped as he brushed a blonde strand of hair out of his eyes. "It will be a little longer before I can get online again. Once I'm up and running I can afford for contractors to come in and properly gut this place."

It was quiet out here, but Ash's presence made it seem normal. Mari thought she'd be uncomfortable if she were alone out here in the gloom. Too many bent trees twisted around the property, giving the place an oppressive aura. She glanced over her shoulder. "I came to see Clover."

Ash glanced up, his expression pensive, before he said, "She's sick, Mari."

"Sick?" Mari blinked, confused. She hated how the word sparked dread in her chest. "What's wrong?"

"I don't know—a cold? She hasn't been out of bed for a couple of days."

Flustered, heat rippled under her skin, that clawing sensation of panic. "Why didn't you call me? I could have come over."

Ash seemed uncomfortable, noncommittal, as he yanked a large bramble from the ground. "It happens sometimes. It's part of her condition."

Mari looked away, hoping that her guilt wasn't written over her face. She didn't want to admit she'd been checking up on them. It didn't seem like fevers or colds were part of Icaria Disorder. Instead, she plastered on a bright smile. "Can I go see her?"

He smiled gratefully. "I'm sure she'll love that. She's in the orangery—waiting for sundown."

Mari nodded, taking a large step over a log. She was about to leave when he called her back. "Go around back…through the ornamental garden, you'll see the doors are open."

Following in the direction he'd pointed, Mari waded through tall grass and weeds, leaving the crypt behind. She spied the low stone wall and a cracked stone path, zigzagging its way through overgrown hedges and topiary. The path was eaten up by moss and grass, crumbling under her shoes. More stone maidens dotted the path in various positions, some carrying urns, some flowers.

Fear licked at her scalp, and she shuddered, pausing near the center of the rose garden. Their faces—all of them—had been gouged and scratched beyond recognition. Wrapping her arms about her waist, she pushed away the eerie sensation. In the center of the garden was a maiden kneeling on the cracked stone slabs, covering her face as though she were weeping.

Mari tiptoed around her edgily, telling herself it was nothing more than the work of vandals. She crept up some steps under an arch of jasmine and honeysuckle, ducking as she poked her head into the orangery. At least there was a breeze filtering through today.

What Mari saw in the fountain made her stop dead, and she shrieked, "Clover! What on earth…?"

Clover lay face up in a bed of lilies, eyes closed, as she floated listlessly on the water's surface. The dark, quiet depths of the pond water engulfed her legs, her nightgown billowing on the surface. Mari hauled her torso over the lip of the fountain and grabbed the girl's arm. Clover's eyes snapped open. "Mari!"

"What the hell are you doing?"

Clover sat up, shivering, spluttering. "I was fine…I was…"

Mari clambered inside the fountain, no more than knee-deep, and hoisted Clover out by the arms. A haze of heat rose off the girl, yet her teeth chattered. Mari looked her over, sunken-eyed, white lips and shark skin grey. "You're burning up. Let's get you to bed."

Weakly, Clover nodded, her nightgown leaving a sopping trail as she hobbled alongside Marianne to the chaise, where she flopped. "I can't walk far."

Ashen, Mari stared at Clover's legs, thin and weak, her veins visible through the skin.

Clover smiled wanly, folding her arms around her chest for warmth. "Ash will carry me up later."

"I'll get you some towels," Mari said, rushing across the room and flinging the door open to the hall. Mari caught sight of a few stray leaves pirouetting from the ceiling in the dreary, moth-eaten gloom of the hallway. Grabbing the worn banister, she jogged up the stairs. The rail was covered with vines growing from between the slats in the floor, and she wondered when they'd grown there, curling up the stairway and into the darkness.

When a board split under her foot, her ankle turned, and she flung herself against the wall in fright. The stairs were rotting. This place was decaying, dissolving into the earth like the ground wanted to claim it back. Reaching the first floor, Mari recalled where Ash's bedroom was, across the faded rug with the frayed edges. She let the door swing open, greeted by the sight of his neatly made bed and the fire crackling in the grate. She darted to the bathroom and grabbed a handful of towels, careful not to linger and poke around. The last thing she wanted was for Ash to catch her snooping.

Bundling them in her arms, she closed the door behind her, her neck prickling as she faced the looming corridor ahead. Her throat caught, and for a second, she remained frozen at the door, one hand on Ash's door handle.

Someone was down there watching. It'd been a moment, fleeting, but she'd seen a shape move, a flash of eyes watching her. She took a heavy step nearer, feeling it there, waiting, and watching her make a move. "Hello?" she called, her voice cracking.

"I've got her, Mari," Ash called from the top of the stairs, his voice jolting her out of her daze, forcing her to look away and lose sight of whatever or whoever was in the shadows. Ash appeared, cradling Clover as though she weighed nothing.

He carried her across the hall and, to Mari's horror, turned sharply to take the corridor where she'd seen the shadow hiding. Her voice withered as she went to speak, and he didn't appear to hear her as he marched his sister down the hall and kicked open a door with his shoe.

Mari was quick to follow, clutching the bundle of clean linen, trailing behind him into a master suite, where a small fire burned in a hearth. He lay Clover in a massive dark wood four-poster, where the duvet seemed to gobble her up. She breathed deeply and shut her eyes, laying her pale hands on her belly.

Mari eased onto the side of the bed, and her brows pulled so tight she could feel a headache forming. "What's wrong with her?"

Ash looked away, biting his lower lip. "A few days and she'll be back to normal—whatever normal is for her. It's the illness…it drains her, leaves her weak."

"What can I do?"

"There's nothing you can do," he said, the hopelessness in his tone gut-wrenching. "Keep her company. Read to her. She'll bounce back—you'll see."

Deeply asleep, Clover looked like a fallen angel against the floral print of her bed linen. Mari crept closer, letting her hand rest on top of Clover's. She jerked in alarm. Clover was as cold as stone, like one of the maidens in the ornamental garden. A knot of sorrow rose in Mari's chest; it clogged her throat and before she knew it, a tear escaped her lashes, dripping down her nose to leave salt on her lips. She wiped her eyes, unsure where that'd come from, as Clover took a long, shuddering breath.

Ash smiled. "It'll do her good just hearing your voice."

Mari spent the afternoon thumbing through the old, worn books on Clover's bookshelf, reading aloud. On the bed, Clover slept, occasionally taking a long, slow breath or expelling a small sigh. Mari fussed and arranged her hair, which had dried in pretty yellow curls on the pillow, the color of wheat, ready to be sheaved. She leaned on the bed, stifling a yawn. The room smelled of jasmine, and with the heat of the fire at her back, it was enough to make her sleepy.

She didn't know she'd nodded off until Ash prodded her and said it was time to go home. They walked silently, both in thought, and when he stopped at Keller's steps, Mari squeezed his hand. Their fingers linked, and she promised him she'd go back.

FIFTEEN

Days passed, with Clover resting, occasionally waking for half an hour. Mari fed her soup she'd found in the old kitchens, heating it on the fire. Ash hadn't exaggerated about the leak; the kitchen floor was covered in murky puddles, and she remembered to bring waterproof boots when she needed to go down there. She did *not* want to spend long in the darkened lower halls of Rosewood, thinking she had heard whispers in the halls, the voices of those who had worked down here years ago. It struck her how the levels below were once a hive of activity and must have been crowded with servants. Now, it was desolate and rotting, and Mari was surprised that she was becoming familiar with the winding corridors.

Still, she didn't linger. Even now, she couldn't shake the feeling that someone was watching from the shadows.

"You look tired," Clover murmured one afternoon from her bed. She'd woken to Mari reading a chapter of Little Dorrit, another leather-bound novel she'd found on the bookshelf.

Mari clicked her tongue. "Worry kind of does that to a girl."

Clover looked stricken. "I hate that this is upsetting you. It upsets Ash, too."

"It doesn't matter—you seem to be getting better. How are you feeling?"

Clover yawned, fisting the covers as she struggled to sit up. Mari took her shoulders, brushing the hair aside as she arranged Clover in a sitting position. A sharp tickle itched in her throat, and she coughed to ease it. Clover looked better. Her skin was flushed and pink again.

When Ash walked Mari home in the evening, she was brimming with frustration. All the accidental hand touches, brushing back her hair, or longing looks were slowly driving her crazy. Things had gone decidedly stale after the mention of taking her out on a date.

"He likes you," Clover had said one afternoon while rain thundered on the glass roof over their heads. She was drinking her tea, a pink hue returning to her lips.

"He has a funny way of showing it," Mari said.

Clover's face lit up. "Oh, he will. Ash doesn't play games. When he knows what he wants, he'll make it known."

Mari flushed as Clover struggled to her feet. "Where do you think you're going?"

Clover stared at her as though she'd gone mad. Mari didn't want to admit that she'd enjoyed coming here the last few days, looking after Clover. It was like having a sister, someone to care for. Someone who cared that she was around. "It's Twilight," was Clover's explanation.

"Don't you think you should rest?" Mari asked with an eye roll. Clover took her hand, and they strolled together for the stairs.

"My rose will bud again any day now," she said, her voice quiet, reedy. "I have to be ready."

Twilight had suddenly become the most intense and fascinating time of the day. Mari would stand in the door and watch while Clover glided around the Orangery, her arms wide as she twirled en pointe, lifting into the air like a feather on a breeze. As the light slowly crawled out of the room, the plant life breathed and bloomed into magnificent scents and an array of colors adorned low walls, metal ladders, and anything Clover had created. Watching it thrive like it were a waking entity, Mari could almost pretend she was in a fairytale. Undeniably magical.

And Clover was their goddess, a young white-haired nymph waiting below the light with her eyes closed and arms held wide. It was short lived, her strength would wane and she'd collapse on a chaise, exhausted.

By the time Ash walked home in the evening, Clover was glowing, but Mari only felt more sorrowful. She told herself that her friend was recovering, but it hurt to see her so frail.

"Don't feel sorry for me," Clover told her, kissing her cheek. "I can see it in your eyes. I'm happy. And I have a feeling the next time this will work."

On the fifth night that Mari stayed past Twilight, she insisted on taking Clover back upstairs to rest. Even though the girl looked healthy and bright-eyed again, a seed of worry lingered, and Mari was happy to tuck her in.

Clover surprised her by scooping her arms around her and kissing her cheek. Mari smiled fondly, hugging her tight. Clover held on tight, anchoring Mari to the bed, and whispered in her ear. "You've been so kind, Mari. I feel like you've given me back some light in my life."

For a moment, the world swayed, and nausea roiled in her stomach. Her mouth filled with saliva as she pulled away.

The smell—decay. Mari rubbed her eyes, coughing into her hand. Clover tilted her head, frowning.

"Are you alright?"

Mari coughed again into her hand and then quickly folded her arms behind her back. "It's fine. It's just a little off color."

"That's because you've been looking after me," the girl said. "You need to rest."

Mari pulled out of the girl's embrace, squeezing her hands before she said goodbye. There was a backup of emails from Eric waiting for her at home, and she had several inquiries waiting to be answered. Caring for Clover had sucked away a lot of her week, but she didn't mind. She wanted to be here.

Shutting the door and alone in the empty corridor, Mari opened her palm, which she'd coughed into. A speck of blood had seeped into the lines on her hand. She rubbed the evidence on her jeans.

It's nothing, she told herself, even though that spark of dread washed her cold. A shape moved in her peripheral, and she stared down that dark, looming corridor where she thought she'd seen the shadow. Breathing hard, she tilted her head, peering hard to see better.

Feet scampered on the old carpet, and Mari sucked in her ribs. There was someone down there.

"Ash?" she whispered, feeling her heart rocket. "Is that you?"

She took a few steps closer as a door swung open and slammed again. Her heart caught in her throat, and ice was on her neck and in her vision, screaming at her to leave right now.

Instead, her feet kept moving, past wall scones dappled with cobwebs and paper peeling in chunks from the walls. The door she'd heard shut was the only door down here as she came to an abrupt dead end. Whatever she'd seen had vanished inside.

With trembling fingers, she twisted the knob, heart vaulting as she broke into a cold sweat. The room was long, one narrow corridor with a door at the other end. It was decorated in faded royal blue paper, and one leaded window let in the light of the moon. Mari stood at the door and listened, but whoever led her here was gone, perhaps out the door at the other end.

Mari gasped as she turned. It was a room of mirrors.

Both sides of the hall had mirrors in many different shapes, frames, and sizes, all hung on royal blue paper. And every single one was smashed so that when she caught her reflection, it was fractured and split, her face cut in half down the center, slashes through the middle.

Like the stone maidens outside.

A beam of moonlight flooded the room and bounced off the mirror facing her, and for a moment, she saw something ghastly in the mirror where her face should have been—a hollowed-out face with coals for eyes, and sunken cheeks, strings of hair on a bald, waxen scalp.

Mari screamed and rushed for the door before she realized the reflection of the creature she'd seen was her own.

SIXTEEN

Bolting down the stairs, Mari's knees buckled on the last wooden slat. Her foot slipped on the loose step, sending her careening forward. Ash's chest broke her fall, and they tumbled the last few steps together. It was a soft landing, but Mari was on her knees, red-faced and trembling.

Ash's wide hazel eyes drew level with her. "What the hell is it?"

"I saw…" her answer died on her lips because she couldn't explain what she'd seen. Panting, she sat on her knees and covered her eyes.

Think, think…

There were broken mirrors—dark shards of glass that fractured her reflection. The drumming in her chest dulled to a normal beat, and she looked up, her eyes watery. Ash lay a hand on her shoulder. "Marianne. What did you see?"

"Nothing," she answered, honestly. "I didn't see anything. It was my reflection…"

…a monster…

"It was my reflection, that's all…"

I don't believe in monsters and things under the bed.

He took her face, thumbs grazing her cheeks, and she went molten. "You look terrified."

She forced a laugh, brushing back strands of hair that had fallen free. She held his forearm, and for a long, frustrating moment, they locked eyes. Mari thought he was staring at her lower lip, his eyes darkening as he wondered what she tasted like.

She hid her face, her knees a little wobbly as she stood, taking him up with her. "It's fine."

He held her face in his hands, his thumb tracing the curve of her cheek, and his eyes darkened. "You can tell me," his voice was deep and hypnotic like she could fall into him, let him capture her, and let the rest of the world dissolve. "You could tell me anything."

Could I? So much lay there unspoken, so much she wanted to say. How lonely she was. In the last couple of weeks, she'd felt like she was part of the world again. That he made her feel alive and that she mattered.

She edged away, afraid of how strong this pull for him was. "Please, I'm okay." She wiped her nose on her sleeve. The dried, dead leaves swept across the hall floor, blowing around their legs as though they intended to bind them forever. Mari couldn't process what she'd seen in that room of broken mirrors.

His lips pressed to a bloodless line, and Mari couldn't read his expression. He looked angry, and confused, and she gripped his forearm. Was he annoyed with her? Angry that she wouldn't confide in him? Mari couldn't admit what she'd seen up there, because then it might be true.

Snapping out of his haze, his eyes met hers, and his face softened, the dimples in his cheeks deepening. "You know what? I'm starving. What about you?"

Despite the fact her nose was running and her hair was stuck to her face, she smiled. "I could eat."

He gave her a look, longing pooled in her belly, and right then, she thought she'd follow him anywhere. "Then it's definitely time I asked you on that date."

He said date, but it wasn't really. Ash felt sorry for her. At least, that's what she told herself as she raced indoors and thundered up the stairs to get ready. Ash said he'd be by in an hour. The heavy thud of her sneakers on the wood made her jolt to a stop mid-step, her heart drumming in her chest.

He's not here anymore. The house was silent, as though he slept below in the darkened room where his hospital bed was still set up. A shadow fell over the window, blocking the light and she turned, spotting her mother leaning on the doorframe, as if it was the only thing keeping her upright.

"Where have you been?" There was accusation in her tone.

Mari stared at her. She was in her bathrobe, her hair in a scruffy top knot, her skin blotchy from sleep.

"Um." She didn't know how to answer that question. Would her mother understand that she was going out on a date?

Before she could respond, her mother shuffled into the glow of the lamp on the hallway table while Mari hung on the staircase. "You need to keep the noise down."

Mari's stomach lurched, and she trudged back down the stairs, meeting her mother at the foot. Remnants of courage bubbled inside her. "Mom…he isn't there."

The slap sent her face flying to the left, the force letting air whistle through her teeth. The sting of her mother's palm was immediate, and her skin flamed. She blinked away tears and looked away.

"I want James," her mother said, her voice cracking as she turned, spinning in the direction of the den. Before Mari could stop her, she crossed the hall and flung open the door, greeted by the sight of the empty bed, and old hospital sheets. An oxygen tank was propped in the corner. Her mouth trembled. "He should come home where I can take care of him."

Despite the throbbing in her cheek and shock coursing its way through her blood, Mari walked up behind her and gently took her shoulders. "Mom...please."

"It was too fast," she sobbed, pulling out of her daughter's arms and grabbing up handfuls of sheets. Mari watched, helpless as she tore around the room, yanking up old linen and pillows and throwing them over the floor. "We didn't have time. He was stolen—stolen from me. And now I can't be with him."

Hot tears pricked her eyes as she took her mother's arms and walked her out of the room. "Have you eaten?" She could guess the truth without a verbal answer. Mari guided her mother to the couch in the family room and hurriedly made a grilled cheese, placing it carefully beside the broken woman. Mari slipped onto the sofa, gently taking her mother's cold hand. She thought about Zara and what she'd said. It pricked her conscience. How long would this living death go on for?

"Mom, we need to talk about getting you help," she whispered. "Help with the grief—more than just medication."

"I need my boy home. In his bed, upstairs listening to music, where he belongs," she said through gritted teeth, and the outburst made Mari's throat clench. "I won't grieve for him yet. I won't…let go."

"Mom…"

"If I let go, he'll really be gone…"

"The hospital bed…the equipment…"

Her mother's eyes snapped up, the familiar glassy blue like hers staring back at her. "What about them?"

"We have to get rid of them...clear out..."

"I will not be told how to manage my son," she hissed through her teeth. The look she shot her was deathly cold, and Mari didn't need to be a mind reader to know what her mother was thinking right then.

It was in the sting of her cheek and the tone of her voice. The force of her stare was cold and unfeeling. Mari could feel it in the print on her cheek.

It should have been me.

Mari stood, clamping her lips shut in case she burst. She needed to get to her room. Her mother seemed to fade, easing into the cushions and staring blankly at the television.

"Bear will need feeding," she said aloud, even though she knew this was where her mother would remain for the night, and she'd take care of him anyway. "But I'm going out now for a couple of hours. I'll lock up. In the morning...I'm calling Doctor Conners."

Her lip twitched, and Mari knew she'd heard. Maybe she'd understood. "You never believed him."

Ice washed through her veins. "What?"

"You didn't side with him. Family is everything, Mari. He was your *brother*, and when it counted...you didn't take his side."

Her eyes went wide. "Take his side? Mom...I don't see Zara anymore. I don't see..." She wanted to say anyone, or any of her old friends, that old life, but she knew how selfish it sounded when James's life was done. "I was there. I supported him."

"You didn't believe..."

"I nursed him!" she barked. "I was there when he died! What more do you want?"

"For it to have been you!"

The cry was anguished, shrill, and came out of her mother like a wail of pain. She collapsed into the pillows. "If God wanted to rob me of one of my babies... then it should have been you."

Numb, Mari backed out of the room. She didn't believe in monsters or God. She believed what she could see and feel. God didn't steal James in the same way Mr. Raggerty was just a pile of straw. It simply wasn't true. The blow cut deep, but it wasn't like she didn't already know. Her mother showed her every day just how she felt.

"I'm going out. Bear will need feeding," she repeated in a low voice, a choked sob before she left her mother staring at the television, where she would stay.

SEVENTEEN

It's not an actual date, she told herself again as Ash drove through the deserted streets of Winstone and out towards the parched open terrain of Lincoln. Mari picked at her nails; nerves bubbling in her belly.

She side-eyed Ash, his hair blowing from the open window, elbow resting on the door, as he stared straight ahead. Bathed in the light of the setting sun bouncing off the hood, she spotted the deep grooves under his eyes. Did he ever get much sleep?

"So…" he drawled, his voice gently prodding her out of her haze. Snapping back to reality, Mari briefly touched her cheek. "Either you have overdone the makeup, or you have a bad rash."

Mari's fingertips brushed her cheek, where her mother's handprint still burned. She made a face, thinking she'd done a decent of job covering it up. Clearly, she had not.

"It was nothing."

"That handprint on your face doesn't look like nothing."

She let unspoken words hang between them. How could she explain that since James passed, her mother was only a shadow of the woman she used to be? How could she voice that dealing with her temper, her outbursts was just a way of life now? That it didn't mean anything.

"It was nothing. She doesn't mean it."

Ash snorted, shaking his head. "Fine, be evasive."

Mari stared at his profile, her cheeks heating. "We don't know one another *that* well."

"I don't know if you realize this, but I've been trying to get to know you. But all you do is push me away."

Mari bit her lip and stared hard out the window, a tear landing on her lower lash. She sniffed it back, imagining how James would berate her and belittle her for crying. "I'm sorry. I don't mean to." She let the silence build, wondering how to make this right, to brush it away like dust under a rug. From the look on his face, he was expecting some kind of answer.

"Marianne," he said, his tone harder than she'd ever heard. "Are you safe in that house?"

Her eyes snapped in his direction. "Safe? Of course, I'm safe."

"Then why did she do that to you?"

Because she wishes it were me underground. "I'm getting her help. She isn't in her right mind and hasn't been for a long time."

"That literally tells me nothing," he muttered, scratching his jaw. "But fine. I just—worry. I worry about you all alone over there."

Warmth filled her chest, making her glow, and the flush traveled up her neck.

His hand on her shoulder made her startle, and when she glanced sideways, his face had softened, eyes amber and gleaming. Heat spilled from his hands, seeping into her skin. "Look, you're right. Trust is earned, and if you ever want to open up….well, you can talk to me."

Mari nodded, relieved when he changed the subject. They chatted about his sister and how she was sure that it was nearly time to test again. Which by his grave expression, he was dreading.

"I'm not sure she'll ever stop trying," he answered her unspoken question. "This time, she's excited. She seems to think enough of the *potion*." He rolled his eyes, "has built in her system."

Mari gripped the seat tighter. "Poor Clover." It hurt to think of what Dr. Conners had said. That in reality, Clover was merely clutching at straws, or in her case, vines.

Mari's stomach flip-flopped when he pulled the truck into the busy lot of a diner outside Lincoln. She looked over the dash at the grimy building outside, with its red and white striped awning, windows dripping with condensation, and a neon sign flashing in the door.

How could Ash have known that this had been their place? Mari and Zara had hung out here nearly every day after school when they were kids, filling up on muffins and pancakes with an unhealthy dose of syrup. A little dizzy, she smiled when he frowned at her, hoping he hadn't picked up on her reaction. Her knuckles were white.

Please don't be in there, she prayed.

As they went inside, the bell above the door tinkled, and she automatically scanned the booths with razor-sharp ferocity, checking all the corners. Letting go of a caged breath when she didn't see her old friend, she relaxed. It smelled of cinnamon and honey, and a strikingly pretty waitress ushered them to a booth in the corner. Mari slid in, a little intimidated by her. She was curvy, with tawny colored skin, and had long glossy black hair. She smiled pleasantly, handing them two menus. "I'll give you a minute," she said with a wink before she spun away, returning to the counter where she resumed her conversation with a red-headed woman in running gear.

"You know this place?" Ash asked, looking around. "I've driven past and always wanted to come in."

Mari avoided his stare. "Yeah, I've been here a few times."

He placed his elbows on the table, steepling his fingers as he watched her examine the menu. Her cheeks grew redder until she laughed and had to look up. "What?"

He shook his head. "You're a puzzle, that's all."

"Am I?" She cocked a brow in sarcasm.

"You are utterly determined not to tell me anything about yourself."

Mari sighed, knowing she'd have the club; it had always been her favorite thing on the menu. "Why are you so nosey?"

"Isn't that what you do on a date? Get to know one another?"

Mari sat forward, her playfulness evaporating. "This isn't a date."

"It's not?"

"No. Because if you *wanted* to ask me out, you would have ages ago. You took pity on me. I didn't even have the chance to get dressed up or do my hair."

"Your hair is fine…and what you wear doesn't matter."

"My makeup then."

"Think you're fine as you are—and this isn't a pity invite."

"Really?" she teased. "I knocked you flying down those steps. I should be buying you dinner."

Ash rolled his eyes. "Call it a thank you then. Thank you for all you've done to help over the last few days. It means a lot to us." He looked out the window, shoulders lifting in a helpless shrug. "I don't think Clo has ever had a real friend."

Mari leaned nearer, tilting her head. "Are you buying me dinner so I keep coming back?"

Ash scoffed. "I would have hoped there were other reasons for you to visit." His eyes darkened and looking away once trapped in his beam was impossible, but he deftly sidestepped the subject again, and it was quick enough to give her whiplash. "What did you see up there, Mari?"

She blushed, feeling foolish. "I went in a room with cracked mirrors and scared the crap out of myself."

"Why…what did you see?"

She snorted. "Myself. I looked *great*."

He laughed, shaking his head. "That old place will play tricks on you. And for what it's worth, I think you look great."

It was her turn to change the subject. "Clover said that once you know what you want, you go after it."

Ash smirked, rolling his eyes skyward. "Ah, did she? She doesn't know what she's talking about. I happen to be pretty reserved—so that's something we have in common."

The waitress was back, smiling, and Mari detected the sweet vanilla smell on her skin as she leaned nearer. Ash ordered the biggest burger on the menu, and Mari ordered her usual club—not that she'd visited here for over a year. She'd stopped going out altogether not long after James got sick.

As if the past was determined to haunt her, to bring her to her knees, Mari's heart squeezed as a girl exited the bathroom at the other end of the restaurant. Zara paused at her booth, chatting to the guy waiting for her. They locked eyes, and the world spun.

Mari let out a shaky breath, her hands gripping the table. Ash frowned, instantly picking up on her change of expression, and cast a look over his shoulder. Mari stared hard at the table and refused to look up.

"Who is that?" he asked as Zara remained motionless, her lips parted as she stared at them. She moved to walk towards them, but Mari ducked her shoulders, and the girl stopped as if sensing the wall she'd thrown up. The guy she was with slid out of the booth, cast them a wary look and tucked his arm around Zara's waist before whispering something to her. Watery-eyed, Zara nodded, her chin wobbling as the guy practically steered her out of the diner.

Mari released her hands, tension ebbing out of her body. Cagily, she glanced up, meeting her old friend's gaze through the window as she got in her car. When they were gone, Ash blew out air.

"Well, that was weird," he said.

"It was…"

"Let me guess…*nothing?*"

Mari looked up, and his mouth was tense, lips pinched. "I'm sorry."

"So I don't get an explanation?"

"It wasn't anything."

Ash threw up his hands and sat back in his chair. "Really. Come on, Mari. You looked like you'd seen a ghost…and so did she."

Mari linked her hands under the table, knowing she had no way out. It could be cathartic to air it out. To finally speak the truth. But it was a truth she couldn't bear and didn't fully understand. Because so much of that last night they'd been together, the last night they'd been friends was hazy and fragmented.

"There is a ghost," she said, her voice dry. Ash looked back at her, almost surprised. "Only it's not me or her. The ghost is my brother."

He frowned, leaning forward. "James."

She nodded. "Zara..." Why was this so hard? "Zara dated him for a while."

"Right."

"It was a casual thing, and if I'm honest—I think she liked him more than he liked her. James was good-looking and had lots of girls interested. He didn't tend to keep them around long...once he...you know."

Ash sucked in air as if he knew exactly what she meant. "Teenage boys are the worst."

"But," her voice trembled, and she was saved by the pretty waitress returning and placing their drinks down. Gratefully, she took a gulp, wetting her lips. "Something happened...only I don't really remember. I..." She looked away, ashamed. "I was drunk that night, and I kind of blacked out. I don't remember anything of what she claimed happened."

Ash slid his hand across the table, finding hers, and she didn't flinch or pull away. It gave her courage to speak, that *maybe*, he'd understand. "Go on."

If he doesn't understand, if he walks away… Mari clenched her teeth, calling back the pieces she did remember about that night.

"It was Halloween—a year ago. It was right before James got his diagnosis…he didn't even know he was sick or what was going to happen to him. We were getting ready for a party at our place, but the weather was bad, and the roads flooded. James's friends were already at our place getting ready…all in costume. My mom was out of town on business…that was back when she was okay."

Tears blurred her eyes. "But everything changed that night."

"What happened?"

"We all…played a drinking game, and things got loud and a little crazy. I remember James laughing and handing out beers. I started to feel sick and woozy, and I ended up asleep on the couch. I woke up, and they were all talking about a stupid game to play outside…in the rain and the dark. James made me drink this glass of wine he stole from mom's stash…and…"

"And?"

"And that's it." Mari shrugged her shoulders. "That's *all* I remember. I was so drunk I blacked out. But I have pieces…tiny bits of memory…of running through the corn, and I was covered in mud. I woke up…" she shivered. "I woke up outside in the morning right below that scarecrow."

"Ah." Ash's brows rose. "Explains why he gives you the creeps."

"I couldn't remember anything. But I went back to the house, and Zara was gone. Her car was gone and the house was trashed. James was in bed, and his friends were spread all over the house. I had to do a mass clean-up before Mom got home."

"Nice of him to help you out," he said, as their food arrived. Suddenly, she didn't feel hungry, and Ash only looked at his plate, uninterested.

"I didn't speak to Zara till later that afternoon," Mari admitted. "I was so busy clearing everything away, getting rid of the evidence, that I didn't think anything of it. I thought she'd gotten sick of James's friends and gone home."

Ash nodded, prodding a fry with his fork. "Understandable."

"She called me and asked to meet here…" Mari looked around the diner. "When I saw her…She looked awful—puffy, red-faced…like she'd been crying all night."

Ash went a little grey but didn't say anything. Mari couldn't stop now. The truth—or what she knew of it— burned on her tongue.

"She said that after I passed out…James…" She gripped the table, and Ash grabbed her hand.

"It's okay."

"She said he let them take turns," she choked out. "That he stood by and laughed. They held her down, did things…"

Mari gulped down a breath. The thought of that happening in her house made her stomach turn. The image it conjured was unbearable, let alone saying the words aloud.

"And what did you do?"

"I didn't *see* it happen. There were no marks on her, no cuts or bruises. I couldn't believe he'd let something like that happen to her…that he'd be that callous…"

Ash looked skeptical, and Mari's cheeks flushed. "You didn't believe her?"

Her eyes filled with tears. "She went to the police. They all denied it happened, and there were no witnesses."

"But did *you* believe her?"

"I didn't *see* it…he was my brother!"

"Did you *believe* her?"

Mari closed her eyes. "I told her she must have drunk too much…that James…she got it wrong."

Ash whistled. "Holy shit."

"She was so hurt…she didn't let it rest. Zara never could let go of anything. Only a week later…James collapsed. Within a few days, we were told he was dying."

"What happened?"

"Word spread, and soon it was everywhere. When the charges were brought my mom hired a lawyer, and they annihilated Zara, picked holes in her story, destroyed her. *No one* believed her.

James was popular…he could do no wrong, and now he was *dying*. It made it worse. Eventually, she dropped the charges…and we haven't spoken."

Ash sat back, dropping his fork. "Jesus Christ."

"I'm sorry." She pushed her plate away. "I don't feel hungry now."

"Me either." He stared miserably at his burger. "So…do you think what she claimed is even possible? Was he capable of something so cruel?"

Was he capable? James was capable of many things. When she didn't speak, he pressed on. "Had Zara ever lied like that before?"

Mari shook her head.

"Then what do you believe?"

"I don't know anymore. I can't believe it of either of them…but…I didn't *see* anything. And I don't remember what happened."

"So…no wonder you've been hiding in that house."

"After the rumors spread and James got sick, I dropped out of college. It was just easier, and my mom….changed. Losing him destroyed her. In her eyes, James was the golden child. He could do no wrong. She can't accept he's gone. After he got his diagnosis, it was a whirlwind. It was so fast. Our lives were turned upside down. The den became a sick room full of hospital equipment. We lived in darkness."

"You still do."

She nodded wordlessly. "It's just easier."

"And the boys she accused? What happened to them?"

"Zara dropped everything. When hate towards her grew…she left Meadowford and worked at her father's gas station. Nothing ever happened to them."

"Hear me out," he said, with an edge of apprehension in his voice. "You didn't do anything wrong, and yet you're living like a ghost, off the grid, out of sight. Why?"

Mari's eyes filled with tears. "Because I'm a *terrible* person. I deserve every bad thing that has happened to me."

"Why would you deserve that?" Ash threw his hands in the air, and she could barely lift her eyes.

"Because…what if it's true?"

It was the question she hadn't dared ask herself since that night. What if the very thing that spiked dread in her heart was actually true? What kind of person did that make her?

He took her hand. "You aren't a terrible person. It seems to me that night, three lives were changed. James, Zara, and your own." He gripped it tighter. "There's more than one ghost in this story."

Ash's car rumbled over the gravel, pulling alongside the farmhouse. Mari found the handle, smiling up at him in the dark. "Some date, huh?"

He half smiled, as if recalling her terrible confession. "We ate in the end."

Inside, she felt raw and hollow but oddly lighter. Maybe it had been good to share. She opened the door, and Ash jumped out from the driver's side, grabbing the door for her. "How chivalrous," she joked, blushing.

"Ah, I'm old fashioned," he said, scratching his neck. Under the moon, his skin looked lighter, nearly pearlescent. She shook her head, thinking she must be losing it. "Walk you to your door?"

She giggled, holding his crooked arm. He hugged her, and she liked his warmth. "Maybe next time we can go somewhere fancier? Free of old memories?" he said. "I wish you had told me you used to go there with Zara."

"You weren't to know," Mari said, reaching the bottom step, standing so she was eye level with him. "And who said there would be a next time?"

He took her hands, her breath stilling in her chest, as he lifted one to his mouth and brushed his lips over her knuckles. Tingles reached down her back, swaying a little nearer as their eyes locked. He nodded to her upstairs window. "Remember what I said," he whispered. Burn a candle in the window. So I know you're okay in there. You've got plenty, haven't you?"

Mari laughed, rolling her eyes. "You're kidding, right? Clover gave me a bag full of them."

"Good," he said, clipped. "Then please, do as I ask. I worry about you in there—"

Her stomach went bubbly, his eyes on her mouth. He was going to kiss her. And it was something she'd fantasized about. But after her confession, she was drained of energy, her bones aching as though she had a fever coming. "Ash…"

He cut her off with his mouth, his lips pressed urgently against hers. It was abrupt, not the gentleness she expected from him, but her mouth parted hungrily, her legs going weak as he wound his arms about her waist. Her chest heaved against his, and it was all teeth, arms, and grappling, grabbing at one another until she couldn't breathe. It wasn't the kiss she'd envisioned, but to feel wanted, hungered for, craved like he was starved of oxygen ignited something so deep in her, something she'd lost. Her hands found his hair, and her heart wilted. She could barely catch her breath.

She couldn't catch her breath. Black dots formed behind her closed lids.

She couldn't breathe.

She whimpered against his mouth, his tongue dancing along her lower lip. Using the heels of her hands, she pushed him away, her lips bruised. "Ash...let me catch my breath."

Dizzy. She blinked. She was so dizzy she needed to cling to him while he held her tight. Leaning back, her eyes met his. His were blazing, so dark, wet, and glossy, and he was still staring at her mouth like he'd not kissed another person in a long time. "I'm sorry," he whispered feverishly, kissing her brow, her cheekbone. His breath sent shivers down her spine, craving more, yet she couldn't see straight. "I've wanted to kiss you since the second I saw you."

She gripped his shirt, trying to steady her breathing. "I need a minute."

He looked at her. "Oh, god. I've pushed it too far, haven't I? I was too...I didn't even ask."

"No, it's fine," she lied, even though those black dots wouldn't fade. What the hell was wrong with her? Sucking in cool air through her nose, she met his gaze and gently pressed her mouth to his, where electricity wove between them. "I'll be fine. I'm probably a little shaken after... everything."

Stroking his thumb over her cheekbone, she leaned into his warm hand. He was hot, pulsing with energy, while she thought her knees might give out. That was some kiss.

"Come over tomorrow," he begged, raining kisses over her face till she giggled. "Clover is desperate to test this crazy theory, and she promised to wait for you."

"I'll be there," she promised, stepping out of his embrace and instantly finding her balance. Bear bouncing at the door distracted her. "Good-night."

"Remember to light the candle...so I know you're alright."

Flushing with heat, she smiled, hardly able to form words as she waved, unlocking the door and heading inside. Avoiding her mother, she headed upstairs and sank into a window seat, watching as his shape trekked through the corn. She hurriedly lit one of Clover's candles, sweet vanilla and Cedar wafting under her nose as it burned. As if he sensed she was watching, he turned and waved.

Mari waved back, dabbing her tongue to her lip. It stung. Did he get too rough?

She stood, a little wobbly, half panicked, and flooded with hormones as she swept to her vanity. She stared at her reflection. Her bottom lip looked swollen, and it hurt to run her tongue over it. When she looked back at herself, she gasped, rearing away from the mirror, and grabbed a handful of tissues.

Dark red blood stained her chin. Somehow, during that kiss, Ash had bitten her.

EIGHTEEN

That night, she dreamed of Mr. Raggerty. He was at the window, peeping through the glass and running his long straw fingers down the pane.

Tap. Tap. Tap.

He looked through the window like he was searching for something, his large button eyes narrowing in his sack head. When he spotted her sitting up in bed, his mouth split in a grin, revealing his sharp teeth.

Mari woke shivering, drenched in sweat. She threw back the duvet, her head swimming like she might throw up. Stumbling from the bed, she threw on the lamp, letting its glow illuminate the dark. The candle on the ledge was practically burned out. Swiftly, she blew it out, the smoke billowing like tendrils under her nose.

It made her sneeze. A deep, violent sound came from inside her body, and when she looked at her palm, she saw the blood. Iced to the bone, she dashed to the bathroom, grabbing toilet paper and wiping away the remains of dried blood up her nostrils.

Images conjured in her mind. Memories of James hunched over the toilet and throwing up till he couldn't stand. Sweat coated her top lip, and she wiped it away, tasting copper on her tongue. She looked at her fingers and gagged at the sight of blood on her lips.

What the hell was happening?

"Why are you awake?" a voice came from the partially open crack in the door, and Mari stifled a shriek, then remembered, she had no one to stifle it for. Her mother stood in the shadows, watching. Mari grabbed a towel and wiped her mouth, forcing a grim smile.

"Nothing, something I ate."

"You were making a lot of noise."

"Sorry, did I wake you?"

Her mother blinked slowly, deliberately, before she said. "I was already awake."

Mari steered her back across the dark landing, where shadows played in the moon's light, spilling through the window. "Get some sleep, Mom."

Mari waited as her mother stumbled and ambled around her bedroom. The room smelled stale, reminding her she needed to change the sheets, at least crack open some windows. Mari crept back to her room and tucked in, staring unblinkingly at the ceiling fan. But instead of trying to sleep, she opened the window, letting a cold draft in, anything to break up the sickly smell from the candle. Peering over the field, she spotted the light in Ash's room burning and remembered their kiss.

She dabbed her tongue to her bottom lip, finding it healed. Funny, she hadn't felt his teeth on her lips; it'd all been heady, and she'd been too swept up in the kiss. Fanning herself, she rose from the bed, deciding sleeping wasn't on the cards right now. She sat at her laptop, legs folded, and thumbed through some edits Eric had made, nodding and humming to herself as she typed some notes back.

She was surprised when her messenger box lit up, her brows flying up as he typed a reply.

"You're up?"

She huffed, resisting the urge to slam the laptop shut.

"Can't sleep…so I thought reading your book would send me off."

"Ha, funny!"

Mari smiled. **"Goodnight, Eric. The book is coming on great, by the way!"**

Now, she shut the laptop, idly tapping her fingers. It must be stress, she told herself. She was tired and stressed, and reliving what had happened between her and Zara must have brought it on. She tucked in bed, hoping to dream of Ash Martin, anything except Mr. Raggerty.

The air carried a chill, wrapping itself around her bare legs as she hiked through the corn fields, paying Mr. Raggerty no attention as she walked, even if he did swing in her direction. Determined to forget the last couple of days, Mari lifted her chin, arms tucked under her arms as she walked, her heart drumming at the thought of seeing Ash again. As she pushed away a limp branch with her arm, she strolled onto the Rosewood property as if she'd done that every day of her life and it wasn't something new and foreign to her.

Like he'd guessed she'd been thinking of him, Ash opened the front door, grinning boyishly as she skipped the stone steps. Without waiting, he pushed her gently against the wall of the stone porch, running fingers up her neck to capture her nape in a firm hold. "I was hoping you'd show up. Thought I'd scared you away."

Mari grinned at him playfully, easing to her tiptoes to brush his bottom lip with hers. He closed the gap, breathing into her as he kissed her senseless, dizzy, until she sensed that odd sensation again. Light-headed, almost like her knees would give way, and black dots filled her vision. Gently, with her hands on his chest, she eased him back. "Where did you learn to kiss like that?"

He quirked a brow, leaning an elbow on the wall by her head, smiling lazily. "Like what?"

Mari smirked. "Like you've sucked all the air out of my lungs…and sense out of my head."

"Is that a good thing?"

Mari laughed, shyly. "I'm not sure yet."

All she knew was that he stole her breath away, in all the good ways and bad. She pushed aside her strange dreams, coupled with the nosebleed. Ash was too perfect to let slip away, and she wove her arms around his waist. He kissed her temple. "I hate to tell you this, but Clover has been waiting for you."

Mari nodded, eyeing the sun piercing through the clouds. "I'm a little nervous."

Ash rubbed at his jaw. "Me too. I hate this. I just hope to god it works…or something happens."

He bent to retrieve the tote bag she'd worn slung over her shoulder, his brow creasing as he spotted the contents. Mari had packed gauze, fresh bandages, and antiseptic. "You came prepared."

"Just some stuff we had in the house," she said, trying to sound airy when things were left over from when James got sick. "I just want to be there if anything happens."

Ash stood to one side, pushing the door open and letting it swing wide. He nodded to the darkness within. "Well, you know where she is."

Mari stepped over the threshold of Rosewood, the dark shadows creeping up the walls to greet her. It still smelled damp, of plaster that refused to dry out, and the hole in the roof was nearly patched up, letting in sharp beams of light. She glanced at Ash over her shoulder, where he stood, backlit in the door. "Aren't you coming?"

He shook his head. "I don't like…." He swallowed uncomfortably. "It's not something I want to watch."

Wordlessly, she nodded, heading across the ballroom until the scent of jasmine rose to greet her. She eased open the orangery door, the glass swinging inward. There was no sign of Clover in the orangery where Mari expected to find her. The heat in her workroom was oppressive, and Mari could taste the rose-flavored tea on her tongue. Clover's pestle and mortar lay used and discarded on the bench, and dried petals of the Night Witch Rose sprinkled carelessly over the tiled floor.

"Clover?" Mari called, heading to the small indoor pond and walking around the chaise, where it seemed ivy and white flowers had bloomed overnight. The greenery, succulents, and eucalyptus nestled in every nook, claiming dead shadowy spaces and filling them with new life. She craned her neck to peer around the pond.

"Here," her voice called, faint, breathy, and Mari pushed through a heavy drape of vines adorned with pink and white buds. A thorn caught her sweater. Clover lay, motionless and quiet, under a vast arch of dark red roses. It wasn't till Mari came closer that she saw Clover lay on a metal claw-footed bed, draped with filmy blankets, staring upward, and covered in petals. Her pale skin pulled tight over her cheekbones, her under eyes almost hollow. Mari gasped. Clover's nails were nearly purple.

"Are you alright?"

If Clover weren't so waxy pale, Mari would have said she looked beautiful, ethereal, like a character from a Shakespearean play. Ophelia drowned in the lake and floating away on a carpet of flowers, with all her blonde hair splayed out on the white pillow. She touched Clover's forehead, and the girl blinked.

"Clover…"

"I'm alright," she whispered. "I just need to prepare myself…for…"

"The test."

"…the pain."

Mari released a pained sigh, dropping to her knees beside the girl and taking her bone-cold hand. "Clover…I don't think this is a good idea."

Clover's pale lips spread white, revealing ivory teeth with startling pink gums. "It's going to work, Mari. I can feel it."

"Clo—"

"I can feel the power of the rose in my blood. It'll work this time. I'm going to be free, Mari." A tear rolled down her cheek. "It's got to work."

Clover fumbled blindly for Mari's arm, and she easily lifted her. A flash, a spike of pain throbbed in her temple as she remembered James, how, in the end, he hadn't been hard to lift. Bones in a skin bag, he called himself. The memory made her stomach turn, and she held the girl tighter. "Help me, Marianne."

"I'm here," she promised, a knot in her throat. "Let's do this crazy thing."

"The chaise…" breathily, she pointed to the red velvet chaise by the pond. "Put me there."

Mari locked her arm around Clover's waist, feeling the girl tremble as she took unsteady steps to the chaise. She fell into the cushions, the white nightgown spilling around her legs. She nodded to the large blackout blind above their heads. "When you open that, it'll let in a beam of sunlight that I can reach." Carefully, Clover stripped off her gloves, laying them beside her.

Mari breathed out a pang of nausea swelling in her stomach. "Are you sure? We don't have to do this."

Clover's eyes flashed, a spark of anger, quick to die as she gasped, "I have to try. It's got to work."

"Alright. Tell me when."

Clover took a few shallow breaths. "Now, Mari."

Mari stalked to the window, finding the velvet cord with ease. Taking it between her palms, she gave it a yank, two or three good tugs, and at once a startling beam of sunshine shot through the open blind, basking the orangery in blinding rays of light. It hit the water fountain, sparkling on the surface like crystals. The lilies, laying dormant in the pond, splayed open, revealing their inner petals. Clover edged near the beam, her fingers shaking as she held out both palms, closing her eyes, her lips parted in a smile.

Please work, Mari thought, her heart stilling in her chest. *Please, please, help her.*

Tears cascaded from Clover's eyes as she held her hands in the beam, holding her breath so still that Mari couldn't take her eyes off her. Blood rushed in her ears. Was this working? A smile broke on Clover's face, her eyes open, exhilarated, a half-crazed grin of triumph.

"It's working," she cried. "Mari...it's working."

Mari looked at the beam of light and Clover's bony fingers. It *was* working. She had to believe what she was seeing was real. Clover was in the light. The girl laughed, her head back in glorious rapture, as tears streamed down the exposed column of her throat. "I did it. It's working. It's real."

It couldn't be true, but it was. Clover was more ashen than Mari would have believed. In the sunlight, she was near transparent. Every line and blood vessel under her skin was exposed, like a cell or an organism growing before her eyes.

It was working.

But there was something wrong—a smell in the air. Mari noticed it first, distracted by Clover's haunting cries of elation, but it wafted under her nose. It was unmistakable and quickly turned her stomach to mush. Her eyes widened, but it was too late. *"Clover!"*

Burning flesh. Mari gagged, retching as she yanked the blind closed. Clover's cries of happiness melded into something else, something Mari swore she'd never stop hearing, even in the depths of sleep.

An anguished scream tore from the girl's throat as she rolled, and Mari threw herself onto her. Clover's head cracked the stone floor, and Mari grabbed a blanket from the chaise, quick to douse the flames. She wept, wrapping her arms around the fragile girl as she wept in pain and sorrow.

"It was working," she cried, holding out her hands, scorched and burned to the bone. "I felt it. I felt the sun. I was *alive*, Mari. I was *real*."

Mari tucked her under her chin, holding her together, and let her own tears fall. "Oh, Clover, I'm so sorry," she whispered. "I'm so sorry."

NINETEEN

Later, when Clover had calmed down and sat with her hands in a bucket of ice, Mari pleaded with her for the hundredth time to go to the hospital. Clover, although shaken by what had happened, was adamant and still determined to sip her rose tea. Ash turned away in exasperation, even though the burns were horrifying. The flesh peeled down to lower layers of skin. The damage, the violence of the burn, was enough to make Mari dizzy.

"I want to show you something," Clover said, her smile returning as she carefully lifted her hands from the bucket. Mari's eyes widened as the girl turned over her palms, revealing her flesh intact, red, *scorched* but intact.

Her mouth dried up. "What?"

"I told you, didn't I?" Clover said with an air of triumph. "It's like magic."

"It's not magic, Clo. I saw you burn."

"I know." Tearfully, she gnawed on the inside of her cheek, crestfallen and stricken with guilt. "I'm so sorry you had to see that, Marianne."

"Stop saying sorry!" Mari snapped. "This has to end. You can't keep doing this to yourself."

She took Clover's hands, and the girl winced, and Mari told herself to be more careful. She traced a finger over the healed skin. "I don't know what this means."

Clover leaned nearer, and there was a scent disguised by the pretty smell of flowers, rot, fetid and nauseating. "Mari…do you believe…?" She stopped abruptly, which only sparked Mari's curiosity.

"What?"

"It's nothing."

"This is not nothing—tell me!"

"Do you believe in magic? And I mean real life magic?"

Mari rolled her eyes. "You mean witchcraft?"

Clover scoffed, casting her eyes at her piles of botany journals, books, and magazines, some so old the pages had faded. "What do you think modern medicine is? Where do you think it came from?"

"I mean…If you're asking if I believe in witches with black cats that fly around on brooms, then *no*. I believe in what I can see, feel, and touch. I spent a great deal of time in hospitals. I watched my brother get flooded by chemicals, things that ripped him apart and destroyed what he was…*That's* what I believe in." When Clover didn't speak, Mari continued. "Medicine. Not plants and flowers."

Clover looked sad. "I understand why you feel that way. But this part of the country is famous for many things, and witchcraft is one of them. I *believe* in nature, which is as real as a hospital. And I believe there were women here who knew how to harness the power of nature. Hospitals and modern medicine have failed me again and again. You must admit for a moment there…it was working!"

It was. Mari couldn't deny it, even though what she'd seen and heard horrified her. For a moment, Clover had survived in the light of day. Spurred on by the silence between them, Clover grabbed a magazine tucked down the side of the chaise. It was hidden away like she hadn't wanted Ash to see this. It was one of her father's old science journals.

Mari peered at it. "What is that you're hiding?"

Clover lowered her voice to a whisper. "You can't say anything to Ash…"

Mari huffed with a heavy eye-roll. "I don't like lying." She didn't want to imagine how he'd react if he found out she'd been writing emails, going behind his back. Thinking of him, the welt on her lower lip stung.

"I read this in one of your father's journals,"

Mari felt instantly guilty and responsible for literally handing this to her. "What?"

"It's an article about a rare and ancient type of Oak tree." She thumbed through the pages till she found a photographer's glossy photo. It was an Oak, but it looked bare, with branches that clawed the sky, naked of all greenery, like it'd been born from volcanic matter. It wasn't like any old Oak she'd seen around here. "It's called a Quercus Robur."

"Okay…"

"Only a few have ever been spotted that still stand today. They can live for two thousand years! The bark is known for its healing and blood-regenerating properties—how it has survived for so long. And back in the old days, it was used for wiccan potions."

"Oh."

"That's not all." Clover beamed with excitement. "I'm sure you've heard of the Mickleford witches?"

Mari fought the urge to snort out a laugh. "Clover…"

"It's ingrained in the folklore around here."

"Yes, that's the key word—*folklore!* It's not real, Clover. Sure, there's a town from here with a strange reputation…and I've grown up with the stories…but that's all it is."

Clover's face fell. "You *gave* me these books. You believe in science, and yet you spend your days proofreading fairy tale nonsense that man writes. You gave me your father's magazines. The facts are right here under your nose, and you won't listen. Sometimes, magic and science can be the same thing."

"What are you saying?"

"There's one of these Oaks here! A few miles away in a town called Cedar Wood. It's been spotted on a few hiking trails. If I could get some of the bark…" Her voice sped up, hurrying through her words before Mari could cut her off again.

"Clover!"

"And add it to the rose somehow…I don't know yet…but it could work. You saw it, Mari…you saw me in the light. Modern medicine had *nothing* to do with that."

Mari rubbed her eyes, suddenly so exhausted that she didn't think she had the strength to fight her. "So, you want me to get you this bark?"

Clover grabbed her hands. "Yes! It will work, Mari!"

"If I do this for you…will you promise me something?"

Clover looked anxious. "Of course."

"If we do this and it doesn't work…please *stop.* Stop hurting yourself."

"And do what? Just fade into the black? Become a shadow?"

Mari understood. She could feel the terror in Clover's voice, hope dwindling to the smallest flame.

"I'm only across the field. I won't let you be alone."

"Alright," Clover nodded tearfully. "If this doesn't work…"

"I want to take you to a proper doctor…a real one. The one James saw."

"Okay, Mari," she said. "I promise."

Mari needed to talk to Ash. The whole event had left her drained, weak, and feeling like she could sleep for a week. Witnessing Clover's anguish and pain was too much, and Mari felt a burning need to make this right. She didn't like going behind Ash's back and roaming the dark, ominous forests of Cedar Wood for a specific ancient oak, not at least without talking to him.

The whole idea was madness. But there was that niggling doubt.

Clover *hadn't* burned. At least not straight away. For a few moments at least, it'd worked.

"Ash?" Mari walked the dark hallways, cradling her waist and staring up into the gloomy heights of the landing. Something moved up there, a shadow darting past the top of the stairs and heavy feet on the wood floor.

Shuddering, Mari held the rail and made her way upstairs. "Ash, I need to talk to you."

Her neck prickled, shadows moved as though they breathed, and even up here, it smelled cloying and damp, the old rugs running alive with dust. Musty drapes hung from the windows in moth-eaten tatters, and she wondered if Ash would ever get to fixing all this. The corridors were lit by oil lamps on the wall, burning with a real flame. "Ash?" she called again, spotting a shadow dart from room to room.

Her blood froze when she heard a man's voice whispering in the shadows, something low and painful.

It's the roof, only the roof, she told herself, taking a wide step back. She whirled on her heels, gaping at where Ash had done a reasonable patch job, only a few specks of light peeking through the gaps in the wood. She tried to forget the reflection she'd seen in those mirrors, telling herself it was her gaunt face staring back at her. She told herself that her curiosity had drawn her to that room, that there had been no one leading her. No one had been watching her.

"Help me…"

Mari rooted her feet to the spot, her ears pumping with blood. As she turned, every hair stood on her arms, spying a figure standing in the shadows down one narrow corridor. Cobwebs hung like drapes, moving like ghosts as she faced the stranger, her voice dying in her throat.

"Mari."

Ash's call came from behind, and she gasped, and then the shadow ran. Ash's hand landed on her shoulder, and a cry ripped from her throat. When she glanced back, the corridor was empty. Ash spun her to face him. He was wet from the shower, his skin glinting, and his robe was open but tied loose at the waist. She blushed, looking away, glancing back where she'd seen the stranger and heard his voice.

"What's wrong?" he asked, his hazel eyes dark, narrowed.

"I saw someone down there!" She pointed wildly in the direction she'd seen the shadow, the eyes. Ash wanted her to open up, and for once, she was too shaken to concoct a lie. His eyes flew wide.

"What? Where?"

"D-down that corridor—no!" She grabbed his bicep as he made to run after the figure. Still sopping wet, his arm slipped out of her grasp. "Ash, it isn't the first time I've seen something."

His nostrils flared, grabbing up a pewter candle stick from a broken-up dresser against the wall. "Why the hell didn't you tell me?" Wiggling out of her grip again, he stalked into the shadows, and Mari's heart plunged into her stomach. "It's probably kids messing around."

He stopped right in front of the room of broken mirrors, flinging open the door so hard it smashed against the facing wall. She called out after him, but it was too late; he vanished inside. Mari ran in after him, facing the long, narrow room with the door at the other end. Light shone from the shattered glass, and a million faces reflected back at her. "Ash...I think he went through that door. That's what happened last time."

She yanked his forearm to make him stop. "Please, listen to me!"

Ash grabbed the handle and yanked it, which was locked and bolted. Fear licked at her heart, and she looked around the room. Was it in here watching them? Whoever it was couldn't escape this time. Ash gritted his teeth. "I don't even know where the keys are for this door."

"But…" she stammered, confused. "Before it went through that door. It was unlocked—I swear to you!"

Ash shrugged his shoulders, throwing his eyes around the dark room. "I've never opened this door, Mari. Nothing could get through here."

She ground her jaw, frustrated tears burning in her eyes. "But I *heard* it."

He further infuriated her by shrugging again, clutching the towel at his waist. "I don't know what to tell you."

"What's with all the shattered mirrors?" she asked, stunned that he didn't seem worried about what she'd seen.

He huffed, humoring her with a tight smile. "I have no idea. I told you…I've not explored half of this place yet. While I wait for you to work through your internal crisis….can I get dried off?"

Mari snapped to her senses, shook her head, and his smile dropped. She'd come up here to talk about Clover, about the horror she'd just witnessed in that room. Was he so blind to his sister's anguish that he could hide and shrug it off?

"I'm guessing by that look on your face, it didn't go well." He nodded to the door, keen to leave this room behind.

Once they were outside in the corridor, she leaned against the wall, her neck aching with tension. "No, it didn't go well." Sarcasm dripped off her tongue, annoyed that he hadn't been there. "She fried her hands."

Ash winced. "I'm sorry. I'll see to her."

"No…it seems to be healing—already. Which is weird…"

What was weirder was that it'd worked for a few moments, but she didn't say that.

Ash pulled his robe tighter. "What's wrong?"

Mari stepped back because the closer she got to him, the dizzier she became. "Look, Ash…you're her brother."

"I know."

"You owe it to her to explore every avenue of this thing. You—*we* can't let her keep doing this."

His brows drew together in a dark frown for the first time, his face tense, like he wasn't happy she was pushing. "Are you saying I haven't tried everything? Gone down every avenue?" He clicked his tongue. "You haven't been there, Marianne. You haven't seen her at her worst. I have."

"I'm not saying that." However, it did sound like she was. "But I need to know for myself. I'd like to see a dermatologist at Meadowford General. My family doctor recommended him. He sounds amazing, very forward-thinking, and open to alternative medicine. If anyone can take what Clover's doing seriously, he will."

He quieted and took a breath, crossing his arms. "You've been researching this? Talking to doctors behind my back?"

Her stomach knotted, a look of regret passing across his face. Regret that he'd let her in, confided in her. Bitterness clouded his voice. "I can't believe you don't trust me—all Clover wanted is a friend."

Her cheeks flamed with embarrassment. "I do trust you—but I need to know if there is anything more we could be doing for her. I want to see him, Ash, and I'm going," Mari said. "With or without you. But I'd like to go with you."

"What do you expect to learn?"

"Ash," she breathed. "It kind of worked."

His pupils widened, that glazed look gone in an instant. "What?"

Mari nodded. "For like a *minute*...it worked. She was in the light. I can't believe I'm saying this, but I think she's onto something. The burns were horrific, but they healed."

Ash turned away, his gaze drawn to the corridor where she thought she'd seen something only moments ago. He stiffened, his eyes narrow, until she touched his arm. "Ash."

He raked his hands through his hair. "That's insane...if it worked."

"It did," she said. "And if there is a possibility that this could be real...then I want to talk to a real doctor. This could be pivotal."

Distracted again, Ash stared into the empty chasm, his lip twitching until he dragged his gaze to hers. "Alright." He gave a firm nod. "I'll go with you. When do you think we can see him?"

Mari didn't want to look down the narrow stretch of the hall, convinced she hadn't imagined it. Something had been there, listening in the shadows, watching them, and the thought stole her breath and her nerve. Ash sensed it, too, but Mari guessed he wouldn't draw attention to it.

"I'll make the call," she said, shivering, and for once, she wanted to go home.

TWENTY

Mari ignored a barrage of Eric's emails and messages, guilt gnawing at her gut as she went home and called Dr. Franks, the dermatologist her family doctor had put her in touch with. He hadn't replied to her email, but it didn't take long for her to dig up his secretary's number online. Rain pelted the window, and Bear snuggled at her feet while she hunched at the desk with her phone cradled to her ear.

She was put on hold, and the tinny music played in her ear, irritating a headache that had begun in the orangery. While she waited, she thumbed through Eric's notes, nodding and talking to herself as she worked, typing with one hand. As if he'd sensed her across the internet waves, his profile picture popped up on her chat page, and she groaned.

"Hey, how are you? I haven't heard from you in a few days."

Mari thought about ignoring it, but he was her best client, and she knew well enough that he'd bug her until she replied.

"Hey. I'm so sorry. I'm sending some feedback through right now. My mom got sick."

It wasn't entirely a lie.

The screen flashed, and Mari's headache throbbed like it was gnawing at the deepest cavities of her skull.

"I'm so sorry to hear that. Hope she's better now. What did you think about the description of the little town? Did it feel eerie enough? The hunting family in the woods?"

Mari rolled her eyes, distracted and annoyed, the on-hold music jarring her nerves. She didn't want to admit that all Eric's town descriptions were the same—small, forestry towns with woods for miles and a spooky mansion thrown in for good measure.

"It was great. Atmospheric," she lied. "But maybe you could delve into the town's history more."

A few seconds later, he came back with. "On it! By the way, I'm thinking of naming my towns after virtues…what do you think of Temperance? Or Mercy?"

Gritting her teeth, she typed back, "Good plan!"

"Hello? May I help you?"

Pain spiked her temples, and she nearly choked and dropped the phone at the sound of the receptionist's voice. She ignored Eric and quickly explained who she was and that she'd already emailed Dr. Franks. When she explained the situation as best she could without mentioning shadows and figures hiding in the dark and a room that was now conveniently locked when she knew it hadn't been before, the secretary made noises of understanding before she replied.

"Yes, he got your email, Miss Fox," she said, kindly. "But he's away in Ohio right now for a family wedding—he'll be back Monday, and we can schedule an appointment for your friend for a few months."

"A few months?" Mari spluttered. Clover needed help now, and who knew how many times she'd try and test this crazy theory on herself in that time?

"Is there nothing sooner?" she begged.

The secretary tutted in sympathy. "I'm afraid not. Dr. Franks is one of the leading Dermatologists in his field, and he's booked months ahead."

Defeated, she hung up and hung her head. Nothing left to do now, but try to sleep off this headache. She'd see Ash in the morning and explain. Exhausted, she lifted from the chair, as Bear jumped and barked at the window. Mari frowned and glanced outside, catching a flash of blonde hair as Ash crossed the field. He was heading for her house, and the look on her face made her wilt. He looked pissed off, probably due to her meddling. Mari supposed he'd be relieved when she told him they couldn't see Dr. Franks anyway. And it wasn't that she didn't trust him. She just needed to know.

She jogged down the stairs and opened the front door. Bear shot past her legs and darted around Ash as he opened the gate. Bear brought him his rubber chicken and dropped it at his feet, but Ash kicked it away, stalking past him. Bear cowered miserably, and Mari scowled.

She met him on the porch while rain plastered his hair to his head. Crossing her arms defensively, she firmed her chin. "Is there a problem?" She was used to standing up to bullies considering she had lived with one. The expression on his face cut deep. He'd never looked at her like that, with his fists balled like he was holding in his temper.

"You railroaded me," he shot back, equally as angry, his nostril flaring.

"Railroaded you?"

"You emailed a doctor without talking to me," he said, and Mari clicked her tongue, knowing she hadn't imagined the sour glare he'd shot her earlier. "Behind my back."

Mari balked. "I only want to help her, Ash."

The handsome face she'd come to love so much contorted with anger, so fierce she barely recognized him. "And you think I don't help her?"

"That isn't a life!" She pointed to Rosewood, shrouded in trees and shadow. "What you're providing... isn't good for her!"

"And what would you know about anything?" he sneered. "Hiding away like a coward because you betrayed someone who loved you."

Mari drained and sucked in air. Tears blurred her eyes, and she'd never felt more like sinking into the mud. Every reason she'd hidden away for the last four months flooded back. Malice sparkled in the depths of his eyes, laced with triumph and knowledge of what she'd done. She shouldn't have told him about Zara. Biting her lip, she finally managed to look up.

"It's not me who is railroading this whole thing."

"What's that supposed to mean?"

In that moment she wondered where her kind gentleman had gone. The man glaring at her resembled nothing of the sweet guy who worried about her that she'd met weeks ago.

"It means…" she took a shallow breath, carefully choosing her words. "I don't think you came here to help Clover, not really."

"I learned long ago that there is no help for Clover."

"Don't you want her to recover? Or at least explore the possibility that there might be life for her beyond that house?"

"I'm the one who takes care of her!" he cried. "Me. I've done it for years. I'm her brother, and I know what's best. And…" he looked skyward. "Mari, don't push me. Don't make me say things I don't want to say."

She snorted out a withered laugh, wiping her eyes. "You already said plenty."

A bitter look of regret crossed his face, and he went to reach for her, but she backed away.

"I just want to help her. She doesn't deserve that life."

"You don't know her. You don't know anything."

Mari took a step back. "You accuse me of secrecy…but you're hiding things. Are you trying to keep her sick?"

"What?" His brows flew skyward, and she knew by the anger in his eyes that she'd pushed too far. He sucked air through his nose before turning away, running both hands through his hair. "Do you think I want this life?"

"Where are your family?" Mari fired. "Why is it just the two of you? How can it be that *no one* is around to help you?"

Startled, as though she'd slapped him, he stepped away. "It's always been us. Just me and Clover. We've always been alone."

"That doesn't make any sense," Mari snapped, quickly losing patience. "Look…"

"I'm leaving," Ash said, filling the gap. She breathed a sigh of relief as he stepped off the porch. She trembled with adrenaline, but somehow, the guilt crept in.

"Ash…please…"

"No, Mari. You don't trust me. For some reason…I don't know. I can feel it. Why can't you accept what I'm saying? That for Clover, this is it."

"I can't accept there's no hope," she said. "I can't."

Ash shook his head, sorrowful as he walked away. "I'll see you, Mari."

She watched him leave, the wind blowing her hair around her face, now more confident than ever of what she had to do. He hadn't even allowed her to tell him about the doctor. He must have stewed about this all afternoon, pent up and angry, ready to erupt like a geyser.

Clover asked her not to tell him about the Oak or her grand scheme. She'd warned her of Ash's reaction if he found out. Mari had pushed, and now she knew, grateful she'd kept Clover's wishes to herself. Mari didn't just need to find that Oak; she *wanted* to.

TWENTY-ONE

It was early when Mari slipped on her hiking boots the following day. Bear wound through her legs, and she clipped his leash. Standing in the hall, she gazed up at the landing, the house quiet and still. Her mother's soft snores came from the open bedroom door, a habit she'd fallen into when James got sick, keeping her door open so she could hear him if he called out.

"Come on, boy," she said, shrugging on her jacket and tugging the leash. Bear scampered happily behind her, wagging his tail manically as he hopped down the path to the truck. She lifted him into the front seat, glancing over the dash to the house shrouded by trees across the field. The rain had let up overnight, leaving the ground a soggy mess, not the greatest conditions for a trek through the woods. The fight with Ash had kept her awake, along with the constant pounding in her head and the rain beating the roof.

She'd pushed him, and he didn't like it one bit. He wanted a friendship for his sister, but was part of that friendship looking in the other direction if someone was in pain? A knot twisted in her belly as she recalled how he'd flung her betrayal of Zara in her face. She wished she'd never confessed, the irony not lost on her. Belting up in the truck, she clipped her cell phone to the dash, typing in the address of the hiking trail in Cedar Wood that Clover had mentioned. It was a nature park surrounded by thick trees and various walking trails for different hikers. Some were only an hour; some longer. Mari hoped she'd find the Oak on one of them.

She had no idea how she'd ever find this tree or if it even existed, but she had to try. She couldn't watch Clover go through that horror again.

It was a Tuesday morning, and the roads were empty and quiet. It took about an hour to drive to the outskirts of Cedar Wood where she parked the truck at a nature park. She spent the morning combing the trails till a sweat broke on her neck. She saw a lot of birches and white-red ferns but nothing that resembled the oak in the photograph Clover had shown her. Bear was having a blast; chasing squirrels and leaping into piles of leaves, enjoying this new terrain to explore. It was quiet, not many other hikers on the trails, and she couldn't shake the sensation that this was the kind of forest in which you could easily lose your way.

As lunchtime rolled around, her water supply was dwindling, and her belly rumbled. Mari trekked back to the lot and drove to the diner outside Lincoln; it was the closest, and right now, she was too tired and hungry to worry if Zara could be in there. Bear was antsy and all too happy to lap fresh water from a silver bowl outside the diner. Inside, he was fussed and petted by the waitress who'd served her and Ash when they came for their date.

He ate treats right out of her hand, winding through her legs until he yawned and stretched out under the table by Mari's hot, throbbing feet.

She guessed she could check the maps and see if there were any trails she'd missed. Hunched over a latte, she scanned her maps, her brow creased as an ache began forming behind her eyes.

That morning, she'd woken with a headache that had made her stomach swim. The pain had been blinding. Right now, she wondered if caffeine was the right decision, but she was bone tired, worse than ever, and it'd taken a monumental effort to get out of bed at all this morning.

"Out for a hike?" a soft voice pulled her out of her daze. She glanced up, tucking hair behind her ear. It was the waitress, waiting with her pad and pen.

"Something like that," Mari said, stifling a yawn. The waitress refilled her mug, peering at the maps.

"Are you looking for something?"

Mari guessed she must be referring to the red crosses and circles scrawled all over the map, places she'd tried so far. Her calves ached from walking, and she was sure she'd have blisters.

"Depends. Have you ever seen a tree like this?" Mari flashed the photo of the rare oak on her phone. The waitress, whose name was *Evan* from her tag, frowned deeply, her mouth twitching in interest. "It's called a…"

"A Quercus Robur," Evan finished for her.

Mari blinked. "Do you actually know what that is?"

Evan slipped into the seat opposite her, glancing carefully over her shoulder in case she might be missed. It was quiet and humid, and the windows were beaded with condensation. "I've seen an Oak like that before. It's in Cedar Wood."

Mari looked up hopefully. "I've been walking all the trails, and I'm exhausted. And someone is getting cranky."

Bear was curled up on the beaten-up seat next to her. The walk had tired him. His caramel-colored mustache ruffled as he snored.

Evan pouted and gave him a gentle scratch between the ears. "You mind me asking why you're looking for a tree like that?"

"It's kind of dumb…probably a little crazy…"

"I understand crazy. We get all sorts in here."

"I have this friend, she's sick, and she believes that the bark from this tree will help her. That she can add it to teas." Mari wasn't sure of how much detail she should go into. The girl's gaze was intense as if she were drinking every word.

Evan looked thoughtful. "That does kind of make sense."

Mari laughed, sitting back in her seat. "Does it?" She shook her head. "I'm not so sure."

Evan leaned forward on her forearms. "Well, you know this whole area has a history with witchcraft, don't you?"

Mari rolled her eyes and Evan laughed. "Okay, well, I see you are a skeptic…but that tree has a nickname. I'm surprised you don't know if you live around here."

"No," Mari said. "I went to a different school near Winstone. Why? What do they call it?"

Evan's face darkened. "It's the hanging tree."

Ice rippled up her skin, and caught in her dark gaze, she trembled. "Oh. I guess I don't have to ask how it got that name."

"Did you ever hear the stories about the Mickelford witches?"

"Of course."

"That's where they hung her—out at the oak at Cedar Wood. I guess they didn't want to make it a public affair."

A witch buried under an old oak tree... Mari's brows drew close. Hadn't Eric written something about that? The coincidence made the hair on her arms prick up.

Mari drained. "I didn't know that," she said, though it felt like she should have. She questioned whether she should be hiking out there at all. The clouds overhead were leaden, threatening rain.

"It's not *too* far from here," Evan said, answering her unspoken thoughts. "It's about an hour's hike..." She turned the nature trail maps towards her, running her finger along the grids till she found the diner on the map. "Most hikers either leave their cars here or park further up. But if you walk in from here and head south, once you reach the old church, head east."

"And it's there?" Mari brightened, pleased this stranger was being so helpful. Evan made a face that could only be described as a grimace.

"It won't be hard to find."

She stood, leaving that hanging between them, and Mari suppressed a shudder. The waitress spun back in her direction, narrowing her eyes.

"Just take care out there," she warned. "You have to keep your wits about you. This forest has teeth."

"What does that mean?"

"Avoid straying off the paths," she advised, nodding to the sleeping Bear under her feet, "And be careful not to let him stray too far. This forest is famous for old hunting traps. We've had many injured hikers here after falling down a pit."

"Right," Mari agreed as nervous butterflies danced in her belly. She bundled the maps back in her pack. "We'll be careful."

Mari walked for an hour and realized that she was incredibly out of shape. Her seclusion at the farmhouse had done nothing for her fitness, even though she'd told herself she got plenty of exercise when walking Bear. He chugged alongside, happily wagging his tail and keeping on track unless he saw something buzzing overhead. Stopping by a mossy stump, Mari paused to stretch her lower back. Everything ached, and she was sure she must have headed in the wrong direction.

Earlier, she'd passed by a massive house, more like a mansion with a huge iron gate. It cast a foreboding shadow, giving her a little chill as her eyes combed the grey walls and empty windows.

She thought she spotted a stained-glass panel in the door, similar to the one at Rosewood, and thought maybe this was the building Ash mentioned.

As she shuffled deeper and further in, she passed a massive meadow expanse before grabbing the map to check she was on course. "Bear, come on."

She jerked her head, mildly irritated that the mutt hadn't moved from his spot. He was standing on the edge of the woods behind, staring at the trees. He whined low in his windpipe, and a burst of goosebumps broke on her arms. "C'mon boy," she called again.

The trees rustled like something large had moved up there, and she narrowed her eyes, her stomach jolting as Bear dropped to his belly. The trees exploded in a flurry of leaves, and a falcon swooped low over her head. Mari screeched and ducked as it soared inches above, circling and then vanishing into the woods. She let out a laugh and clutched her chest. "Jesus Christ."

After another hour of hiking dragged slowly by, Mari was about ready to give up. Her calves burned, and she was sweating under the layers she wore. She wound her hoodie about her waist, staring through the dense canopy, a vibrant map of oranges, yellows, and greens, and thought she saw a grey cloud. When a splat of rain hit her forehead, followed by a torrent, she ducked for cover, crouching under a bush.

Bear snuggled closer. "May as well check the maps and wait it out," she said. The sound of her voice provided some comfort, that she wasn't alone out here in a spooky forest, on a crazy mission, to find an ancient tree, where a witch was hanged. Mari shivered, huddling into her jacket. Then she froze, disturbed by a rustling noise from above. Craning her neck, she peered through the leaves.

It was the falcon again. It was small and delicate, and it cocked its head to watch her in her hiding spot. Its little yellow eyes narrowed with interest.

Mari smiled. It was pretty, with speckled white and brown wings. "Hey," she said, giving Bear a nudge. He whimpered, drawing closer to her. "It's just a bird, doofus. Since when were you scared of a bird?"

A low growl rumbled in his chest, and Mari frowned, patting him between the ears to shush him. She lifted her eyes to the falcon, who watched with interest, hopping from branch to branch until it was eye level. Mari laughed nervously. The way the bird looked at her, it was almost... Mari shook herself, thinking she'd been alone with Eric's words and inner monologue for far too long.

"Don't suppose you've seen a creepy-looking tree out here, have you?"

She'd been joking, anything to break the heavy silence. To her surprise, the bird cocked its head, spread its wings, and flew away.

Mari snorted, getting to her feet. The rain had stopped. That was kind of weird...almost like it'd understood her.

Now you're losing it, she thought. Going a few yards, she paused, spotting her new friend in the trees. It took off, flying a short distance and then stopping to wait for her.

"Okay…" she said, her hand tightening on Bear's leash as she followed the falcon through the undergrowth. At one point, she hit a steep incline, and she winced, going down haphazardly on her ass, before she dusted herself off, only to look up and see the bird still watching her.

"If I *believed* in magic, then I'd say you were leading me," she joked, keeping pace and a little out of breath. "But then, I don't believe in magic."

Bear stopped, his tail dropping and ears flattening as he tugged hard on the leash. "Hey," she called, "What's wrong, boy?"

It was no use. He wasn't going any further. Part of her didn't blame him. Under the thick Cedars, it was quiet and cool, the ground mossy and knotted with old, dead roots. A narrow path wound through a patch of dense Cedar trunks, making her shudder. A low mist crossed the path. She went ahead, peering through the trees, finding they were on the edge of a meadow.

Bear was under some brambles, and Mari backtracked to him, scratching his face. She carefully wound his leash through a stump, aware the falcon still had eyes on her. "Okay, I'll be back in a minute," she promised. "You stay here."

Straightening, she hoisted her pack over her shoulder, turning as the falcon shot off the branch and flew down the path. Drawing her shoulders to her ears, Mari followed, unable to shake the odd, creeping sensation of being watched. It was only a few yards until she broke through to daylight, and air filled her lungs, the heavy sensation lifting. She looked back over her shoulder, wary of eyes watching her every move.

She turned and gawked in awe. It was there. A giant, naked oak stripped of any finery, with its gnarled roots knotted into the ground. Its branches stretched to the sky like hands praying to an unseen god. *A hanging tree.* This thing was every inch a witches tree, like something out of a kid's fairytale.

The falcon rested in one of the branches, observing as she approached. Mari set her pack on the ground in the long grass, circling the oak with interest.

"Is it supposed to look...*dead*?" she asked herself and the falcon, as if it would actually give her an answer. And yet something about the oak was alive. It kind of hummed. She could feel the ground vibrating through her sneakers.

Someone died here.

Of course, that was ridiculous as people died in all sorts of places. But in this spot, an execution had taken place, a woman's life ended in a ghastly fashion. If she closed her eyes, she could almost imagine the scene and how disturbing it must have been. Shivering, she backed out of the oak's shadow and into the sun's rays, forcing their way through the cloud.

She whipped around, her hair flying as she thought she'd heard feet behind her. Staring at the treeline, she swore...

A man…a man in a hood. It was so fleeting, she wondered if she'd imagined it.

This forest has teeth. It had to be a fellow hiker.

"Okay, I need to get out of here," she said, dropping to her knees and grabbing the plastic tube and knife Clover had given her. Lunging for the trunk, she used the knife to shave several long cuttings off the bark. Clover had advised her to cut deep so the oak's flesh could be revealed under the dark, knobbly bark. But what she saw made her gut roll. Thick, tar-like treacle, welled from the cut, oozing down her hand. It was black, sticky, and smelled foul. Mari gagged and shoved it in the tube. More substance drizzled out of the tree, dripping down the trunk.

Like blood.

A coughing fit overtook her as she gagged, her throat closing. She coughed and hacked until she saw those familiar black dots, her knees trembling.

Her nose itched from the stench, coating the inside of her nostrils. Shoving the tube into her pack, she took off, aware of the falcon watching her as she trekked back through the shadowy path to where she'd left Bear.

Had he sensed it? Was that why he didn't want to go near the oak? Mari wondered if Clover knew what she was getting herself into. The sap from that bark wasn't normal…thick and dense, like tar.

"Shit!" she cried, stopping in her tracks as she rounded the corner.

Bear had a friend. A man was kneeling beside him, stroking his head and scratching behind his ears. Bear's tail wagged in appreciation, happy to have company. The second her foot cracked on twigs, the man bolted up and spun away, quick to replace his hood. Mari gaped, her voice dried and gone as the man fled. In that brief instant, she'd spotted a flash of white blonde hair, and he'd been carrying…

A crossbow. She grabbed Bear's lead, who was pining and whimpering after the stranger. What the hell kind of place was this that men just randomly hiked with weaponry like that?

What kind of animals lived in the woods that were so dangerous that you'd even *need* a crossbow?

Whoever it was, he was gone, and he hadn't hurt Bear, only given him some kind of comfort, so Mari guessed he wasn't dangerous. Still, the whole thing had left her jittery and her head swam from her coughing fit. She wiped her mouth, and blood came away on her fingers.

Shit...what is happening? Mari logically guessed her bout of coughing was to blame. But did it explain her nausea? Her headache? Splintering pain wracked her bones and she wasn't sure how she would make it back to the truck.

Above, the falcon had followed her in, and she smiled at it gratefully. Spots of rain pelted her jacket, and she guessed it would be a good couple of hour's hike back to the diner where she'd parked.

"Don't suppose you know a shortcut to the diner?" she asked, not expecting the bird to jump into action, watching fascinated as it soared through the trees.

She followed, a little nervous to pass by the creepy mansion again. But to her surprise, the falcon took a different path. "I'll be your best friend if this is a quicker route."

She was *joking*, because Mari didn't believe in magic. But the falcon got her back to her car, watching her the entire way until she strapped herself in and settled Bear before driving away.

This forest had teeth alright. Mari swore that would be the last time she'd ever visit.

TWENTY-TWO

When Mari arrived back at Rosewood, she was relieved that Ash didn't seem to be anywhere in sight. Telling herself she wouldn't be long, she parked the truck and left Bear in the seat with the window rolled down. The evening was becoming humid, and she was bone tired. Wiping her nose on the edge of her sleeve, she was relieved when it appeared clear.

The glass panel in the door greeted her, and she carefully edged it open, peeking around the corner into the dark, shadowy hallway. The scaffold remained in the middle of the hall, and as she stepped inside, a loud clanging from above signaled that Ash was up there somewhere, working, and probably still pissed off at her after their argument.

She sidestepped around the scaffold and headed to the orangery, where the familiar cloying heat quickly greeted her and left a film on her skin. "Clover?"

She headed to her workroom, which was empty. The room was densely hot and smelled strongly of perfume, a floral scent tickling her nose. She sneezed, suppressing the terror as she looked at her hand and saw it was clear of any blood.

"Clover?"

She headed to Clover's floral bed chamber, now a draping canopy of climbing white roses and honeysuckle. Deep green eucalyptus hung in clusters around the bed where the girl lay. Mari's heart leaped. For a moment, she thought she was gone. Laying so still, unmoving and unblinking among the leaves, like a fallen angel.

She touched Clover's ice-cold hand. "Clo?"

"It's alright," she said, in a reedy breath. "I didn't die yet."

Mari's eyes filled up, horrified and hollow. "Don't say things like that. You aren't going to die."

Clover's thin, parched lips twitched. "Not today, maybe. But if I don't make this work, then soon…"

"Don't!" Mari knelt at her side, fumbling in her pack. "I got the bark, Clover. I found the tree."

As though an entity had breathed life back into the girl, her skin flushed with color, and she turned her head, her blonde ringlets moving on the velvet pillow. "You found it? Was it really there?"

"Oh, *yes.* I found it alright." She revealed the glass test tube with the cuttings inside. Since removing them from the tree, the black color had oxidized, turning a nasty, deep shade of red. Mari hoped she was imagining things, but she swore the liquid bubbled. "And let me tell you, that was one creepy forest."

Clover sprang to life, lifting from the mattress in frightening speed, so fast Mari blinked in shock. She grinned, revealing pink gums as she snatched the test tube. Something about her expression made Mari's eyes darken, and she stepped back. "Did you know?"

Clover didn't seem to be listening. She was studying the contents of the vial, turning it over in her hand. Mari bristled. "Clo, did you hear me?"

Snapping back to herself, the girl looked up. "Know what?"

"Did you know it was a hanging tree? That the Mickleford witch was executed there?"

Clover gave her a coy, innocent smile. "I heard rumors." Her answer made heat blast under Mari's skin, her temper rising.

"Did you know the forest was full of traps?"

"Didn't *you?* I thought everyone knew that!"

"No, the waitress at the diner told me. You could have warned me, Clover."

Clover's elation drained from her face, her big eyes filling up, and she grabbed Mari's hand. "I'm so sorry...of course you're right. Please don't be angry with me. You don't know what this means."

Clover's breakneck pivot in personality was enough to give Mari whiplash. Instead, a dull ache formed behind her eyes, her head pounding. She wanted a shower and her bed. Plus, she'd avoided Eric's emails all day and was sure he'd been waiting on her response.

"I should go," Mari stood as Clover's fascination with the vial and its contents took over. Her neck prickled as she walked away, and it wasn't until she darted a look over her shoulder that she spotted the girl in her peripherals. Clover moved unnaturally, darting around the fountain and heading to her workroom. The way she'd moved made the hairs stand up on Mari's arms. Hadn't the girl been lying supine on her back moments ago?

Leaving the unpleasant sensation behind her, she hurried to the hall, preferring the darkness to the heat of the orangery. A flicker of movement in the corridor caught her eye, and for a moment, she stood rooted, her feet on the edge of the pool of light by the scaffold. Dust motes breathed around her, glittering like stars.

Someone was there. She remembered the figure she thought she'd seen, the thing she hoped her mind had conjured from Eric's stories. Stories that bizarrely mirrored the place she'd just visited.

"Mari?" Ash called from above. "What are you doing here?"

Her mouth dropped, and she reluctantly dragged her gaze from the shadows. Maybe Rosewood really was haunted? She glanced up at Ash, watching her from the second platform, his hair hanging in his eyes. He flexed a hand in her direction, and she touched it, letting him guide her up. She followed him carefully to the second platform, where only a tiny patch of sky remained in the roof.

"I'm sorry," he blurted, hands on her arms to steady her. He tucked a hair behind her ear as the breeze tried to steal it away. "I'm sorry I was off and weird about everything."

Weird was an understatement. He smiled, and she hated the way it tugged at her heart. It was so easy to forgive him, to look away and forget the malice she'd seen in his eyes.

Mari was done looking the other way. Still, if he wanted to talk or explain, she'd listen.

She couldn't tell him why she was here, where Clover had sent her today, so instead, she held his arms, hoping to forget their quarrel. Leaning forward, he kissed her jaw and quickly found her mouth. She whimpered, the bruise on her lip throbbing. "No, Ash."

Hands like iron clasped her shoulders, ignoring her refusal as he clamped his mouth to hers, kissing her as though he were oxygen-starved. Mari fought, squirming under his grip, her heart pounding with fear. She pushed him away, and his eyes shone.

"What's wrong?" He licked her blood off his lips, and she touched her mouth. Her head swam.

"I said no...I thought you were going to apologize." She felt like an idiot for climbing up here with him.

Ash licked his lips, frowning. "Mari...you're bleeding."

"Oh." Embarrassed, she wiped her nose, swaying on her feet. "I have a headache, that's all..."

"You're as white as a sheet," Ash worried, taking her hands. "Let's get you down."

Thick, coppery blood made her gag as she swallowed it down, and by the time she reached the bottom step, she was faint, a chill spreading up her neck. "I don't feel so good."

"I'll put you in bed."

"No, I want to go home." Who knew what would happen if she stayed here overnight? And that thing, the shadow in the halls, was watching her. She didn't want to be anywhere near it *or* Ash Martin. "Please..."

She swayed and collapsed in Ash's arms, and the last thing she heard was him promising to get her and Bear home and in her own bed. She allowed herself to be carried, undressed, and folded into her own clean sheets only because she was too pathetic to help herself.

Bear nuzzled her cheek, and she didn't protest as Ash forced her to drink water and take an aspirin. "God knows someone needs to take care of you," he said, his shadow moving around in her bedroom. She heard drawers opening, the noise of the window cracking open, and fresh air filling the room.

"I'll light the candle," he said before she dozed off. "When you wake, blow it out and I'll know you're okay."

Just go, she wanted to shriek. This helpless version of herself was annoying, unable to walk without getting dizzy or wanting to vomit. She just wanted him out of her room and her life.

"Thank you," she mumbled reluctantly.

"I don't want anything to happen to you," he whispered, his breath on her forehead, lips brushing her brow. "I'll go, but if you need anything…"

"I know," she whispered as he kissed her head, wrapping the covers around her chin.

TWENTY-THREE

She woke with her vision swimming. Stabs of white hot pain spiked in her temples and she tumbled from the bed, her stomach about to unleash everything she'd eaten at the diner earlier. Stumbling to the bathroom in the dark, lit only by the moon pooling through the window, she collapsed by the toilet and threw up till she couldn't see straight.

On her knees, she found the light switch and her horrific reflection in the mirror. Gaunt and dark eyed, the front of her shirt was soaked in blood. It dripped in constant torrent from her nose, dribbling down her chin. Waves of panic took over, but she knew this. James used to get nosebleeds, mainly when he played football.

Wadding pads of toilet tissue in her hand she mopped at her face, trying to scrub it off with cool water.

Hunched over, she shuffled out of the bathroom and across the hall, careful not to wake her mother. She could hear her soft breaths from the open bedroom door. James's room was opposite, and as Mari found the cool handle with her hot hand, she took a moment to think. Her mother didn't like her going in here.

No one had been in here since the day she'd gotten a suit for him to be buried in. Her mother didn't want the room disturbed. But she knew James had saline medication. He'd wandered around the house with it, stuffing a squirt of nasal spray up his nose if he'd had a rough game.

It stopped the bleeds, and Mari was sure it was still in there. He kept his meds by the bedside cabinet. She let the door swing open to the humid, stuffy room. It still smelled like a teenage boy; stale aftershave and unwashed sheets. Padding across the room, she plopped onto the edge of his old bed; his striped sheets cool and unused. There was still an indent from his head in the pillow, and her heart lurched.

Switching on the bedside lamp, the room glowed with amber light. The drawer squeaked as it opened, but it didn't take long for her to find what she needed. Among an array of old painkillers, condoms, and used batteries, sat the saline solution. She hastily undid the lid and squirted the liquid up her throbbing nose. She winched through the sharp sting, feeling a tingle as blood glugged down her throat, blinking as her eyes watered.

Pinching the bridge of her nose, she waited for the pain to subside and her vision to stop swimming. Dabbing her nose carefully, she was relieved when the tissue came out clean.

"Thank god," she muttered, her voice hoarse from where she'd thrown up. She needed to sleep for a week. Her body ached from her hike, and she promised herself she'd bathe and sleep in late tomorrow.

She didn't want to think about work or Eric. Or even Ash and Clover. Or that weird-smelling crap in that vial. Mari wasn't sure what that was; but it wasn't normal.

She didn't want to think about the falcon who'd practically led her back to her car, or the man she'd seen with Bear. Or the shadow lurking in the halls of Rosewood.

Staring around James's bedroom, she could close her eyes and imagine him here. His work out gear and dumbbells in the corner. The porn stash she was sure he kept under the bed. The clothes he'd bought with his birthday money, still in a bag, never worn.

What use does a dying kid have need for new clothes? He'd been so furious, and Mari remembered his bitter, defeated tone. How he would lash out.

Sitting here was like facing his ghost; she'd had enough of those. Leaning to switch off the light, a glass bottle of pills caught her eye. It was hidden, way back in the drawer among some unopened letters and an old phone. Narrowing her gaze, she plucked it out, brushing off the dust and squinting in the low light to read the faded print on the bottle.

It slipped from her fingers the second her brain caught up with her eyes.

Rohypnol.

Mari clutched her throat, and she shook. Sitting on the edge of her dead brother's bed, she questioned why the hell he possessed a bottle of Rohypnol. James never had sleep issues. He was one to fall asleep in a chair, his energy burned out, leaving him to nap where he fell.

"I don't remember anything." The world peeled at the edges. *"I didn't see anything."*

"No," Mari whispered. "Oh my god…no." She threw the bottle back in the drawer. Then, she thought better of it and took it out, wrapping it under her arm as she hurried back to her room.

Thoughts spiraled in her head. This couldn't be real. This couldn't mean…

"Do you believe he would be capable something so cruel?"

Mari collapsed on the bed, tears clogging her throat. She hadn't believed her. She'd turned away from her best friend. It was true. It was all true. She didn't need any more evidence than that. James was *capable.* James could be cruel, vicious, the *man* of the house.

James hurt her best friend. He'd made sure she was out of the way that night. She remembered waking in the mud below Mr. Raggerty.

It's almost like he's watching you.

Mari's blood ran cold. The scarecrow knew. She didn't know how it was possible, but knew it to be true. He knew what she'd done. He wanted her to remember. He was out there, watching, taunting, and following her every move because he was waiting for her to remember. He knew how Zara had suffered, outcast and alone, because he was the same.

You turned away from her.

Shaking violently, Mari did something she thought she would never do, even though it was nearly five in the morning, and the sun had yet to rise. She took out her old cell and switched it on.

TWENTY-FOUR

Meet you in the diner, came Zara's reply as soon as seven am hit. Filled with nerves, Mari showered and dressed, scraping her hair back vigorously with a comb. Her scalp pulled and itched. Standing under the hot spray, she washed off the remains of the blood, sticky and coating her chest, soaked through her old shirt. Lathering her hair, she gave her scalp a good scratch, the deep itch begging for relief. When she removed her hand, she shrieked. Tufts of her dark hair came away in her hand, entwined with her fingers. Staring at her bare feet, she watched in dismay as it swirled and eventually sucked into the drain.

What was happening to her? She ran a comb carefully through her locks, pulling it into a damp bun at her nape, terrified of brushing too vigorously.

Her mother still slept as she left the house, and she gave Bear a quick scratch and cuddle before she dashed outside in the rain. It hadn't stopped since early this morning, the pattering on the roof keeping her awake. The truck grumbled to life, and Mari flicked on the wipers, heading through the deserted streets of Winstone and finally pulling into the diner's gravel-paved lot.

Mari gripped the wheel, her knuckles white, and took some calming breaths, even though no part of her was calm. She was going to face her old friend after a year of silence. They couldn't spend a day without calling or messaging when they were kids. Zara's absence in her life had left a gaping hole. A hole she'd dug herself, dived into, and then allowed herself to be buried.

Mari caught sight of her gaunt reflection in the glass of the diner door, her hollowed-out cheeks and dark circles. The smell of honey and cinnamon made her stomach knot, and she didn't think she could face eating right now. Evan, the pretty dark-haired waitress, beamed when she spotted her lurking in the doorway.

"Back so soon?" She jogged to greet her, scooping up a menu. "Did you find what you were looking for?"

Mari managed a chuckle, followed by an eye roll. "Yeah, you could say that."

Evan glanced over her shoulder, eyeing the only other customer in the diner this early. "Do you…?"

"I'm meeting her," Mari stated, her stomach backflipping with nerves. All of a sudden, her feet were as heavy as lead. Zara glanced up from her menu, stray blonde hair falling over her brow. Mari closed the short distance between them, sliding into the battered leather seat opposite, linking her fingers on the table.

Evan breezed around them with a coffee pot. "Can I get you anything?"

"Coffee would be good," Zara said, her voice throaty. There was no mistaking the redness in her bright blue eyes. Evan returned after a few moments, sloshing hot coffee into mugs, possibly the longest seconds of Mari's life, while neither spoke, only stared at the other. Zara was dressed for work at the gas station, in a uniform shirt and torn cut-off shorts, her hair piled up in a messy bun.

When Evan left, Zara leaned in the chair and shook her head. "Mari—you look like shit."

"Thanks."

"No—I mean it. Are you sick or something?"

"Just a stomach thing," Mari lied, waving it off, even though every muscle in her body begged her to crawl back to bed and sleep. "Thanks for meeting me this early."

Zara shrugged. "My shift starts at eight. What's up? I thought you didn't want to speak to me again…and after the way, you looked at me while you were on that date the other night…"

Zara's pink lips smacked closed when Mari placed the small bottle of yellow pills on the table between them. It took her a few minutes to register, take the bottle, and read the label before licking her dry lips. Then she took a swig of coffee. "Is this a joke?" Her blue eyes flashed.

Mari balked. "No! I found it in James's bedside cabinet."

Zara slammed the bottle down hard, loud enough to make Evan glance over from the counter where she'd been chatting with a tall, red-haired woman in running gear.

"Is this your *proof?*" Zara leaned over the table, lowering her voice to a deathly whisper. "That I was knocked out and made it all up?"

Mari sat back in shock, her lips parting. "No."

"That this made my way into a drink, and I somehow concocted the whole thing?" Her eyes filled up with tears. "You think I haven't heard that before? Trust me, I remember *everything* that night in *great* detail." A tear fell and she swiped it away. "Everything."

"Zara…"

"Everything, Mari."

"I believe you!" she blurted, grabbing her hand across the table. "It was me who he drugged—*me!* I never lied to you when I said I didn't know what happened. All I remember is waking up in the mud underneath the scarecrow. But when I found this…I *knew*. He did this….and I'm so sorry, Zara." She clutched her hands together, their fingers weaving as she burst into tears. Zara sobbed, using her free hand to wipe at her eyes.

"I know I'll never make it up to you," she said. "I let you suffer alone. When James got sick…it was so fast. It was over so fast, then he was gone, and I couldn't let myself believe that my dead brother could have….*God.*"

Zara slipped her hands from under Mari's, folding them in her lap. "It wasn't just him. Jenson and Tyler were there." She sniffed, roughly wiping her nose until it went red. "They got to carry on like it never happened."

"You dropped the charges," Mari said, which only inflamed Zara more.

"I had no choice. Your mother…she put so much pressure on me. She came to college…. sent emails…"

If it was possible, Mari went a paler shade of white. "What?"

"Oh, I bet she never mentioned that did she?" Zara snapped. "Your mom is a piece of work—like her son. She threatened me, Mari. She made my life hell and because James was terminal I let it go. I had no one, Mari. You dropped out of college…"

"I couldn't stay there," Mari tried to explain, knowing how feeble it sounded. "The rumors…"

"Yeah, no shit. I remember."

"I'm sorry. I can't say it enough. What I did…"

"You turned your back…but I could have forgiven you. Your piece of shit brother died, and you had your mom to look after…but you locked yourself away." She choked on tears. "Like *you* were the victim."

For a while neither spoke, both too lost in grief. Zara's breathing was slow and shallow like she was holding on by a thread.

"James was cruel," Mari admitted aloud, and it hurt, it physically *hurt* to say it. The truth burned on her tongue. "He was favored, and he deserved none of it. He could be mean and spiteful, but I wanted to believe he was good after he died. Dying elevated his evangelical status—in my mother's eyes at least. We live in the dark, like he's still in that front room dying. She won't let him leave."

Zara sniffed, her eyes softening. "I'm sorry, Mari."

"I was alone too. I missed you."

"I missed you too."

Mari leaned her elbows on the table. The road ahead was rocky for them, and Mari didn't dare to believe she could be forgiven. "How can we go forward from this? I don't—want to live like this anymore."

Once again, a red mist seemed to fall across her friends eyes and her mouth pinched. "Well that depends."

"On?"

"On you. You believe me. So, are you going to stand by me?"

Mari swallowed dryly. "What do you want?"

"I want those fuckers to pay for what they did to me," Zara spat acidly. "They get to graduate college and I'm left in the dust working at my dad's gas station? This wasn't the life we planned, Mari."

She smiled sadly. "No, it's not."

"James is gone, but they're still *very* much alive and if we stay silent they'll do it again. So…" She took a deep breath. "Are you going to stand by me?"

Mari sat back, lips pressed to a bloodless line. She looked away, and Zara laughed, like she'd already guessed her answer. "Fuck you, Mari."

"Yes…I'll stand by you," she promised in a hurry. "It's just reopening the case will reopen everything with James. And I know you must hate her…"

"I don't hate anyone."

"…but my mom is sick. She needs help. And I need to be the one who decides for her. I need to get her help. Can you let me do that first?"

Zara mulled it over, her features softening, and Mari glimpsed a little of the old friend she'd known, the feisty, headstrong girl she'd been. Loneliness had eaten away at them both. "Alright," she said at last and Mari breathed a long sigh.

"But Mari…I can't promise we'll go back to what we were…like the old days."

Tearfully, she nodded, her throat bobbing. "I understand."

"Too much water under the bridge and all that…and we have a lot of water around here…"

Mari thought of Dan Wheeler, the poor runner who'd gone missing. Zara cared for her. The day of the storm, she'd called her to make sure she was okay. "I know."

Light a candle and I'll know you're okay…

Zara had always been there, but Mari had looked through her like a ghost.

When she glanced up, she caught Zara staring at her in curiosity. "I wondered what had happened to you that night." She jerked her chin at the bottle of pills on the table. "I guess that explains it, you had a date with old Mr. Raggerty."

Mari shrugged, feeling a chill cross her neck. She linked her fingers under the table. "Hmm. That thing still creeps me out."

"It always did…do you remember the old stories that my Gran used to tell us…that he was the old owner of that creepy mansion over the cornfield and he was cursed by a witch?"

Mari blinked in confusion. That was the second time in her life she'd heard that story, first Ash and now Zara. "I never heard that story in my life."

Zara grabbed her jacket. "Sure, my Gran told me…I was sure you must have been there. I mean, we *were* always together."

Warmth filled her chest, and the friends locked eyes. Mari smiled wanly. "We were."

"Who was the guy you were with the other night?" she asked, a flash of playfulness returning.

Mari breathed, listlessly. Her mind was elsewhere. In the field with her old raggerty friend. "Just someone I've been seeing."

Zara slid out of the booth. "I've got to get to work—but thank you. This….means more than you know."

Mari smiled up at her hopefully. "Can we meet up again soon?"

Zara looked away, biting her lip. "Maybe…give me time. I hope you get everything settled with your mom. Maybe try keeping your phone on?"

Mari didn't believe in magic, witchcraft or curses, but as Zara left the diner and the bell tinkled above the door, her mind was drawn to that night and the moment she'd woken in the wet mud underneath the scarecrow.

I think you have a stalker…

Mari followed Zara's truck with her eyes, watching as she sped out of the lot. She didn't believe in magic, in potions or spells. She'd seen too much death, the medical scent of hospitals and wards haunted her dreams. The despair and loathing in her brother's eyes when he took his last breaths and the tear that had fallen down his cheek.

She believed in what she could see, smell, and touch, but these past weeks, it seemed magic had flung itself like a blanket around her shoulders.

Clover had shown her things she wouldn't have believed a year ago. She'd seen something in the dark at Rosewood, and she felt in her gut that waking up that night at the foot of the scarecrow wasn't only a coincidence. The blood on her shirt was real last night. Something was wrong with her.

Mari shuffled out of the booth, suddenly wide awake. She paid Evan and added a tip.

"Where are you off to?" the girl asked, swishing her long black hair over her shoulder. "Not another hike I hope. If you don't mind me saying, you don't look so good."

"No," she replied, glancing cagily at her haggard reflection. "I feel like doing a little sightseeing."

Mari wasn't about to return to Rosewood until she had some answers, and she couldn't suppress the feeling that the truth lay somewhere hidden in the past.

TWENTY-FIVE

Mari pulled the truck alongside the curb at the large red-bricked museum in Lincoln. Parking, she yanked on the brake and gazed up at the building, her stomach still a little watery.

Sunlight beamed off the hood, making her squint. Shielding her eyes from the glaring sun, she hopped out of the truck. It'd been cloudy when she left home, and it rained all morning. The asphalt glistened under the sun, desperate to burn through. Her eyes throbbed, and she could barely tolerate the light.

She promised herself she wouldn't dally long. The building was old, built in the colonial era of red brick, and cast an imposing shadow over the empty old quarter of Main Street. Mari thought she'd been here before on school trips over the years, but it'd been a long time ago. She was unprepared for the bright, airy, and modern interior as she walked through the door. Catching sight of her reflection, she looked away, a horrible taste in her mouth that she couldn't place.

At the reception desk, a woman glanced up from a stack of books she'd been cataloging. She had dark eyes, warm skin, and glossy black hair tied in a bun at her nape. "Hi. Welcome. It's just a donation to get in."

"Oh…" Mari rummaged in her pocket and handed over several dollar bills. The woman smiled warmly.

"Is there anything in particular you were looking for? We have a new farming and horticulture exhibit in the Guild Hall."

"Um." Mari scratched her head, her scalp itching. Strands of hair came away in her fingers, and she fought down a wave of panic, stuffing her hand in her pocket. "I was wondering if you had any information on local architecture. I live near a pretty old manor, and I was hoping to do some research…" She stammered as the woman glanced over her with concern, and Mari guessed she must look dreadful. "I fact-check for an author."

When the woman's brows rose with interest, Mari felt compelled to keep filling the silence. "He writes horror and fantasy."

Partly true, she supposed. Eric loved a good haunted house story.

The woman tilted her head thoughtfully, tapping her chin with her pen. "I mean, I don't think we have information on all the famous houses around this area…but I do believe there's a small section on the first floor about Eilhard Ghast."

Mari looked perplexed. "Who's Eilhard Ghast?"

"He was an architect from the southwest of Germany. He sailed here in the 1800s to draw up the plans for three of the big houses in this area. It's upstairs behind the local textile mercantile exhibit. Keep to the left."

Mari nodded, letting out a shaky breath. "Thanks."

She took the flight of stairs to the first floor, avoiding the sun streaming through the long windows and headed in the direction the woman had suggested. She passed various paintings and local exhibits. They even had a huge stuffed wolf in a large case at one end of the building. Her shoes squeaked on the floor as she came upon a small area set up like an architect's desk, with a large oak drawing board filled with plans and blueprints sprawled over it in a messy fashion. She hovered over the desk, arms folded, and tried to read the almost illegible scrawl. It kind of reminded her of Clover's workroom.

Pinned to the makeshift board were three enlarged blueprints for three different styles of houses—all gothic and sprawling with towers and porthole windows, sweeping porches, and overhanging roofs. The grandest of the three was named 'Mercy,' and her eyes widened. That had been the old creepy place she'd seen on her hike with the fountain and topiary trees. Another one looked a lot like Rosewood, but it was labeled 'Temperance'. The last house was an imposing building that almost looked like it'd been built with no real design in mind. It was a tall, thin house with a porthole window at the top and a crooked porch. It's like someone deliberately designed it to look a little off-kilter.

After a while, a man with glasses approached, eyeing her curiously. "You look a little lost?"

Mari smiled, and her face cracked. Her skin felt parched and papery. "Are these real?"

"They're replicas—the real ones are behind glass in our basement. But we wanted to make a little display…no one ever really asks much about Eilhard Ghast."

Mari's brows rose. "Who was he?"

"A German scholar, inventor and brilliant architect." The man's eyes twinkled. "There was even a rumor he was a magician."

Mari leaned closer, peering through the glass at Ghast's erratic, scrawled handwriting.

"The Reverend who sailed here to minister the towns lived in Cedar Wood and had Eilhard shipped over to plan these for him."

"All for him?"

The man shrugged. "I think they eventually were sold. All except Mercy. The original family still owns it."

"That's insane...what about this one?" She pointed to the building that vaguely resembled Rosewood. "Temperance?"

"Oh, that one...it was sold to a local man who eventually became a big name in farming around here. The Rosewoods?"

"So it *is* Rosewood Hall? It got renamed."

Temperance. A chill broke out over her arms as she recalled the stained glass window in the door of Rosewood Hall. Eric's last message to her, the one she'd barely paid any attention to when she was on hold for the doctor, came to mind.

"I'm thinking of naming my towns after virtues...what do you think of Temperance? Or Mercy?"

Mercy. Temperance. It had to be a coincidence—it *had* to be.

"What about this one?" Jutting her finger toward the design for the house that looked like it'd been built by someone wearing a blindfold, he nodded.

"Patience," he said. "It's still there, the oldest of the three, and that's where the architect chose to end his days. It's in a little seaside town called Fallows Watch."

Mari trembled, gripping the edge of the desk, and hoped he didn't notice. She glanced again at the design for Rosewood. Was this just the strangest coincidence that Eric would pick names of local famous buildings, one right across from her own home? She shuddered.

You don't know anything about Eric, she thought. And that had been her choice. She didn't want to know, determined to keep him at arm's length and professional at all times.

"You know it?"

"I live right across the field from it."

The man's face lightened with interest. "Ah, I guess you know all about the old Tobias Rosewood story?"

"Actually that's kind of why I'm here. I didn't go to school around here. I always knew that he'd vanished suddenly."

"1804," he answered matter of factly. "Right before the Mickleford Witch was hung for murder."

"But there was no evidence that she killed him?"

"No evidence…but the rumor was she was sleeping with him. They'd been seen at the local tavern on many occasions, and I guess once she was tried and found guilty and he was nowhere in sight…"

"….people came to that conclusion," Mari finished. "Well, I guess that makes sense."

"There's a family portrait right down the hall here. I'll show you!"

He was enthusiastic, and Mari fought an eye roll, wandering down the narrow hallway behind him. He paused, waving his hand at a medium-sized gold-framed portrait, showing a handsome, stocky man in his thirties with dusty blonde hair posed next to a dark-haired, pale woman with hazel eyes and thin lips. The two other figures in the portrait made Mari's flesh crawl, and she backed up against the wall in fright. The curator looked at her aghast. "Are you alright?"

"Who are they?" She lifted a shaking hand. "Who the hell are they?"

His brows drew close, glancing back at the painting. The taller young man stood behind his father with one hand on his shoulder and the other holding his mother's. He was handsome and gentle, with pensive eyes and a thin-lipped smile. With her hand in her mother's lap, the girl in the chair had waves of long bleached hair, her sharp gaze piercing through the canvas.

"Who the hell are they?" she repeated.

"I believe they are Ashley and Clover Rosewood," he said. "Tobias's children."

The woman at the front desk hurried after Mari as she fled the museum. Hurling herself down the stone steps, Mari found the nearest trash can and vomited up bile. Her head swam as she sank to her bottom on the pavement, ignoring the curious stares of passers-by. Her cheeks flushed hot.

"Oh my goodness," the woman exclaimed. "Are you alright? Can I call anyone for you?"

Wiping her mouth, Mari stood on shaky legs. "I'm fine. I just need to get home."

"I'm not sure you should drive."

Mari wasn't sure about that either. "I need to get home."

Convincing herself that if she just got home and crawled under the covers, she would be okay, Mari drove slowly and carefully back through the winding roads to Winstone. When the grass grew high on either side of the streets, and she spotted Kellers Farmhouse overlooking Rosewood on the brow of the hill, she licked her cracked lips, sighing with relief. Bear was eager to get outdoors, winding through her legs and chasing her through the kitchen with his leash.

"Not right now, boy," she stuttered, shivering as she crawled upstairs and headed across the landing to her bedroom. She collapsed face down on the bed, her head hitting the pillow. Bear whimpered and climbed up beside her, licking the palm of her hand. Mari barely felt him; she slipped into a deep sleep, and behind her closed lids, she saw the haunted faces in the portrait. A portrait that couldn't be real. But it was. And how could those two people be right across the field in Rosewood Hall and hadn't aged a day?

TWENTY-SIX

S omeone was yelling.

Mari's eyes cracked open, and for one second, she panicked, her heart vaulting in her chest when she thought that she'd lost her vision. The room was dark, bathed in moonlight, and she sat up blearily, her stomach still a little watery.

The yelling was getting louder. Mari blinked, shuffling out of bed and into the hall. It wasn't yelling, it was Bear. He was barking, running in circles in the hallway below.

Mari sped down the stairs, holding on tight to the rail, still in the day clothes she'd slept in. Bear was at the door, leaping at it over and over. Then he bowed low and growled at the door.

"What is it?"

Mari grabbed his collar. "Shush, boy. What's wrong?" He wriggled free, scratching and barking at the front door. It set a chill down her spine. Numbly, she grabbed the keys from the dresser, shaking as she twisted them in the lock. She stood wooden as the door creaked open. She grabbed Bear's collar as he went to bolt through the open door. "No! What's wrong with you?"

The open door revealed an empty porch with chipped paint and scattered dry leaves. Breathing hard, she stepped into the cool night air, casting her eye over her shoulder. The clock ticked in the hall, showing it was past midnight. She'd slept the whole day. Hadn't her mother noticed she wasn't around?

Bear struggled in her grip, and she yanked him indoors. "There's no one there," she said through gritted teeth as she slammed the door closed and locked it. Still, it didn't stop her feeling jittery. This wasn't like him at all.

Mari padded through the living room, habitually keeping all the lights off. It wasn't like she was scared of the dark; she was used to it now.

She huddled on the sofa and coaxed the dog to join her, but he was too busy in the hall sniffing around the door.

"It was probably a fox," she said, more to herself. For the first time in a couple of days, the fog had cleared, and she thought about everything she'd learned.

Mari didn't believe in magic, or ghosts, or family curses. But something was wrong at Rosewood Hall. There was no mistaking the figures in that portrait; somehow, Ash and Clover were Tobias Rosewood's children. It wasn't possible, but she fought for any other explanation. Relatives, doppelgangers…lookalikes? They had no history or background and were both off the grid in a house without phones, electricity, or heating.

She paused midway on the stairs, the open door of the den catching her eye. Mari hadn't seen her mother since she'd come home, and she guessed where she was. Pushing open the door, it squeaked, and she spotted the familiar lumpy shape huddled on James's hospital bed.

Mari's mother was sound asleep, propped on her side, and she couldn't fight the urge to be with her. Crawling onto the bed behind her, Mari linked her arms around her mother's waist, cheek against her shoulder. "I'm sorry, Mom," she whispered, tears dampening the material of her mother's nightgown. "I'm sorry I can't be what you want."

In her sleep, Mrs. Fox gripped Mari's hand, holding her tight, breathing easy and slow as she whispered, "Did you have a bad dream, baby?"

Mari smiled against her back. "No, Mom. I'm okay."

"You need to listen to your father," she mumbled, her voice thick with sleep. "And look for the rational explanation when you get scared."

Safe inside a dream, her mother drifted further away. Far away where nothing but her little family of the past existed, where James was here, she was still married, and death had never found them. Mari fought away tears. "I'm going to get you help, Mom. I swear to you."

I just need to get through this without fading away.

She sniffed, and something wet tickled her nose. Blood coated her fingers. Mari gasped and grabbed for a tissue. What the hell was happening to her?

She thought of everything she'd experienced since meeting Ash and Clover. Ash's too-eager kiss was how he'd caught her lip with his teeth. The way she couldn't *breathe.*

Leaving her mother soundly asleep on James's hospital bed, she tiptoed out of the room, surprised Bear's barking hadn't roused her. Mari took out her phone and stared at it in her hand, heading back to the living room. There was only one person she could turn to. But how could she ever begin to ask for Zara's help? Would she even listen? She thought about writing an email, but it seemed cold, so she called and prayed her old friend wouldn't pick up. Thankfully, it went to voicemail, and Mari's voice was hoarse.

"Zara...hey," she whispered in the dark, the only sound of Bear sniffing and scratching the door and her lonely voice. "It was good to see you. And I want you to know how sorry I am…for everything that's happened between us."

Mari took a deep breath, a tear catching on her lower lash. "I have no right to ask—I have no reason to believe you'd even want to help me. But I'm in trouble, Zara. I think…the guy I'm seeing might be dangerous. He has a sister, and I think something is wrong. They're staying at Rosewood, and I've been getting to know them…" She broke off, saying this out loud made the whole story sound insane.

Mari wouldn't have believed her if the roles had been reversed. "You said today that I looked sick…well…since I've known them, I've been getting sicker, having nosebleeds and headaches and….my mom doesn't even know I'm in the house half the time."

Saying those words aloud made it real, and she struggled to speak around the lump in her throat until eventually, she broke off and sobbed into the crook of her arm. When she recovered, she wiped her face.

"I think Ash is hurting Clover." There, she said it. "And I know you don't know them or care about her like I do, but I have to help her. I have to save her from him. She's so helpless…I have to do *something* right, Zara."

"Look, I know I deserve nothing from you…but I could use someone to talk to. Even if you tell me, I'm just crazy. Even if you tell me to get lost." She paused. "I just need to hear your voice. I didn't know how much until today."

Bear's incessant whimpering made her cut off and hold the phone to her chest. She hung up, debating if she should just delete the message. Instead, she let it slip from her hand onto the couch, distracted by Bear, who'd padded into the living room and barked at the window. "For god sake," she muttered, getting up, every bone in her body aching and heavy. "What the hell is up with you tonight?"

She glanced at the window. The dark pane of glass captured her haggard reflection. Bear's noise pounded in her ears, and for a second, as she locked eyes with the thing staring through the glass at her, she couldn't register what she was seeing.

For a moment, she swore the thing with the hollowed-out eyes and skin stretched over bone was her. It pressed its long, skeletal hands to the glass, and Mari screamed so loudly that the thing made a choked, unearthly noise and fled, vanishing into the corn.

Mr. Raggerty was *alive.*

TWENTY-SEVEN

Mari screamed and fell away from the window. She landed ass down on the hardwood floor, and a spike of pain shot up her spine. Bear frantically scraped and barked at the window pane relentlessly, before he dashed past her and into the hall. He growled at the door, and Mari gaped at him.

She got up, every nerve on edge, half her mind refusing to believe what she'd seen. There was no going back. She had seen it and knew some part of her would never shake that image.

Steeling herself, she hobbled to the kitchen, threw on the light, and ransacked the drawers for a flashlight. When her hand landed on one, she paused.

Call the police. You can't go out there.

Mari was done hiding in the dark, and whatever was out there looked terrified. Maybe it needed help? Unlocking the door, she let it swing open, holding the flashlight like a weapon, the beam of light trembled in her palm.

Whatever that thing was, it wasn't a scarecrow. Scarecrows didn't come to life, no matter how many nightmares you had about them chasing you through the cornfields.

The creature she'd seen, waxen, hollowed eyes, and bent double in pain, wasn't a bale of hay. It'd been a man, a real flesh and blood human. The terror in its helpless eyes was enough to convince her of that. Holding the flashlight at chest height, she carefully stepped onto the boards as if the wobbly light could protect her. "Where are you?" she called. "I want to help you."

Bear raced past her legs, and Mari scrambled for his collar, but it was too late. He bolted into the corn, and she yelled after him, stamping in frustration.

"Dammit, Bear," she muttered, a knot wedged in her throat as she rushed through the swinging gate and faced the corn, grown way over head height in the last couple of weeks. She flashed the beam through the corridors.

"Bear," she croaked, her voice cracking. "Please."

Sweat beaded her forehead, the back of her shirt sticking to her as she wandered the narrow corridors of corn, the sense of eyes on her making her skin crawl. Something scampered beside her, and she shrieked, aiming the beam in the direction the sound had come from, only to find nothing. When she swung back, straight ahead, something crossed the corridor. Mari caught it with the light, and the thing hissed.

It was grey, shrunken, with long limbs the shape of bone and wisps of black hair on its bald, waxy head. It stared at her, terrified, in shock, like a rabbit caught in headlights as its coal eyes darted nervously from left to right, deciding which way to run.

Mari took a gentle step forward, but her shoes cracked on a broken stem, and the thing flinched in terror. It looked away, shielding its eyes as the beam drew closer, and she lowered it.

"It's alright," she whispered. This thing was in agony. What the hell was it? "I can help you."

It shook its head, and as she got closer, she saw it wasn't wearing a shirt. Nodules of its spine protruded through alabaster skin as it recoiled. Overpowered by a wash of pity, she couldn't understand why her chest was tight.

It covered its eyes in shame, and Mari remembered James the day he'd got his diagnosis, the look of hopelessness on his face. It would never stop haunting her. The night he'd died, how a tear had rolled down his cheek in his final moments. Now, she wondered if he thought he was being punished.

James hurt Zara. He let his friends hurt her. Mari didn't know if she could pity him anymore.

The creature stooped, crying, holding its long, spindly fingers over his face. Mari saw the back of its pants, yellow and black lycra.

Running gear. Every hair on her neck stood up as she gently knelt beside it. Tremors shuddered through its body as she laid a hand on its cool skin, hiding her revulsion.

"Dan?" she whispered. "Are you *Dan* Wheeler?"

At the sound of his name, the thing's huge eyes flicked to her face and for a second she saw a spark of hope. It was over quickly. Bear scrambled through the corn, rushing at the thing, howling loud enough to wake the dead.

"Bear, no!" she screamed, but it was too late. The creature took off, hobbling out of sight into the corn. His eyes flashed, and he was gone.

He was the one hiding in the shadows at Rosewood. The cries for help. He'd been there the whole time.

Mari ran after him, arms battling through ears of corn, scratching her face and limbs as she called after him. Breaking through to another corridor, she aimed the flashlight up and down, sweat trickling down her back.

"Where are you?" she cried. "I want to help you!"

Movement up ahead caught her attention, and she took off running as Bear overtook her. He was tracking him, and Mari let him. He'd likely find him quicker than she could. Overhead, spots of rain fell, dotting her shirt, the coolness giving her respite from the heat in her body. A streak of lightning zig-zagged across the sky, followed by a low rumble of thunder.

Mari was still weak, and her limbs ached like bone on bone.

Is this what they did to him? She thought wildly. *They drained him. And now they're draining me?*

Ash's kiss, Clover's touch. One minute, they looked grey, then the next, bright-eyed and sparkling. Clover could dance around the orangery one moment and then collapse on a chaise in the next. *Energy*, Mari thought wildly. *Like they're draining energy.* Her rational mind searched for answers but circled back relentlessly to this one conclusion.

Mari was sure she must be running in circles. In the dark, buried in the claustrophobic walls of corn she couldn't make out what route he'd taken.

A scream of pain and terror broke the silence. Mari screeched to a halt, her heart hammering so hard she could feel the blood pulsing in her ears. What the hell was that?

"Where are you?" she cried.

He screamed again, pain, agony, and terror all in one haunting cry. Something she knew would imprint on her memory for life. "Dan!"

Where the hell was he? She shoved and scrambled through the corn, her clothes sticking to her. She tumbled free on her ass, rolling to her knees in the middle of an empty corridor. She lifted her chin, feeling that familiar gaze.

On her knees in the mud, she looked up, her neck heavy, disoriented, the way she'd woken the night of Halloween.

Mr. Raggerty watched her, his button eyes gleaming in the moonlight. Mari stared right back, determined not to be afraid. Because he wasn't real. There was no *soul* in that thing, stuffed with hay, with its long scraping twig fingers.

He wasn't real, and there were no witches or curses. Mari believed in science and fact. Those things were only stories, tales that Eric made up, and she fact-checked and edited them.

Dan Wheeler was real, and she had to find him. She sat up on her knees, cupping her hands over her mouth. "Dan! Where are you?"

It was too quiet. Rain pelted the corn, a gentle sound that should have been soothing. Mr. Raggerty swung and Mari gasped. There was no wind, no air; it was humid. Yet he swung away from her, lolling left on his pole, his spindle arms almost pointing down a wide corridor that opened on its left.

Mari got to her feet, unable to take her eyes off him as she passed. She stared down the dark corridor, and unbelievably, Bear poked his head out between the stems. Then he vanished down the hall, and Mari cried out, stumbling as she chased him.

"Bear, wait!" she screamed as lightning split the sky. The mutt ran full pelt, head low as he hunted, and she struggled to keep up. Rain fell in sheets, and seconds later, she was soaked, her hair plastered to her head. The corridor widened, and Bear scrambled to a stop, whimpering before he turned tail and dashed in the other direction. Mari's brows rose. "What the hell, Bear?"

He vanished, leaving her with whatever he'd seen to cause him to flee. Mari clicked on the flashlight, but it sputtered and went out, engulfing her in darkness. She stepped into the clearing, shielding her head as a lightning bolt lit the night sky.

Her heart stopped. But it couldn't have done because she could still feel it in her veins, as every cell in her body froze with terror. On the ground lay the prone, stone-like body of the thing that used to be Dan Wheeler, his eyes wide in shock, mouth open from his last scream.

Ash and Clover sat over him, their hands buried fist-deep in the cavity of his chest, scooping out what remained of its heart and sucking it into their mouths.

They were eating Dan Wheeler.

TWENTY-EIGHT

Ash was the first to spot Mari. Standing frozen, her feet unable to move, and her brain refusing to believe what her eyes saw, she gasped.

He was dead. Dan was dead.

They killed him. Ash looked aghast, his teeth and gums stained with blood, stark against the white of his skin. "Mari…"

He *swallowed*. Swallowed down whatever remnants of Dan he had left between his teeth, and she gagged, clapping her hand over her mouth. Clover looked up, doe-eyed, imploring. "Please don't hate us, Mari."

She let out a choked laugh. Hate them? "What the hell did you do to him?"

She didn't need an answer, really, she could *see* what they'd done. It was making her stomach swim. She finally found the strength to step back, her feet squelching in the mud. Ash held out his palms, stained with blood.

"Please, Mari. We can explain…"

"Don't turn away from us, Mari," Clover begged, her big eyes full and watery, managing to appear angelic even with gore dripping down her chin. "If we don't take the heart…we die."

Mari shook, panting hard. "What *are* you?"

Vampires. It was the first absurd notion to spring to her mind. But everything she knew from books and television…every movie she'd ever watched—was false. Ash had stepped into the light. He hadn't burned. No, they were *something* else.

Ash stood, mirroring her stance. Instead, he had one foot pointed in her direction, and somehow, she guessed he wouldn't have trouble catching up with her if she ran. "Mari. We don't want to live like this. We don't want this life."

"What are you?" she repeated, tears flooded her eyes. Betrayal stung deep, and she was so confused. He'd lied to her from the start. He edged a little closer. "Tell me, now."

"It's not what you think," Clover said with a promise. How could she sound so sincere and sweet, even after what she'd done? "We didn't want to kill him. We never *want* to hurt anyone. It's just...what we are."

They'd done this before. Mari's mind raced to Ash's bleak Instagram profile, views from all the places he'd lived. *Never does the sunshine here in Fairbanks.* The missing teacher article she'd skimmed over, not seeing, looking straight at the truth even if the truth was terrifying.

Mari thought of the portrait in the museum. "You're Tobias Rosewood's children?" she accused. "That would make you over two hundred years old. It's not possible."

"It is possible," Ash said.

"I don't believe it." She squeezed her eyes tight. "I don't believe."

"It's real," Clover said. "Our father vanished in 1804. We never found out what happened to him—but there were horrible rumors...terrible stories. About the Mickleford Witch. Our mother threw herself from the top of the tower the following year, convinced the witch was haunting her...she hadn't the strength to carry on."

"But you...?" Mari pointed at them. "How are you alive?"

"Ten years later, we started to notice that something was wrong—that we failed to age like our peers," Ash explained. "I tried to manage the Rosewood estate alone, but everyone was terrified to work for us. They believed we were cursed, too, when local villagers started to notice. We left..."

"Why did you eat....?" Mari looked away, squeezing her eyes, unable to shake that image of them feasting on Dan like he was a Thanksgiving dinner.

"If we don't eventually take the heart, then *that's* what we become," Ash said, unable to meet her eyes in genuine shame. He stepped a little nearer. "Blood—human life carries energy. *Life force.* It's an urge we cannot ignore. We learned the hard way…we see ourselves differently."

"What you see isn't what we see in the mirror," Clover said tearfully. "But then if we don't take a heart. The mirror becomes…"

"Reality…" Ash finished her sentence, something Mari guessed he'd been doing for centuries. Mari's eyes widened—the room of broken mirrors…the stone maidens with gouged faces.

"You locked away all the mirrors," Mari gasped out. "Covered all the portraits…"

"The eyes watch me," Clover said as a tear caught her lash. "They know what we are. Mother said that vanity is a terrible sin."

Mari backed away, her blood running like ice. "How…?" She waved to Dan's ruined body at her feet.

Ash stepped closer, holding out his hands. "I found him out in the storm that day…not long before I ran into you. I rescued him. He'd tumbled into the Grenfell and hung onto the grate for dear life…I brought him back here, and we nursed him back to health."

Everything in Mari's body screamed at her to run. They rescued him, nursed him, healed him, and then they sucked him dry. She'd heard of something like this in one of Eric's many tales.

Dan had been a man with a family who loved him, who mourned him. And they'd taken him with no remorse. She choked on tears. She'd heard him through the walls, crying out for help, and she'd ignored it, looking away, like she'd done with Zara.

"Alaska?" she asked. "You took someone there."

"And then it was time to leave," Clover finished, almost in a sing-song voice. "If you keep taking from the same spot repeatedly, the locals start to get edgy."

Mari tasted blood on her lips, and she licked a dry crack where it stung. "Is that what you've been doing to me? *Draining* me?"

They exchanged a look, heated and troubled, an unspoken truth passing between them. Eventually, Ash looked at her. "We didn't mean for any of this to happen. I...I like you, Mari."

She nearly fell sideways. The heart-eating monster liked her. She choked. "Was I going to end up like him?"

Ash shook his head vehemently. "No!"

"Then why am I sick?" she argued. "The nose-bleeds...the headaches?"

"Accidents happen," Clover jumped in. "We can't help what happens to those around us. We can't help what we are....the energy we steal."

She looked heavenward, shaking her head as rain pelted her face, matting her hair. She'd been a meal. Recalling how after Ash had kissed her, he'd glowed with radiance while she couldn't catch her breath. "I need to go." She nodded at Dan's remains. "You need to bury him properly. You can't discard him out here like he's trash. He was a person before you sucked him dry."

She went to leave, but Clover moved with lightning speed. Mari barely blinked, and she was right beside her. Catching her hand, her eyes big and watery and full of remorse. She flung her arms around Mari's waist and sobbed into her chest. "Oh, Mari, please don't turn away from us.

You're right—we'll bury him. Can you be there? Besides, it's time to test the latest hybrid…I can't do this without you. You made me promise to wait for you."

Mari gaped down at her, equal parts intrigued and terrified. Clover's wide eyes revealed nothing but sincerity. "Please, Mari. We're sorry. You don't know what it's like…to live in the dark."

Yes, I do, she thought but said nothing. Gently she prised Clover's arms from around her, hating the sight of blood on her teeth and lingering on her breath. It was sour.

"Alright," she said, backing away. There was still something unsolved playing on her mind. "Is the light allergy part of your curse?"

"I was in my mother's womb when our father vanished. The Varga Witch came here, confronted her, to reveal what our father had done—their affair. She touched my mother's belly and said I'd never see the light of day. My mother believed she'd killed me in the womb—in a way, she did. When I was born, she thought it would all be okay until she tried to take me into the light." Clover wiped her face. "It turns out many things wither and die in the shadows…my mother was one of them."

Ash stood straight. "It's always been me and Clover."

"The hybrid will work this time," Clover insisted. "After you took that sample from the hanging tree I mixed it with the soil, and the rose turned completely black."

Mari deflated, horrified at her stupidity. "You *knew* about the oak. You already knew what it was when you sent me there."

"I couldn't go, obviously," Clover answered, her sincerity switching to clinical so fast it made her heart stamp. "Ash had to stay and look after…him."

She glanced at Dan's ruined carcass. He'd fought.

"He kept getting out," Ash said miserably. "And tonight was the final straw. We were arguing about the hybrid…and he broke free. We knew we had to end it."

Dan had fought to live with every last ounce of his being. He'd broken out and come to her because he'd seen her inside Rosewood. He came to her for help. It didn't do anything to ease Mari's gut. She lifted her chin as overhead the rain broke.

"Alright," she whispered again. "I want to bury him." God knows the authorities couldn't find out about this. It was too awful. She told herself that Dan's family were settled. They believed him to have drowned, and that was better than the truth. It'd kill them to learn the truth. His wife on the television, begging anyone to come forward with news. Dan had fought to get home to them, destroyed, deformed. He'd *fought*.

"And then you'll be there to watch me test the hybrid?" Clover beamed. "I want you to be there when the sun comes up. I want you to be there, Mari."

Mari wanted to run. Every ounce of her rational mind was telling her that she had to turn around right now. Go home, call the police, lock the doors. Hide under the bed and pretend she hadn't seen this. She wished she could force back her rational mind and tell herself this wasn't real.

Would Ash come find her? If she didn't see this through would she ever be safe, or would she always be looking for candles flickering in windows across the field? She had to know the outcome, otherwise her mind would never let her be. If this thing failed, as she guessed it would, then she'd see Clover burn and feel nothing this time. She balled her fists.

"Okay," she said. "But I swear, once this is over, I'm *done*. I never want to see either of you again for as long as I live."

TWENTY-NINE

I t might have been a mistake to venture back inside Rosewood Hall. The moment Mari's feet crossed the threshold, the cloying scent of Jasmine caught in her throat. Seized by a coughing fit, she rounded, aware of Clover and Ash's eyes on her. Wiping her mouth and hiding the blood spots, she hurriedly wiped her hands on her jeans.

Ash touched her shoulder, but she flinched away from him. He looked crushed, and she couldn't pretend it didn't hurt. "Are you—?"

"I'm fine," she snapped. "Let's get this over with."

In his arms, Ash carried the dead body of Dan Wheeler, his ruined carcass looking as if it weighed nothing. Ash set him down on a plush sofa in the hall, before he glanced at Mari. "I will bury him, Mari. I swear to you."

She didn't reply, unable to look at Dan's remains any longer. The two Rosewood children exchanged a look between them, their eyes downcast, crestfallen. Mari refused to feel anything for them right now.

She wondered how many friends they'd lost over the years. How many unsuspecting acquaintances got unknowingly sucked dry of their life? How many ended up looking like Dan Wheeler?

Mari wrapped her arms around herself like a shield. Spotting one of the veiled portraits in her peripheral, curiosity got the better of her and she darted for it. Clover gasped. "Mari, no!"

The black veil rippled as Mari tugged it free, revealing a slashed portrait of a man with a neat, grey mustache, cleanly parted hair. He wore a cravat and dark morning suit. Clover shrieked and spun away in horror, running for the safety of her brother's arms. Mari stared at the deep slashes over the man's face.

Ash massaged his sister's shoulder as she wailed into his chest. "It's alright, Clover."

"*Who* covered these up?" Mari asked.

"Clover did," he said with a long sigh, reliving a past he had no fondness for. "She covered them all."

"Why?" Mari's brow rose. "Did you kill him?"

Ash nodded grimly. "All of them. We took their hearts." He nodded to the man in the portrait. "Our Uncle…he was the first."

Mari stared at him in shock, and when she didn't speak he continued. "We realized that we were draining them…even if we never meant to. It gets to the point where we can see the heart, beating—failing."

"Dying," Mari whispered, her hand on her breast bone, checking that it was still beating in her chest. Ash looked away in shame.

"Once we become too weak—we can't fight it anymore. We *have* to take the heart to live. It's not something we want, Mari."

She locked eyes with him, and he was the first to turn, as if he'd already guessed her train of thought. "Can you see *my* heart right now?" she asked tearfully, her hand gripping her chest. "*Can* you?"

They shared a glance which only made Mari's stomach churn, and fear flutter up her throat. Clover bit her lip and looked away, and Mari didn't need to hear him say it outloud. She was dying. They were going to take her next, and if she didn't get far away from these people she'd shrivel up like Dan and die in this house.

Looking over her shoulder, Clover must have sensed her apprehension, as she scuttled to Mari's side. "Let me test the rose, Mari. And then." She looked downcast. "We'll never see eachother again."

Caught in the depths of Clover's haunted eyes, Mari relented. What would happen if she tried to leave? She was weak, in pain, and didn't think she could outrun Ash if she tried. "Okay. Let's do this."

Find a way out of here, she thought. *Get this over with, and find a way out.*

"Follow me then," Clover said, a melancholic look in her eyes, glancing at the ticking clock on the mantle. "It's nearly sunrise."

Mari followed behind Ash, telling herself this was a mistake. She should run, get as far away as she could. But she'd promised to be there for Clover and part of her needed to see this through. If true magic really did exist, then she would need to see it for herself. Whatever substance she'd scraped off the oak tree in Cedar Wood hadn't been natural.

Clover led her across the shadowy ballroom, and Mari followed, dread building with every step. She recalled all the times she'd watch Clover dance and play piano while her musical box tinkled along. She wished she could return to that time, when she'd remained in the dark. The truth of it all now left a bitter taste.

The orangery was dim and humid, and instantly, Mari felt sweat bead on her top lip. In Clover's workroom, papers and notebooks were thrown everywhere in a frenzy, like the girl was some tortured genius. The room was a mess:

smashed vials, candles upturned, and wax pooling on the floor.

Clover took a wide step, holding her hand to the rose in the cabinet. There were three buds, but only one in bloom, and it was ready, its petals stretching as if it'd woken from an enchanted sleep. It was indeed black. The petals were like fine, immaculate leather, so dark they sparkled silver in the moonlight flooding through the workroom window. Mari stepped closer to the glass in awe.

"It's beautiful."

Clover beamed with excitement. "Mari, this is the Night Witch Rose...my invention." She opened the glass. "And it's my cure."

"We don't know that for sure, Clo," Ash said through gritted teeth. The scent was overpowering, so heady and floral that Mari swayed on her feet. Like a drug, she felt intoxicated. She had the urge to escape, even though she couldn't get enough of the scent, engulfed in its aura.

"Well," Clover said with a wicked gleam in her eye. "I think it's time we tested."

Clover plucked the rose from its root, thorns pricking her skin. Mari and Ash's gazes held, bound by concern. Blood pooled on Clover's skin, but she didn't notice as she held it up to the light, twirling it in her fingers. "It's perfect." Pride flooded her voice, like a parent admiring their child as they accepted an award. Mari almost opened her mouth to tell her that *pride* was also a sin, but the manic look on Clover's face made her clench her teeth.

"So what now?" Mari was keen to get this done. "Do you dry it and put it in a tea?"

What the girl did next set Mari's teeth on edge, and she couldn't pull her eyes away. Even Ash looked horrified as his sister plucked every single petal from the bud and stuffed it in her mouth. Black juice ran down her chin like tar, making her teeth sooty as she chewed. Choking and coughing as she ravaged each petal.

"Is that a good idea?" Ash asked.

Clover nodded, stuffing them in her mouth until the last petal was gone. "No point in waiting. That's what I've been doing wrong. I need to go straight to the source. Her essence is in the rose."

"Who's essence?" Ash barked. Now he was the one in the dark. "Clover!"

"The Varga witch. I learned long ago that the one who cursed me is the one who can cure me." Clover looked too pleased with herself, with her ruse. Mari saw what she was for the first time. Unhinged, and dangerous. Clover jerked her chin in Mari's direction. "Blame her—she's the one who got me the bark from the tree."

Ash's eyes swung to Mari, who wilted, all too aware of what she'd created, of how she'd been lied to. Of course, Clover hadn't asked Ash. He wouldn't have dared to go to the hanging tree of the woman who'd cast their curse. "What did you do?" he whispered.

"I didn't know!" Mari cried. "How could I have known this is what she'd do? I had no idea…"

Clover said with a wink, "I really couldn't have done this alone, Mari. Thank you."

Ash spat in anger, his nostrils flaring. "Clover…you of all people should have known better than to delve into the occult—with the devil. That's what got us into this mess."

"Our father got us into this mess—him and his wandering eye. We were the victims, and now her essence will be the one to set me free. I *will* walk in the light, Ashley!"

Stepping back, Mari shook her head, the weight of her guilt settling on her shoulders. "Ash, I'm sorry."

He shook his head, stunned as Clover began ramming the stem into her mouth, biting and chewing at the thorns that pricked her tongue, her gums. She coughed and choked as it went down, and Mari drained of color. "God…"

"You didn't know," Ash said. "She knew that I'd never go to Mickleford for her. I'd have never let her deal with witchcraft."

Clover licked her lips of black blood. "We are born from a curse, Ash. It's what we are. I see no harm in using it in our favor?"

She walked briskly past the two of them, leaving them to gape after her. Gone was the spindly, frail girl. Clover's white hair bounced on her shoulders, her nightgown billowing around her as she headed into the orangery, circling the small ornamental fountain.

"What are you going to do?" Mari asked. The room was nearly covered in flowers. Overnight, it seemed they'd filled every nook, every crevice, and vines hung from the stairwell. The smell was overpowering, and she blinked away the water in her eyes.

With a satiated, contented look, Clover lifted the hem of her gown and crawled across the lip of the fountain. Her dress floated on the surface, yards of silk puddling like moonlight as she carefully stepped into the middle of the water, the inky black enveloping her lower half. She lay down on her back, floating between lily pads, her hair splaying on the water. Her gaze locked above, and Mari followed her. The drapes were already open.

"I just have to wait for the sun," she whispered, in a dream-like state. She floated like she was on a canopy of leaves.

"Jesus, Clo, don't do this," Ash begged. "The sun…"

Was already peaking through one corner of the long rectangular window. Mari's heart sped. "Clover, please don't do this."

"It's going to work, Mari," the girl said. "I believe. Don't you believe?"

Mari flung herself toward Ash, fear thick in her voice. "What are you doing? Haul her out!"

Grimly, Ash shook his head. "Just let her be."

"What?"

"She'll try again—one way or another. It was always going to end this way."

"She could die, Ash!"

Ash stuttered a sigh. "Then she'll be free, won't she?" For the longest beat, their eyes collided, and there was that look, the one she knew well. The one she'd seen on James's face. Resignation. It was over. He was done caring for, and protecting this girl—someone who'd driven him to the brink.

Mari gasped, staring at him in horror. "I'm not leaving her to go up in smoke!"

Mari dashed to the fountain. She had one sneaker in the water when he grabbed her around the waist, tugging her over the lip with a force she'd not expected. His arms were like an iron grip as he wrestled her to the stone floor. "No, Ash—she'll die."

"We're already dead, Mari," Ash gasped in her ear, holding her tight. "Let the light take her if that's what she wants."

He squeezed, and she stopped struggling. Light pooled in through the window, an orange-pink hue lighting the way. Every flower retracted, wilting, inching away from the sun as though it burned. Maybe, now, she did believe. Beauty really could thrive in darkness.

"It's coming," Clover cried, elated. "It's coming, Ash. It's going to work."

Mari's eyes filled with hot and salty tears as they clogged her throat. Some part of her couldn't bear to look, but her eyes remained transfixed. She couldn't watch Clover die, no matter what she'd done.

Light bathed the girl, and she sparkled, laughing and crying. Surrounded by petals on the water, she looked like a radiant angel. Slowly, she stood, her dress soaked through, as she raised her hands to the sun. "Thank you," she cried. "Thank you, Vecula."

"It's working," Ash breathed beside her, his eyes filling up. He grabbed Mari's hand. "Mari…is this real?"

God, she wanted to run, but her feet were glued. "I think so."

Clover was crying and laughing hysterically, praying to the light, letting it bathe her closed lids while tears streaked her skin. "I'm going to live, Mari. I'm going to walk in the light."

"Are we forgiven?" Ash asked more of himself. "Is this real?"

The water swirled and writhed around her legs, and one by one, each lily in the water shriveled and died, fading to green stalk. Like a light, each one withered and vanished below the water's depths. Mari grabbed Ash by the wrist, but he'd seen it too. "Clo…"

With her arms splayed wide, Clover didn't notice, as vines as black as ink crawled up her thighs, curling around her ankles and waist. She didn't notice, until they linked under her arms, entwining around her wrists.

"Clover!" Mari screamed.

Clover's eyes went wide in horror, grappling with the deadly vines as they dragged her down. She screamed, water flooding her mouth, her hair the last thing to vanish below the surface as she kicked and flailed.

"Clover!" Ash yelled, hauling himself over the lip of the pond as her hand shot to the surface, grappling with his. It slipped in her palm, and Mari watched as her friend's face surfaced, gasping for help, taking a lungful of murky black water.

The skin rippled off her bones, stretching and turning the shark's skin grey. Her eyes rolled and morphed into inky black. Mari dashed to the fountain's surface, trying to grab hold of any limb Clover exposed. A slim, bone-like hand grasped for hers. It was cold, like touching death, and slipped in her grasp.

Mari sobbed. "Clover, I can't hold on."

Mari watched it happen. She saw Clover submerge, the water crossing over her head. Within seconds, she was gone, and the water finally stilled. "No," Ash moaned. "God, Clover—no!"

Ice flooded Mari's blood, and she glanced at him across her shoulder, her hands still wrist-deep where she'd fought to hold on to the girl. Had he known? The tears on his cheeks shone in the bright light of the sun. His emotion was real…wasn't it?

She wasn't sure anymore. She'd seen that act before. The remorse, the fake crying. She knew it all too well.

No…

"It's over, Mari," Ash said, sniffing, wiping his eyes with the heels of his hands. "It's over. She's gone."

"Ash…"

"She'll be at peace now…in the light."

Standing straight, Mari glanced at her empty palms, wet and stained with the black substance. She lowered her voice, glaring at him. "Did you know?"

"What?"

"Did *you* know?" She annunciated each syllable like a punch, her throat was raw and tight. "Did you know this could happen?"

When he didn't answer, she rushed ahead. "Did you know the whole time? What her plan was?"

Ash backed up as she stalked nearer, her nostrils flaring. With Clover gone, the walls shrunk inward, bright light spilled in, lighting every crevice, and all the plants and vines shrunk away in the shadow. She could almost smell them burn. Her eyes filled up.

"Please, Ash. Tell me the truth…"

"I didn't believe, Mari," he said, his eyes darkening. "I didn't believe she could pull it off. But I didn't know….that would happen." He glanced at the dark water.

"But you knew? You knew what the rose might do. You let her go through with it."

Ash backed up against a railing. "Sometimes too much hope can kill a person, Mari. Clover has been doomed since she opened her eyes, destined for a life in the shadows. Now she's free."

Mari shook her head. "And so are you."

"It wasn't like that—but yes. I suppose that's true."

She snorted a nasty laugh. "Oh—you *suppose*?"

"We can have a life, Mari. We could leave this godforsaken place, finally let it be. We can walk in the light…together."

"You're sick…" she spat. "If you think for a moment I could—"

A sound behind them made the words stick in her throat. A sound she couldn't unhear. A wretched gurgling noise, the sound of lungs full of tar and muck, preceded the creature that rose inch by inch out of the fountain.

Mari's world spun on its axis. She believed now. The horrible truth was staring right at her, hauling itself across the lip of the fountain on arms as thin as spindles. Strings of white hair hung from its waxen head. Clover lifted her eyes and gasped, pools of black water dribbling through her teeth. "Ashley...help me."

Ash went white, backing up. "Clover...?"

The thing thunked to the ground with a crack, a Gollum dressed in white. It was a nightmare. Things like this didn't exist. Clover spat up mucus and tar, stretching out her hand. Ash cried, tears streaking his face. "Oh, God, Clo, I'm sorry."

"Help me..."

Mari couldn't take a full breath. "Ash..."

Clover twisted her head, finding Mari standing there watching. She crawled over the stone using blunt nails, leaving a wet trail behind her. Choking, retching, and dribbling black water through her teeth.

"Help me, Ash. Her heart..."

Mari's legs buckled. What the hell did she just say?

"I need her heart, Ashley."

Mari wasn't fast enough. Her heels skidded, turning as she tried to run, but instead, she ran into the path of Ash Rosewood, holding a spade above his head. Pain blasted her vision into blackness, her head cracking the ground as she fell.

THIRTY

It hurt to swallow, and her eyes felt gritty like they'd been glued shut. The most feeble amount of light touched her irises as she forced them open, and a pulse through her skull left her nauseous.

God, what was that smell? A foul stench filled her nose, and she jerked her head as if she could wriggle away, but it was everywhere—rot and death. When her vision cleared, the white shape in front of her took form, and she knew where that smell was coming from.

Her skin burned like she was stuck with a thousand needles, and when she craned her chin to look, she saw why. She was on Clover's ornate bed of flowers under the iron canopy. Only what had been jasmine and roses was dead, browned, and rotting; all that remained were the thorns digging into her skin. She wriggled her fingers, but they were numb, bloodless, and bound to the bed. And there was Clover.

Clover. Clover with her hands on either side of Mari's head.

Mari screamed, or at least tried, her voice scratchy and weak. The thing, the monstrous creature that had been Clover Rosewood, let her lips part in a toothless, black smile as she could see right through to the back of her head. Strings of blonde hair fell lank over her knobbly shoulders. The sight of her induced a terrible sense of pity, and Mari's gut tightened. What the hell had happened to her?

A black shadow crossed her vision, and her head was heavy, like she could sink into whatever was propping up her head. Clover's long fingers were cool, bony, and like spindles as they traced over Mari's brow. Mari couldn't keep her eyes open.

When she startled awake, she could see Clover's pupils, the hazel flecks in her eyes, and once more, that spark of dread took hold.

It's me, she thought. *She's draining me.*

Mari flinched out of her way, and Clover drew back. "Hmm. Maybe you have had enough for now? There is no use taking everything at once. Not when you have *so* much to give."

"Why are you doing this?" Mari whimpered raspily.

"Like I said—this was never personal. We could have managed with the other for a while. He would have sustained us. But you were—*unexpected.* So full of grief."

Tears blurred her eyes. "The *other* had a name. Dan. And he was a father…you killed him."

Where was Ash? He wouldn't let her do this. Clover's knobbly fingers unbuttoned a few buttons on Mari's shirt, exposing her sternum. Mari wriggled frantically.

"What are you going to do?"

"I need your heart, Mari…or at least someone's. Is there anyone you'd be willing to volunteer?"

"Are you kidding me?"

"It seems you're too strong at the moment," Clover said, a bitter edge to her voice. "I need to drain more from you. You were already weak—it shouldn't take long."

"People will notice I'm gone!" she argued. Clover's horrible face cracked in a skeletal grin.

"Really? All of your friends?" she teased, and it stung. "Your mother? I doubt she'll notice you're gone until she needs to refill the liquor cabinet."

Mari screamed in frustration and anger, not fear. She kicked her legs, and Clover giggled softly, brushing away strings of her old hair. "There's still too much fight in you."

She placed one clammy palm across Mari's mouth and nose, and she fought, smelling death on her skin. Writhing against the bindings on her wrists and ankles, they slit her flesh. The coolness of Clover's skin sickened her, slick and grim. Clover shuddered, licking her parched lips like she'd tasted chocolate for the first time, as a cold spread of fear washed through her blood, and she went limp. Closing her eyes, Mari felt her heartbeat dim.

I have to get out of here.

Clover laughed, trembling as she shuffled away. She fell onto a plush violet chaise by the bed, panting softly and closing her eyes. "She's good, Ash," she whispered. "I know why you wanted her."

Ash? He was here? Mari could barely turn her head; it made her temples spike with pain, but she sensed he was nearby, his shape lurking in her periphery. Her stomach swam with sickness, bile racing up her gullet before she swallowed it down.

"We don't have to do this," he whispered, his voice floating out of the shadows. "We could take another…"

"Who exactly?" Clover argued. "We were so lucky when that runner just fell into our hands. It was too easy to keep him. And look at me! How can I *go* anywhere?"

"This wouldn't have happened if you just accepted your fate—all this with your stupid flowers…"

"The rose *worked!* I have two more left, and one will bud any time…I'll try again."

"You're wrecked, Clover. You've destroyed yourself."

"I need her heart, Ash." The statement sent chills down Mari's spine. "And she's perfect— to think she was there all along. So full of regret, grief, and misery…her heart is bursting with it." Clover cast a maniacal glance at Mari bound on the bed. "I don't think she'll be missed…and by the time someone notices, we'll be gone."

"And where to Clover?" Ash's voice peaked in tone, sharp, angry as he got closer. "Where are we going to now? This was going to be it. Our last move. You promised it would be over."

"Ashley…"

"I won't do it," he said, and for a moment, hope rose in her chest. But Mari knew well that hope could be a terrible thing. She'd been wiggling her fingers at her sides, willing blood back to her hands, the needling sensation a comfort as she chased for freedom. "I won't be the one to do it. I won't taste her heart."

Clover rolled those horrible black eyes in her sockets. "Fine then. But it doesn't make any difference. I still need her weak. And I need to rest."

Bone cracked on bone as Clover, bent double, hobbled from her seat and shuffled from the room, leaving Mari to stare at the dead canopy of flowers over her head. A tear dripped down her cheek, and Ash caught it with his knuckle. She flinched away from his touch.

"Don't do that," he whispered.

"You make me sick," she spat with what little strength she had. Her voice sounded so far away, and her blood pounded slowly in her ears. Her heart was dying. Every part of her was numb, anchored to the bed. Still, she wiggled and twisted her wrists when he wasn't looking.

He came to hover over her, his eyes shadowy and hollow, lips bloodless and white. He looked ghastly like he'd not slept in days. "I'm sorry, Marianne."

"It was all a lie." She thought of the candle in her room. *Burn it, and I'll know you're okay.*

He brushed his fingers over her temple. "I didn't lie about the way I feel. I never wanted to hurt you. But…"

"Accidents happen," she finished for him acidly. "I get it."

"It could have been different."

"You were *draining* me," Mari said. "It was never going to be any different. I was getting sicker and sicker…when would you have stopped?"

Ash looked away, anywhere but at her. "It wouldn't have stopped." He rolled up his sleeves as if he had work to do. There was mud under his nails and dusting his palms. There was a light sweat on his forehead. Mari guessed he'd kept his word and buried Dan Wheeler. It made her sick to think of him trapped in these walls, lonely, afraid, and now he was buried here, forever to be forgotten.

The crypt—her innocent joke about burying someone in there. Mari felt so foolish.

"At least Clover was right about something…you won't be missed. At least not straight away." That hurt more deeply than the thorns digging into her wrist as she worked her way loose. Maybe he was right. "You're such a friendless creature, Marianne. You even turned your back on your best friend to protect your brother."

Mari's eyes blurred. God, he was right. Ash smiled sadly. "That's right. You don't tend to believe things unless you see them with your own eyes. Not in monsters or magic…or that your brother could be capable of hurting your best friend, even though you knew deep down. You *knew.* You simply looked away…"

"I didn't know…"

"And claimed ignorance…well, maybe now you believe? Some things are out there, hiding and waiting in the dark, lying in wait under your bed. That beautiful things can grow where the light cannot touch…people don't tell you what they are Mari…they show you."

He leaned closer as sweat trickled down her neck, his breath cool on her skin.

"How could you do this?"

"It's just survival, Mari. Clover and I are the damned children of a sinner, and we're cursed to remain immortal. The Varga witch knew how to make a punishment last…the only thing my father did was fall for her."

Mari had done it. One hand was out, and prickles of blood rushed to her newly freed veins as Ash cradled her with his upper body, leaning closer, one hand on either side of her face. She twisted her bound wrist in agony, the sting of thorns unbearable as she worked. He came closer, and she knew he was going to kiss her. And his kisses packed a punch.

His lips brushed hers, gentle at first, and her eyes flew wide. Her neck paralyzed as he deepened the kiss, opening her mouth with his lips. She made a choking sound against his mouth, but his eyes were closed, enjoying the feast. Tendrils of silver lit the air, like threads leaving her body.

That's me…he's draining me.

Her eyes fought to stay open, the engulfing pull of sleep hard to resist.

Fight! You need to fight. She couldn't just die here. He was wrong. There *were* people who loved her. She had pushed everyone away, but she could make it right. She swore she would.

Mari bit down hard, and his eyes flew open as blood from his lip spilled into her mouth. He roared, but as he pulled away, she only clamped down harder until flesh tore, and she spat out what she'd ripped off. Blood coursed from his mouth as he whirled away, and Mari wasted no time. Struggling to sit, foggy headed, she slipped from the bed, and with as much strength as she had, ripped her hand free.

Thorns tore her forearms, ripping the skin and leaving rivulets of blood. She swayed, copper coating her tongue as she left him bent double and screaming. She limped through the orangery, dragging her body like she was wading through thick tar.

She needed air. She needed to get out of this heat and this house. The flowers in the orangery were dead, curling, and wilted, brown vines retreating into the dark.

Mari burst into the ballroom and stopped dead. Clover was asleep on the chaise, her body stiff and gaunt like she'd passed out at an awkward angle—a real life stone maiden. Mari rushed past, risking rousing her from sleep. It would be seconds, and Ash would be behind her.

Clover's eyes sprung open, and the creature flew for her, hauling Mari to the shiny, polished floor and grasping her legs. Mari yelped, flailing to free her legs, and landed a solid kick in Clover's ribcage. The wraith yelled in pain, and Mari heard the distinct sounds of bone cracking as Clover shrank to the ground.

Panting, Mari picked up running. She fled Rosewood, dragging open the heavy door and slamming it behind her, a torrent of rain sticking hair to her head as she fled into the storm and through the corn.

THIRTY-ONE

The rain coursing from above bought Mari a little time. Nerves ran like shredded tissue under her skin, and every step she took with her bare feet brought eye-watering agony. Ash's kiss had left her feeling like she was suffering from the worst flu she'd ever experienced, her skin so hot she felt like the rain was sizzling where it touched.

Painfully, she ran into the corn, and her arms stretched to keep the wet leaves and branches off her face. A way behind her, she heard the familiar slam of wood, the glass panel in the frame smashing as it flew open.

"Mari!" Clover screamed, her voice shrill and terrifying as a lightning bolt lit up the sky.

Mari's stomach turned watery, and fear made her wobble as she crouched in the mud, desperate for respite and to catch her breath. Ice filled her lungs. Clover would find her; she had to keep moving.

"Marianne!" Ash's voice joined Clover's on the breeze. "It's no use running—we'll find you."

Calves cramping, she held her breath, gasping in pain as she tried to get to her feet. When pain shot up her bones with knife-like splinters, she fell on her knees, elbows on the ground.

She wasn't going to die out here in the rain; alone and with no hope. Unable to run, she crawled. Mari willed every ounce of strength to her limbs as she dragged herself through tall ears of corn, her clothes muddied and soaked. She dug her nails into the ground when her knees gave out.

Keep going, she thought, *you have to keep going.*

Lightning filled the sky, a jagged light cutting through the inky black like a scar. For a brief moment, she thought she'd seen eyes watching her—Clover's hollow black holes where her beautiful hazel eyes once were.

Marianne curled into a ball, pelted by rain, and sobbed on her knees. After a few moments, she opened her eyes and shook herself. She had to get back to the farmhouse. Sensation gradually returned to her legs, and she hauled herself upright, able to limp and hobble through the rows of corn.

Had she lost them? Was she alone? A terrible sense of dread built in her chest. Or was this all a game, and they just let her tire herself until she collapsed? They wanted her weak, after all.

She still tasted Ash's kiss on her mouth, his blood on her tongue. Suddenly, the bile she'd fought down earlier rushed up her throat, and she bent double and vomited. She stared dismally at her bare, bloodied feet, scraped by rock and stone. She licked her lips, tasting blood in her bile.

"Mari—*Anne!*" Clover bellowed in a sing-song voice. "Just you keep running. The more you run, the weaker you get."

Mari collapsed onto her bottom, hugging her knees. Clover wasn't wrong. Her skin was on fire, a fever rapidly spreading around her body. By the time they found her, she'd be nothing but a husk. Tied to that bed for hours, enough time for a whole day to pass, they'd taken their fill.

God, did she look like poor Dan? A Gollum, something out of a nightmare?

Keep moving. Mari got up and gradually put one foot in front of the other, over and over, until she gained a little speed. The corn crowded closer, and she wasn't sure what direction she'd come. Maybe she could outrun Clover till the sun rose? But that didn't take care of Ash.

Something rustled the leaves ahead, and she halted, her breath caged in her lungs. Clover's face moved in what should have been a smile. But it practically split her deformed face as she crept out of the corn.

"There you are," she beamed, revealing a mouth becoming more toothless.

Mari wasn't going to die here. She bolted left into a thick, dense patch that practically tripped her up, so high she had to climb over it. Scrambling through, she pushed thick stems aside,

Clover only yards behind. Pain tore her scalp, as Clover grabbed a fistful of hair, yanking Mari's head so hard her neck cracked. Mari twisted, balling her fist as she let it fly, and it smacked Clover in her jaw.

Clover screamed, her entire lower jaw dislodging and falling loose. Mari wriggled away in horror, scrambling through the corn as the girl struggled to hold the lower half of her face in place. "Bitch," she screamed.

Sweat dripping down her spine, Mari broke free of the corn, tumbling into a clearing. It was only when another streak of lightning sliced the night that she saw Mr. Raggerty swinging limply on his pole. She was nearly at the farm—she was nearly home!

Clover fell free of the corn, righting herself. Like some kind of unhinged puppet as she grinned demonically. Mari rose from the ground, panting, glancing behind her at the farmhouse in the distance and the sun slowly peeking over the roof. The sun was coming up.

Clover didn't seem to notice the sun. She gaped at something behind Mari, her eyes wide, filled with terror, and she seemed to wince and shrink, turning her head away. Confused, Mari looked behind her, finding only the old scarecrow on his pole.

The scarecrow? Mari nearly choked on a laugh. She was scared of *him?* Of…

Mari went cold. Tobias Rosewood. But that was impossible because she didn't believe…because if that really was true…

Clover sobbed into her hands and fled, running back the way she'd come, as sunlight slowly trickled across the field, leaving Mari breathless. She glanced up at the old scarecrow, its button eyes glossy and empty as it swung in the morning breeze.

"Thanks," she whispered.

"I never liked to imagine what he'd think of me," Ash's voice came from behind her. Shit, she'd forgotten he'd even existed for a while there. A whack split the air and Mari dodged a blow from behind. Her hair flew up as a huge spade hit the dirt beside her. Ash growled, blood still pouring from his mouth as he lifted it and lunged for her again. His face was ruined, blood soaked his shirt. He panted, lifting the spade higher. "We all get what we deserve in the end—sinners do. He certainly did."

"He made a mistake," Mari choked out. "We all make mistakes, Ash. No one more than me."

"Well, you'd be right there. Toby Rosewood never heeded the warnings of the three virtues—he even changed the house's name to his own. Vanity is a curse, maybe the worst of the sins. Now he gets to watch life pass him by."

Mari was weak, tired and wouldn't be able to dodge him for long. Her ankle gave way, cracking as she stumbled. Her arms lifted to shield her face, squeezing her eyes shut but the blow never came.

"Mari…for god sake, get up!"

Mari blinked up at her rescuer. "Zara?"

Her friend hauled her to her feet, dragging her across the mud. "C'mon." Mari looked over her shoulder at Ash, lying unconscious at the base of the scarecrow's pole. Zara was pale, shaking all over, and the rock she'd been clutching slipped from her trembling fingers. Mari's heart swelled with gratitude, adrenaline coursing through her body.

Zara snapped to attention, grabbing her under her arms, pulling and dragging her along, and relieved tears filling Mari's eyes. "How did you find me?"

"You left me that garbled message on my cell," she said, huffing as they stumbled through the maze. "I didn't listen to it for a day, but then I drove out here, and the house was empty and..." Zara looked at her profile. "Your mom was out of it. I called her an ambulance."

Mari sobbed. "Thank you."

"I found Bear running around the house going crazy, so I came out here..."

Mari grabbed her friend's shoulder, begging for respite even though Ash could wake any minute and come after them. Breathing hard, she hung off Zara. "She's gone back, Zara. She'll try again."

Mari thought of the remaining buds left on the Night Witch rose. Two left. Two more chances.

"We have to go back," she said.

Zara's blonde brows flew skyward. "What?"

"I can't believe I'm saying this...but we have to destroy what's left...I'll explain but you have to trust me. She'll try again...she'll come back."

Their gazes locked, and Zara looked cagily over her shoulder at the old ruin of Rosewood in the distance. "Did she do this to you?"

"They both did...but if I get rid of the rose then maybe...this will end. She won't have any more chances to..."

"*Or,*" Zara put a lot of emphasis on the word. "We could call the police and get you the hell out of here."

Mari shook her head, holding onto Zara's arm, pleading with her to see the truth. "No, Zara. It won't help. I can't explain it...but they're..." She didn't want to say monsters, or vampires or whatever it was. That wasn't the old Mari. "I've seen things to make me question..."

Zara snorted. "What happened to the Mari Fox, who never believed in fairy tales or monsters under the bed?"

"She believes now." The look on Mari's face must have been enough for her old friend, the haunted eyes staring back at her as they locked gazes. Mari didn't like to guess how haggard she must look. Zara brushed a stray hair off her friend's face. "Jesus, Marianne. What did they do to you?"

"Zara—I need you to trust me. I have to go back." She looked away, ashamed she was asking this of her friend, someone she'd betrayed deeply. "I can't ask you to come with me."

Zara let a long silence hang between them before gritting her teeth and nodding. "You don't have to."

THIRTY-TWO

"This is crazy," Zara muttered as she heaved Mari over a nest of brambles. They kept low, backs bent double as they circled the property. Rosewood was dark, with no lights on inside the house, apart from one flickering candle in one of the topmost windows.

Ash's room. Mari's throat burned as they crept through the overgrown yard towards a tiny back door nestled in the rear of the building. Her brows rose. "How'd you know this was here?"

Partially covered in vines, the small wooden door had been busted open, hanging on its hinges. It looked like someone, maybe the police had attempted to break it up at one time. Zara rolled up her sleeves and snuck under the boards. "James used to take me here. I guess he thought it was kind of romantic." She rolled her eyes at the memory. "He and his friends used to play here when they were kids."

Mari frowned, feeling a little confused. "How come I didn't know about it?"

Zara's lip quirked in a smile as she held out her hand for her friend. "You were too sensible."

Mari squeezed under the splintered board, and something tugged on her hair. She wriggled free, a spark of panic lunging up her chest. "This isn't sensible."

"I agree," Zara whispered, ushering her into the darkened corridors of the old servant's quarters, deep below the house, where it smelled like stale water and mold. After the leak in the old kitchen, the stone floor was dotted with murky puddles, and Zara was careful to step around them. She cast Mari a glance over her shoulder. "Don't get wet feet—prints!"

Mari gestured to her bare, bloodied feet covered in mud. "Little late for that."

They listened for noise from above. Clover must be in here somewhere. "Tell me why we aren't calling the cops again?"

Mari tiptoed past, brushing away cobwebs. She spotted the pantry and old leaves chasing down the empty corridor, blown in from the outside. There was a chill in the air, and her shoulders rose. "The cops are no use—not here."

Zara crept close behind. "What are they?"

In the dark, the quiet broke, a gentle tingling of piano keys coming from above. Mari's arms gave off goosebumps, and Zara paled, her eyes drawn to the ceiling. "What?"

"It's Clover." Mari thought of the many times she'd been enraptured by Clover's playing. Enchanted. Maybe that had been the plan all along. Her mouth tasted bitter.

Zara gaped at her in the dark. "Marianne…what the hell are they?"

A beat of silence passed before she answered. "They're immortal," was her only explanation. "And they remain looking young…by sucking the life and energy out of us. I think they thrive off grief…trauma." She thought of Ash's kiss, how it'd stirred emotions and need in her. She looked away in shame.

Zara didn't even bother to hide her amusement. "They must have thought they'd hit the jackpot when they met you."

Despite everything, they met eyes and sniggered. Mari clicked her tongue. "Yeah…well…"

"You've always been so….serious…."

"I can't help that!"

"We can't be the same—my mom always said that was why we got along. We were opposite ends of the same scale."

It hurt to look at her. Remorse tugged at her gut, and she looked away until Zara grabbed her hand. Maybe they'd never balance that scale together again?

Mari's skin crawled as Clover's melody became more erratic, fists banging the keys. "We have to get rid of those roses," she whispered.

"What's the plan?"

Mari jerked her head toward the small room off the main corridor. It was the pantry where she'd found the old first aid box. "Matches…candles…find anything we can use."

They split forces, rummaging in cupboards, carefully opening drawers. It didn't take long for Zara to land on a box of matches. "Will this do?"

On her hands and knees, Mari glanced up, withholding a shriek as a spider shot across her foot. Zara was holding a large kitchen knife. "And this?"

Mari nodded. "Perfect."

They followed the winding corridor through to where Mari had first found the set of stairs—a few stone steps to the house's main hall. She thought of where she'd seen Dan in the shadows, but at the time, she had no idea it was him.

Get out of here while you still can. Dan had tried to warn her. Guilt ate at her gut, trying to force away the image of what he'd become. If that was happening to her…

Zara lay a hand on her shoulder, and she flinched, her skin sensitive. Zara's blonde brows drew together. "Mari…you're burning up."

She wiped her brow. "I'm sick…they did this to me."

"Will you be alright?"

She let the question hang between them and paused at the edge of the footwell in the dark. "I don't know." It was the truth. She had no idea of what was to come. Maybe it was her fate—to end the way James had.

"Well, I'm not giving up. You stay behind me, okay?"

It would have been a touching moment if she didn't feel at the brink of collapse. Mari could only concentrate on keeping upright—a fever burned under her skin, setting nerves aflame. The fight to lay down and close her eyes was intense, and she battled to put one foot ahead of the other. The thought of Ash loomed like a shadow, enough to keep her going. Knowing she'd unwittingly drawn Zara into this mess, she couldn't help the seed of guilt that had ripened the last hour.

Zara put her arm out in the dark as if she sensed her thoughts, keeping Mari steadily behind her. "Which way?" she hissed.

"Up the stairs," Mari said. "We should come up in the hall."

From this angle, it was strange to see the great expanse of the lofty hallway, as someone who once worked here would have seen it, treading the darkened, winding hallways that twisted and seemed to change direction—a house ever on the move, blooming like a rose. Mari gripped the back of Zara's shirt, her eyes adjusting to the oil lamps burning low. The old wool rug was rotted, filthy with water, and dirty from the fallen debris. Light pooled through the hole in the roof as leaves fell in a macabre dance to the ground. The scaffold was packed up and gone. It all smelled of wet plaster. The storm had ravaged the roof, and rainwater puddled through in drips.

"I can smell…" Zara sniffed. "Flowers."

"That's the orangery…" Mari crept behind her, her hand reaching for the handle of the large oak double doors. Zara bolted in front of her. "I usually go through the ballroom."

"Isn't there another way? We can't walk right by without her seeing us."

The melody built to a frustrating, liberating crescendo, as though Clover were chasing the notes higher and higher on a wave of anger and despair.

Mari thought hard. There must be. As she'd seen Clover and Ash come and go so often. "I think the library has a door."

Silently, Zara nodded, and they tracked left back across the hall and through a slim door that opened up to the great library. A window had blown in the room, and the stacks had been destroyed, hundreds of tomes ruined by rainwater and devastation. It looked like several books had been ripped apart. Mari glanced at the plush sofa, ruined by deep claw marks, as though some mad dog had ravished it like a toy. A lump clogged her throat. *Clover.*

"This way," Mari whispered, preferring not to look at the once grand room as she hurried to another door, which was closed by dark oak paneling. She eased it open with her fingers, and the humidity of Clover's workroom seeped out to greet them.

Zara went first, holding her kitchen knife at chest level. Mari noticed it wobbled a little. "What do we do?"

Mari gaped around the room in shock. It looked as though Clover had already done the job for them. Every vial was smashed to oblivion. Her workbooks strewn over the counter, in shreds. Her diagrams, drawings, and precious notes on paper crumbled into balls. It was like Clover had gone through here like a storm, in a frenzy. Mari could almost feel her despair.

The dirty windows were smashed, glass fragments littering the ground. Zara stepped on glass and it crunched. "Careful," she warned.

The only cabinet that remained untouched was the glass house for the Night Witch rose. Zara had spotted it first, her blue eyes wide as she tiptoed nearer. "That's incredible—it's entirely black."

Clover's remaining roses had bloomed in the space of twenty-four hours, their petals wide and spread. The rose looked beautiful, housed in its case, but Mari knew the sinister heart that lay in the center, buried under the beautiful, delicate petals.

"We have to kill it," she said, and Zara made a face.

"Really?"

"Yes," Mari insisted. "This thing destroyed Clover. She thought it was her cure."

Mari swayed, staggering under the room's scorching heat. Zara nodded, grabbing a pair of of pruning shears from the bench. She flung the case wide and snipped off the remaining blooms.

Abruptly, the piano stopped, almost as if Clover had banged the keys with her fists. A distinct slam on the top, shutting the lid and feet dragging along the floor.

Mari froze in panic. Zara plucked the blooms, hissing as a thorn caught her finger. She threw them on the ground and stamped them into the stone floor.

From the shadows, the sound of Clover's scream shriveled any strength Mari possessed. The sound chilled her to the bone as she stared at the bruised petals under Zara's sneakers. The smell the rose emitted made her bend double and cough, hacking through her bones.

Zara gagged and choked. "Oh…god."

It was vile, rotten, like death itself. Mari covered her nose with her sleeve. In the soil, the rose roots oozed a pustulous red substance. The roots left in the soil pulsed and started to grow. Mari stuck her hand in the soil, grinding her teeth and screaming as she yanked the roots free, the thorns embedded in her skin as she tore them out.

On the ground, the roots leaked fluid, and Zara jumped clear as it seeped through the cracks in the stone.

"What have you done?" Clover wailed from the door.

THIRTY-THREE

Both girls turned, and Zara let out a terrified shriek.

Not one strand was left on Clover's scalp, her skin stretched and transparent. She crawled on the floor and wept over the bloodied remains of her creation.

For all she had done, Mari's eyes still filled up, her throat burning with unshed tears. "Clover, I'm sorry."

"I only wanted to walk in the light," the girl wailed, blunt nails dragging over the stone. "Look at what you've done."

Falling to her knees, Clover gathered the ruined black petals in her withered hands and cradled them to her chest.

Zara gaped at her, swallowing soundlessly before she glanced at her friend. "Mari, come on…we did what we came to do."

Mari hovered over Clover's shoulder, her fingers aching to comfort her, but they curled away in disgust as the girl's neck snapped in her direction. It was too late before she realized Clover had pinned her gaze on Zara.

She moved too fast, knocking Mari sideways, so her ribs cracked on the workbench, and she crumpled. Clover flew for Zara, her cloven fingers finding a pair of pruning shears on the ground. Metal flashed, there was a slash and rip of flesh, and Zara screamed. Blood pooled on the floor.

Mari scrambled to her feet. "Stop!"

Clover coiled in her direction, and they faced one another.

"It was my heart you wanted, wasn't it?" Mari said, her voice quivering. Zara crawled away, clutching the gash in her calf, gasping in shock and pain.

Mari let out a short, breathy laugh. "I mean…look at me. It won't take much now to finish me off."

Black tar from Clover's lungs dripped through the cracks in her teeth as she crawled closer, and Mari closed her eyes, the kitchen knife buried under her arm. It'd clattered to the ground as she'd hit the work surface. The creature lunged, mouth gaping and fingers splayed as she landed on Mari, bracketing her with her long arms. Sweat beaded Mari's brow, forced to her back, the knife wedged under her forearm; squirming against it, the blade sliced her skin. She fought to hide the pain on her face.

Fetid breath filled her nostrils, and she gagged as Clover pressed closer, her lips dripping with that horrible black venom, the same ooze that'd leaked from the rose. She tilted her head, assessing Mari like prey, with an almost playful gleam in her eye.

"I know why he liked you so much," she said, inhaling as though Mari smelled like roses, and she couldn't get enough. "That heart of yours is full to bursting with remorse." She flicked her black gaze at Zara, who was holding her bleeding leg. "It's even better with *her* here. She gave you something dangerous, Mari. She gave you hope."

Mari blinked under her, her rigid against the cold floor. "Hope?"

"You're full of it. It radiates off you. She forgave you…and now you're whole again. Or at least you're a good portion of the way there."

Mari's eyes filled with tears, shaking her head. "You want my heart, Clover? You think it's so full? You're wrong…my heart...it's dead."

Clover snorted, slowly absorbing what she'd said. "I can assure you, it beats. I'll prove it when I show it to you."

"My heart isn't full," she said, tears choking her voice. Underneath, even with her shoulders pinned by Clover's spindly hands, she worked the knife free, curling her fingers under the handle. "It died a long time ago. I turned my back on someone I cared about—someone I don't deserve."

Clover laughed, but Mari kept her face neutral, feeling Zara's eyes hot on her face. "So you're wrong. And you can take it. But it won't be a cure. It won't make you what you were. My heart was already dead."

Clover touched a delicate finger to Mari's sternum, jabbing it hard enough to make her wince. Then she licked her lips. "We'll see. I'll let you know how it tastes."

The world slowed. Zara screamed as Clover bared a row of pointy yellowed teeth. Mari wrenched her shoulder out from under her, the knife flashing in the morning sun as she sank it fast under Clover's ribs. Her bones crumbled like chalk, so frail it went in with ease and a crunch. Clover's black eyes went wild, and she moaned, tumbling sideways.

A shadow passed over Mari's eyes, and for a second, she thought Clover had rounded on her, but Zara hauled her up. "Come on," she yelled, hobbling as blood drained from the wound in her calf. "We need to leave."

Pain splintered every cell of her body, as Mari and Zara dragged themselves out into the hall. Hobbling and panting they headed for the door, wide open and letting in sheets of rain. Mari froze, her heart thumping.

"Wait…" No sooner had she uttered the words did a crack fill the air and Zara shoved her to the floor. Careening to the ground, Mari spotted Ash's muddy feet. He dragged Zara backward by her blonde hair, and she kicked and yelled.

"Mari, go!" she screamed. On her feet, Mari stared at the door but knew he'd only chase her out there and drag her back. And he needed her alive for his sister.

Ash smacked Zara's head against the ground, leaving her in an unconscious heap. Mari bolted for the stairs. The last dregs of energy she possessed powered her journey upward into the shadowy hall. A board under her foot split and she screamed, flailing for the banister rail as an entire section of the staircase crumpled and disintegrated. Ash was on the steps below, glaring at her in fury.

He glared up at her, as she breached the first floor, shaking violently. "There's more than one staircase in this house," he warned.

He darted into a corridor below, and she panicked. On the ground, Zara heaved herself to her feet. Blearily, she looked up at Mari hanging over the railing. They locked eyes tearfully, and Mari hardly believed she was alive.

"Go, Mari…he's coming," Zara called, dragging herself to her feet. Mari swiveled left, wondering where the hell she could hide. Limping, she clambered along the corridor, her hand landing on the doorknob of the room of mirrors. Ash's footfalls grew louder as he approached, and Mari held her breath, carefully opening the door, creeping in, and closing it quietly behind her. Ash's feet thundered down the corridor, and sweat broke on her temple as she held the knob hard on the other side of the door, willing her lungs to still in her chest. If he discovered her, she was no match for him. He'd kill her.

He stopped outside the door, and she muffled a whimper. Backing away, she had no choice but to hide. She crept over the damp carpet, finding a mirror turned to the wall, leaning at a right angle. It was massive and heavy, gilded with a thick, gold frame. The angle left just enough room for her. She squeezed in behind it, the glass on the other side smooth, and she saw her haggard reflection in the dark. Dust tickled her nose, but she tucked herself in tight, holding her breath tight as the door flung open. She jumped, squeezing her eyes shut.

"Marianne," he chided playfully. "I'm going to find you eventually."

Her stomach went to water, fighting a terrified scream that wanted to rip up her throat. He passed her hiding place, and she went rigid, eyes wide in terror. The tread of his feet faded, heading away, and she let out a whimper.

She screamed as the mirror was thrown so fast it fell and hit the dining table, revealing her hiding spot. Ash lunged, his face contorted and twisted with pain, his lip ruined, and blood matted in his hair. On all fours, she scrambled out of her hiding space right when he grabbed her ankle. She fell, chin smacking the floor with a thud, and he roughly flung her to her back.

Mari saw his teeth and screamed. Any trace of the Ash she'd known was gone—black eyes like coal, wild and feral. Freeing her ankle, she kicked out, catching the gilded mirror's edge. It swiveled, tumbling sideways, hitting his temple with a dull thud. Momentarily stunned, he clutched at his head, buying her enough time to wriggle away. Ash roared as she ran around the dining table, clattering across overturned chairs. When she reached the door, it was bolted. Fingers slippery with sweat and blood, Mari didn't have a second to think as he chased her, and she ran back where she'd come, jumping the discarded mirror wedged between the wall and the dining table.

Cowering behind it, she watched helplessly as Ash stalked in the other direction, running at her. Mari grabbed the mirror, her biceps straining as she lifted it to head height.

Ash's scream of terror made her pause with the mirror held mid air.

Mari would never know exactly what he saw in the mirror, but he reared in fright, stricken as he flung away. It bought her seconds, the mirror weighing a ton in her hands, and as he spun to face her, she brought it down on his skull. A dull thud filled her ears, and Ash dropped to the floor.

"Zara," she whispered, stepping over the fragmented mirror and unbolting the door. How the hell would she get back downstairs? Half of the staircase was in a heap on the hall floor. Dashing through the upper halls of Rosewood, she flung left and right, flinging open doors wildly until she found a spiral metal staircase that took her straight down to the library.

"Zara!" she screamed, dashing into the hall. "Where are you?" Her feet skidded on the old boards as she ran into the orangery. "Zara!"

"Here!"

Zara hobbled over the stone floor, the box of matches falling out of her bloody fingers. She was ashen, panting hard as she landed in Mari's arms. The air was filled with smoke.

The orangery was alight with flame. Fire crept up the blackout blinds and twisted through the rafters. "What did you do?"

Zara grabbed Mari's hand as heat licked at their skin. It burned, and everything went white and hot. The flames quickly took up the dry, dead leaves and roots of Clover's once beautiful haven. "Clover...where is she?"

Clover had crawled to her bed under the canopy of dead flowers, leaving a trail of black ooze in her wake over the polished stone. The girl closed her eyes and lifted her arms to the sun, waiting for it to take her. Mari's throat thickened. "Clover."

A stone pillar groaned and crumbled, falling like a felled tree and blocking their path. Mari stared through the flames, but the girl was gone. She would never see Clover Rosewood again.

"We need to leave," Zara begged tearfully. "I called the cops, Mari."

Zara grabbed Mari, and they struggled to the door. Sweat dripped down their faces, grimy and sooty, as they ran through the house. Mari grabbed the railing, staring over her shoulder.

Flames took the second floor, and somewhere in the ballroom, a window smashed. The fire was engulfing the house, and it groaned and creaked like an old waking giant. "Ash!"

She saw him, his shape against the backdrop of burning orange. For a moment, they locked eyes, before he vanished into the shadows. Zara's hand found hers.

Together, they stumbled out into the night air as sirens wailed in the distance, heading closer. A huge fire truck pulled onto the property, and Zara hauled Mari to a safe distance, where they watched as the once magnificent house crumbled in on itself. The roof cracked, whining as it fell inward, glass shattering as windows exploded. Smoke rose to claim the building, enveloping it in an eerie mist as if the ground was claiming it back.

Mari watched it burn, but Zara held her hand the whole time.

THIRTY-FOUR

Zara huddled next to Mari on a mossy stone bench. From a safe distance, they watched plumes of smoke rise above the once-grand house. Mari winced as jets of water tore the lower floor apart. Zara massaged her shoulder.

"Are you okay?" Mari sniffed.

"Yeah. It's a deep gash, that's all."

"I thought…" Mari coughed dryly, shaking her head. "If she'd have hurt you…after everything I've put you through. You came to find me."

"Come on," Zara side-hugged her. "It's the past, Mari. We have to move on now. But the best bit is we can do it together."

Mari smiled shakily. "Like we were supposed to."

It seemed crazy to be talking about their future when, only a short while ago, Mari didn't believe she had one. Now the warmth of her best friend's arm bled through her sweater, and she remembered old times, movie nights, and staying up late on the phone. They'd been inseparable through school and had meant to go on through college, navigating the world of school, boys, and careers together. But James had torn them apart. Now, she saw him for what he was. Mari didn't know if they could claw back what they'd been, what they'd meant to one another. But she was willing to give it her all.

The shape of a female firefighter with umber skin and black hair appeared through a haze of smoke, and Mari rose off the bench, her bottom numb with cold. The woman's face was grave and pensive as she trudged through old nettles and brambles with her boots.

"Did you find them?" Mari's heart leaped to her throat.

The woman's thick brows drew closer. "We didn't find anyone in that building."

"Are you sure?" Zara asked.

"There were two of them…a man…" Mari broke off, wondering how to describe what Clover had turned into at the end. "There was a girl."

"We'll keep looking," the woman assured them. "But both of you need to rest…we can sort out this mess. However, it doesn't look like anyone lived there for years."

Mari eyed the bundle that the firefighter carried under her arm, something wrapped in cloth. "Does this belong to either of you? We found it at the foot of the stairs…kind of an odd place to leave it."

She unwrapped the bundle, and while Zara only looked perplexed, Mari drained to a new, paler white. The remains of Clover's music box were charred and damaged, and the ballerina's left foot was missing. She shuddered, stepping away. "No, it's not mine." She never wanted to look at the damn thing again. She could still hear the piano while Clover danced, the music box keeping time as she pirouetted over the polished floor. Had that happened? It felt like a lifetime ago.

The woman shrugged. "Never mind. Maybe stay out of old derelict houses next time, huh? That place was a nightmare."

Zara cast Mari a look, linking arms as they both wandered the uncared-for grounds of Rosewood. Mari found she couldn't be on the property another moment, walking among the stone statues, wondering if somehow Clover was still out there hiding. If Ash had somehow survived...

"I know you liked him," Zara said. "Before you found out he was an immortal piece of shit."

Mari hugged her friend's arm. "People show you what they are," she repeated Ash's sentiment. "The trouble was I wasn't looking hard enough."

Zara unlocked her car, and they climbed in. She jostled the engine to a start, and gravel spit up under the tires as they drove through the estate. "I'll take you home."

Mari thought momentarily, and before she could turn to Keller's farm, she touched her friend's arm. "No…I need to go somewhere else first."

Ten minutes later, Mari was standing in front of the police department in Winstone, staring at the grey squat building, her nails digging into her palms. She looked over her shoulder, where Zara sat in the driver's seat, watching her. Maybe to see if she'd go through with it.

She should let the dead be. It was time to let James go. Hadn't everyone suffered enough? But as she locked eyes with her friend, she saw the bitter anguish below the surface. Zara could only move on once she made this right.

She pushed open the door, greeted by the smell of fresh coffee as she went in. The halls were buzzing with activity. It was busier than the last time she'd come here. Probably, news of Rosewood's fire had caused a bit of a stir. She waited in the foyer, her feet becoming wooden as she stood. Every second that passed it got harder to keep strong. Finally, the guy she'd seen before, the old coach, beckoned her with a wave and a curt nod. "Can I help you?"

Mari looked at him, her words sticking in her throat. "I need to report something." She sucked in a breath, and a tear rolled down her cheek. She had to make things right. James was gone, her mother was taken care of, and she had a life to lead. And both of them were stuck.

"Miss...are you okay?" he asked when she couldn't speak for the longest time.

Shakily, she nodded. "I need to report something that happened a while ago...something my brother did. And his friends. They hurt someone I love."

The man's frown deepened, and he set down his coffee. "Aren't you Marianne Fox? James's sister?"

"That's right." She swallowed, and her mouth tasted like smoke. "It's true. What he did—it's all true."

He shrugged, and she clenched all over. Would he dismiss her? Would he believe her over James? If she knew one thing, she'd fight. She would fight for her friend the way she'd fought for her. The same way Dan Wheeler had fought his captors. Marianne wouldn't stop until things were right in the world.

"Why are you reporting this now?" he asked, that dismissive, skeptical tone clouding his voice.

She was doing this, there was no turning back. "Because," she whispered. "It's time I came into the light."

EPILOGUE

Three Months Later

The coffee was good. She closed her eyes and allowed herself to wallow in the taste, leaning back in her chair. Her taste buds had healed, the damage to her lungs was repaired, and her bones no longer creaked or ached when she walked Bear in the evening.

Healing from the scars Rosewood inflicted on her had taken time, but she knew the scars from James would be longer. Beside her on the chair, her phone lit up, and for once, her face didn't contort in fear when she saw the caller ID. She swiped it up, smiling as she answered.

"Before you ask—*no*. He isn't here yet."

Zara tutted at the other end of the line. "He's late. That's hardly a good start."

"It's not a date, Zara. I'm meeting a client, that's all."

Her friend snorted. "Oh, come on. This mysterious guy has been dying to get you into a face-to-face meeting for ages. I hope he's paying."

Mari made a face, replacing her coffee on the table just as the waitress, Evan, swished by with a smile and refilled it. Mari mouthed a thank you.

"Well, as soon as you're done, you need to tell me all about it."

"This won't last long, it's not a thing," she insisted, despite the fact that she was more than a little curious about this author. Still, it was good to have Zara to confide in, and a reason to call her. Even if their chats were brief.

"Maybe *try* to have a good time," she teased, knowing Mari would be eager to get home.

Licking her lips, Mari's eyes expectantly scanned the lot. "Are you coming home from college this weekend? I thought maybe we could meet up."

There was a pause, like her old friend was thinking fast at the other end of the line. The wounds between them were still raw, and more time was needed before Zara could trust Mari again. Mari accepted that, knowing she needed to earn that trust. They'd had a couple of movie nights at Zara's house under the blanket with Bear. But Zara wouldn't step foot inside Kellers, and Mari would never ask her.

James's old friends were under investigation and suspended from college. It was slow, but moving in the right direction. Mari's mother was finally getting the help she needed. Their moments together were brief, slowly, tentatively working their way toward a healthier relationship. Mari guessed it would never be harmonious as resentment still lingered between them. Zara had been by her side when they'd moved her into the new place, and for that she was grateful.

It was baby steps forward, and Mari found she didn't mind the quiet of the farmhouse. She'd thrown open all the curtains, unlocked the doors, and cleared out James's room. She let the light back inside.

"Um, I think there's a party in one of the halls this weekend—but soon! I miss, Bear!" Zara promised. Mari smiled, even though it made her feel hollow. Zara was enrolled in Meadowford and having the life she deserved.

Mari's shoulders tensed as a silver-grey Rolls Royce Phantom pulled into the lot of the diner. Her brows flew skyward, and she let out a shaky laugh. *No.* That couldn't be Eric's driver hopping out of the front seat and heading to the passenger door. That was some car! She didn't think she'd ever rode in anything that fancy. "Uh, I *think* he's here—either that or the king of England just turned up."

Zara squealed in excitement. "What does he look like?"

Mari peered through the grimy window, feeling her shoulders rise. God, now she felt embarrassed bringing him to a diner at the back end of nowhere. The guy had a driver! She grabbed up her paperback copy of Eric's latest publication, aptly titled, *The Grey Witch,* and she thumbed through to the author bio at the back, scanning for his photo. It was a round-faced man with thin ginger hair and a nice smile. A forgettable face, and one not belonging to the debonair man who climbed out of the Royce, hurriedly putting on sunglasses. Sunglasses, even in the dead of winter?

She bit her lip, remembering she still had Zara hanging on. "That doesn't look like him—at all!"

"*Tell* me he's good looking."

Mari had sworn off dating for a while, and she was about done with handsome, charming gentleman. The man who emerged from the back of the vehicle was gangly, lean, and probably reached about six foot two. What she saw first was his shock of grey hair, not silver grey, like gunmetal, and an unmissable white streak straight down his parting. From first glance he looked young, around thirty, and Mari's stomach flipped as he briskly walked to the diner steps. He wore a crisp pinstripe suit and gloves, head to toe in black. "I've got to go," she hissed before she hung up.

The bell tinkled over the door, and he came inside, gazing around the room from behind his dark glasses. Spotting her lurking in the corner, he lifted his glasses and peered over the top, his eyes flashing with recognition. Once he reached the table, a scent of fiery aftershave preceded him. He looked down at her. "Mari?" he asked gently. "Marianne Fox?"

"Um." She bit her lip. "Yeah. I'm waiting for Eric Summers—the author?"

He lifted his glasses, tucking them into the briefcase he carried. It was shiny, leather, and embossed with a crest. A large letter G engraved among thorns, ravens and skulls. Mari's eyes widened as he slipped into the booth opposite. He met her stare and she struggled not to gasp. His eyes were near colorless, the color of sea glass. Framed by dark lashes and along with the gunmetal hair and pale skin, he was startling. "That would be me."

Her eyes flicked to the author photo. "This isn't you?"

"I find life a lot easier if readers don't find out what I look like." He raised his brows. "I tend to give people a bit of a shock."

Did this guy get struck by lightning?

"Hmm."

"This is *charming*." He looked around the diner as Evan approached, laying out a menu in front of him. "I can see why you like coming here—it's very cozy."

Marianne sat straight, folding her arms on the table. This guy was a little off; his eyes were strange, his mannerisms, and the ancient vehicle looked like it chauffeured around royalty. Mari didn't think he was a famous name. He wasn't a New York Times Bestseller or a celebrity author.

After the ordeal at Rosewood, Eric had asked, begged, pleaded and bribed her for a face to face meeting. After all she'd been through, she didn't see why not.

Life was better, and she was stronger. She hadn't gone back to college, preferring the quiet of her family home. Meeting her client face to face seemed like a breeze compared to what she'd been through.

"At last, we meet, Miss Fox," he said with an eccentric clap of his hands. "I'm so pleased you finally said yes."

"Well, you wore me down," she joked. "And I was intrigued." She picked up the latest book, and he blushed bashfully.

"I would have bought you a copy—here let me sign it!"

He produced a silver fountain pen from his pocket, slid the book toward him, and signed his name with a flourish. Mari grinned. "Thanks."

"And what about the book had you so intrigued?"

Mari leaned her chin on her palm, unsure of where to begin. "Well, for one thing…the witch buried under an old Oak tree…it kind of feels familiar."

She wasn't sure because his eyes were so pale, but she swore they twinkled. "Really?"

"Yeah. And the town names you chose…are you aware that in this area, there are three very prestigious estates with the *exact* names you chose for your towns?"

His eyes widened in shock, and he clutched his heart comically. "*Really?* You don't say—what a coincidence!"

"Is it though?"

"Well you tell me—you're the one who doesn't believe in things that go bump in the night, Marianne."

She snorted a laugh, and they locked eyes. It was worrying how well he seemed to know her. "Do you know this area? Like, have you lived here before?"

He mirrored her pose, hand on her chin, and innocently shook his head, looking very young—almost playful. "No."

"Then how did you get those names? Did you just make them up?"

"Maybe someone told me*? People*—like to talk to me. To whisper in my ear. I get given a lot of information and need to get it out. Writing has always been my outlet." He cleared his throat, and she sensed he was about to change the subject. "Tell me, Mari. Do you think the fire gutted Rosewood Hall entirely?"

Goosebumps broke out on her skin. "How did you know about that?"

His smile dropped and he leaned closer. "Did they survive?"

Looking into his eyes, she swore she knew him. Maybe that was his talent as a writer—extracting information. He said people opened up to him. But how could he know about Rosewood? Her mouth went dry and she sipped her coffee. "No," she answered finally. "There was no one in there."

He sat back in his seat. "Well, that's a relief. I worry about you living across the way from Temperance. It's seen its fair share of sorrow over the years. Ash and Clover are where they belong now, where they should have been centuries ago."

Mari slapped the table. "Wait—*what?* How the hell do you know all this?"

He folded his arms, smiling mischievously. "Oh, I know a lot of things, Mari. Why do you think I hired you? There's more to you than being the most irritatingly nitpicky proofreader I've ever worked with. It didn't take long to figure out where you lived and who you were—and the danger you faced."

When she didn't speak, he placed his warm gloved hand over hers on top of the book. "I'm so proud of you for doing right by your friend. And your decision about Dan Wheeler—was the right one."

She gasped, her heart stuttering with guilt. She and Zara had suffered over the decision about Dan. If they told the police where he was buried, what kind of monster would they find? They decided to let him rest, and when the cops and police had cleared out, they found his remains. Ash hadn't done the best job of burying him at the time, so he wasn't hard to trace, and the cops weren't looking for bodies in the yard. Ash had discarded Dan's body in the crypt, with no intention of ever burying him. They dragged him to a quiet spot in the adjacent wheat field.

Mari didn't want to leave him in the grounds of Rosewood.

She was glad never to see that crypt or those creepy stone maidens again.

"Who would ever believe us?" she whispered, as Evan whisked past and refilled their coffee. "They wouldn't have found a man in the ground, or anything that looked like a man. I didn't want his family to know what became of him…who would believe it?"

Eric squeezed her hand. The gesture was warm and kind. "I would."

"Who *are* you?"

Eric smiled, flashing even white teeth, a charming smile lighting up his face. "Well. I guess the ruse is up. My name…my *real* name." He held out his hand for her to shake. "Is Gabriel—Gabriel Ghast."

Mari blinked, taking his hand and shaking it. "Ghast…as in *Eilhard* Ghast…the architect?"

"That's right," he said in a low, melodic tone. "And I live in Patience, in the old crooked old house he built in a town by the sea…called Fallows Watch, with my brother and sister. And I write all the stories the dead tell me."

"The *dead?*"

His face was utterly serious, and she had no idea how to read him. "Yes, the dead. They have a great deal to say—and I write it all down. They make for wonderful stories. And this place...well, it's got a *lot* of stories."

Mari smiled, hooked, as she leaned on her hand. "Really? Is there anything you're working on?"

"Well that depends. Do you happen to know of a town called Cedar Wood?"

She laughed. "Of course."

"Do you know the woods?"

"I had a hike in there once." She recalled the falcon and the man with a crossbow. She took her coffee and gazed at him over the top, finding herself warming to him. He was odd, and a bit eccentric but she was enjoying this more than she thought possible.

"You're lucky you got out of there in one piece," he joked. "That forest has teeth."

Mari glanced up at Evan, surprised to see she'd been watching them the whole time. Ignoring the odd sensation, she looked back at Eric—Gabriel. "I'd love to hear more about it."

His smile was infectious, and his voice was so good she could listen to it all day. "Oh, you will, Miss Fox," he said. "You will."

Later, when Mari drove the truck home, tires snagging on the old potholes, she spotted one of the local farmers in the corn. He was installing some kind of machine—it looked like a small cannon in black—right in the spot where Mr. Raggerty had stood. She threw the truck onto the grassy side and ran through the field.

"Hey?" she cried. "What happened to Mr. Raggerty?"

The farmer lifted the brim of his hat, smiling. "Who knows?" He gestured to the sky. "He's gone where the wind took him. So, I thought it was time to modernize and get a real crow scarer."

"Oh." She rubbed her arms against the chill. "That's a shame. I'm going to miss him."

He turned away, shaking his head like he had better things to do with his time. Mari unlocked the house and set Bear free, where he ran in circles around her legs. Sitting on the porch, she looked out over the corn, a gentle breeze in her hair. It was going to feel strange not having Mr. Raggerty around anymore. In the end, she guessed maybe he was looking out for her.

She watched as night fell around the gutted remains of Rosewood. When the light became low like this, she always imagined she'd seen a flicker of a candle in the window. Bear was content to sit by her feet, as the sun dipped below the trees, shrouding the old manor in shadow. Mari went inside, throwing on the lights, and grabbing a coffee while she worked on her laptop under a blanket, with her Bear beside her on the couch. She fought pangs of loneliness, the house quiet and empty, even though she'd been alone here for the longest time. James was truly gone now.

A message from Eric—*Gabriel*, popped up on her screen.

It was good to finally meet you, Marianne. I've got a feeling we've got plenty of tales between us to share.

Mari's mouth twitched in a grin, glad she'd agreed to meet him. He was nice, kind, and a bit eccentric. She wasn't sure about the whole speaking with the dead narrative he spun, but she liked him.

She typed. **Goodnight, Gabriel. I'll look forward to those pages you promised.**

Gabriel certainly had Mari intrigued, and after an afternoon spent combing the net, she'd found painfully little on the Ghast family. Gabriel mentioned a town where his ancestor Eilhard had been born, and when she'd typed it into the search bar, her eyes went as wide as saucers.

The Black Forest. As she'd read, every hair on her neck stood to attention. The Ghast family hailed from the black forest, one of the most infamous areas of Germany, where the line between fairytale and nightmares wove together like a tapestry. Maybe that was why Gabriel was so whimsical, so eccentric. If she was going to work with him, she thought it was just something she'd have to get used to.

She wanted to keep working with him, and even though she'd never believed in fate or divine intervention before now, it felt like she was meant to.

Settling on the couch, she glanced at Rosewood, her heart stamping with relief to see it in darkness. Bear got his walks earlier these days. Mari would never go out at this time of day when the sun died, and an unearthly pink glow would light the sky.

She no longer cared for Twilight.

Night Blooming Flowers

NIGHT PHLOX

JASMINE

EVENING
PRIMROSE

QUEEN OF THE
NIGHT

MOON FLOWER

GARDENIA

CASA BLANCA
LILY

MOCK
ORANGE

NOCTURNAL
ORCHID

AUTHOR'S NOTE

If you have been affected by any of the themes in this book, please don't struggle alone. There is always someone out there willing to listen, and take your hand.

Mari's story has been living in my head for a long time. All through the Wild Spirit years, this tale of loneliness, loss and human frailty existed inside my head but I never knew how to get it on paper. This story was born off the back of ending a long book series, and inventing new characters was a challenge. I didn't quite want to leave the world of Cedar Wood just yet. There are parts of this story that were hard to digest, and for me, especially hard to write. I hope you enjoyed the journey.

Thank you so much to Chris Kenny, Bethany Votaw, and Bethany Russo for reading this and all my crazy notes. You guys keep me on track and have shown so much love and support over the years. Thank you Hayley Anderton for all you do in indie author community, and me. We are lucky to have you.

Thank you Kim Campbell, my rock, friend and proofreader (I swear Mari wasn't based on you!) However if you need a caring, thorough proofreader who always goes the extra mile, Kim is your woman!

The Wild Spirit Series

The Curse of Win Adler * Huntress* The Last Hickory* Curse Born* Blood Moon* White Phoenix

Other Books by Victoria Wren

Night Blooming—A gothic horror

Ghastly—A tale of Sorrow (Fall 2025)